April
CRUEL

D1291438

KATHERINE H. BURKMAN

outskirtspress
DENVER, COLORADO

April Cruel
All Rights Reserved.
Copyright © 2016 Katherine H. Burkman
v4.0

Cover Photo © 2016 thinkstockphotos.com. All rights reserved - used with permission.

Outskirts Press, Inc.
http://www.outskirtspress.com

ISBN: 978-1-4787-6725-1

Library of Congress Control Number: 2015918099

Outskirts Press and the "OP" logo are trademarks belonging to Outskirts Press, Inc.

PRINTED IN THE UNITED STATES OF AMERICA

ACKNOWLEDGMENTS

Thanks to Don Nigro, Donna Gooch, Noreen Felzer, Jane Cottrell, and Mark Auburn for their helpful suggestions. I am also grateful to WILD WOMEN WRITING (Carole Dale, Ann C. Hall, AnneMarie Brethauer, Marilyn Rofsky, Laura Zakin and Christiane Buuck) for their input.

CHAPTER I

The knife penetrated the flesh, reached the bone, twisted…
His body turned, inadvertently forcing the assailant's knife
to twist as it entered the flesh…

Several short jabs of the knife, in-out, in-out, in…

No matter the details were hazy. The fact was that Paul was
dead. The fact was that his unknown assailant, either unaware
or uncaring that Paul would gladly have parted with whatever
money he had carried on that rainy night in London, had coupled
robbery with murder.

How awful for him. She could feel the pain, the surprise, the
horror as if it were happening to her. It was unbearable.

Or had Paul actually courted death? Had he protested,
refused, taken on his adversary at that midnight hour, bringing
down a heavy destiny on them both? If so, it had been cruel, the
very first cruel gesture he had made toward her, a gesture which
reached across the ocean and touched her life so that she was not
sure that she could ever repress the rage that mingled with her
self-pitying tears. Surely he had not risked his life only six short
days before their marriage. No, she could not believe that of him.
It must have been from behind. He was taken unawares–the pain
was brief.

But Erica Berne could not stop her pain. She lay taut on her bed. Paul's death scene, played out in all its possible forms, kept moving on the ceiling before her half-closed eyes and mingled hazily with her dreams of their future life together. Finally, her eyes closed, her muscles relaxed slightly, and her angular body seemed to lift, then float, then sink into a sleep of grief.

⟫⟪◉⟫⟪

Jim Strand walked to the college slowly, enjoying the fresh smells of April. He saw a rabbit scamper behind some bushes on the corner and for some reason it made him laugh. Poor David, he thought. His best friend on the faculty, David was so invested in his manuscript on Kafka and so sensitive about the course of his career at Huston.

Both of Jim's parents were professors. His mother was a mathematician and his father a historian. It had seemd natural for him to follow their footsteps into the ivory tower. And his scholarship to Harvard had only cemented their hopes for his academic career. Harvard, however, had not been Jim's idea of a blast. Coming from the Middle West, he found himself among a lot of eastern kids, many of whom had attended prep schools. He found it difficult to connect with them. In fact he was only in touch with about two people who did become his friends. The Professors were great, on the whole. He had no quibbles about his education. The Shakespeare course he took was particularly exhilarating and was no doubt the reason he had chosen the Renaissance as his field of interest. Close readings of the texts had made the plays became really his. But he had been lonely. Graduate school at the

University of Iowa had been much more to his liking. After his Harvard experience, he happily turned down Yale and the small stipend they had offered in favor of a teaching assistantship in Iowa. Indeed, he relished going into what he imagined would be the boonies. He had to admit that the courses weren't as difficult as his undergraduate courses had been, but he had connected with his fellow students almost immediately.

Of course the Harvard degree had helped him get this job. How beside themselves would his parents be, he thought, if they knew he was thinking of resigning at the end of the year. Giving up security. Giving up health benefits. Dancing out into the unknown. He didn't, for heaven's sake, even know yet what it was he wanted to do. But he could always get a dumb dumb job for a bit to sustain himself until he figured it out.

It wasn't that he didn't enjoy teaching. He was good at it and very popular with the students. He rather enjoyed shocking them from time to time and they enjoyed being shocked. And it wasn't that he was in any way, shape, or form bored with the Bard. Shakespeare had been something of his bible since he read *Julius Caesar* and *Hamlet* in high school. In fact, he could almost see himself being an actor rather than a teacher, though he certainly knew that was more than a long shot. To go from security to a career which would probably have him waiting tables on the side was not exactly what he had in mind.

The birds were really noisy today. They apparently had a lot to say to each other. What a slew of eccentrics made up their glorious department. At least, he thought, he had one buddy on the faculty, David Stein and Susie Marsh, the departmental secretary. He enjoyed talking to her. In fact, he had promised to lend her his copy of *The Iliad*. He would have to find it. He took it out and read some of it every fall for some reason. And then he would put it away for the year.

Susie was such a quick learner and so eager for his guidance. And yet he certainly didn't think of himself as her teacher. He found her attractive, liked the freckles that almost covered her face, admired her slim figure, and… unlike some of his students, she was growing before his eyes. Her mind that is. Heaven knows, she was otherwise fully grown. He felt strongly and somewhat mysteriously drawn to her. He could just hear his parents saying, "What, a secretary?" They weren't really that snobbish, but they did tend to dwell on him as a Harvard graduate and a professor. Oh well. He had mentioned Susie in his last letter to his sister though. And when she responded there was no reference to Susie the secretary. Elsie was a good kid.

Jim arrived at his office with minutes to spare before his Intro to Shakespeare class. *Hamlet.* Imagine reading the play for the first time, which he was sure was true for many of his students. It was quite a responsibility, he thought. And, he had to admit, an opportunity. Where to begin, that was the question.

———⊙———

David Stein checked his mail box in the main office, picked up his cup of coffee, black, and his *Collegian* before settling down in his own office to prepare his face to meet the faces he would meet. Nothing but junk mail. No word yet from The University of Chicago Press about his Kafka manuscript, but at least there was no polite letter of rejection.

As he listened to the birds singing in the tall birch tree directly outside his half-open window--Jasper must have been in to air the office--, David noted on his calendar that it was Tuesday, April first. Good grief. He had totally forgotten. He had been warned that the department members, faculty and staff, took great glee in making April Fool's Day an unforgettable experience, and not always a pleasant one. He didn't know why this suddenly made him nervous. After all, what could they do? he thought. Or rather what could they not do? Well, he would be wary.

David's pipe, which he had automatically removed from his jacket pocket and put in his mouth, felt smooth and familiar between his lips. Let his colleagues and the secretaries tease him about his chewing on an unlit pipe–he was enormously pleased with himself for giving up smoking. He knew that by not giving up the pipe as well he was probably clinging to his image of himself as a distinguished-looking, if not particularly handsome, prematurely greying assistant professor of English, but so what. Stretching out his long legs, he put his feet on the desk and half concentrated on an article on student unrest, half thought ahead to his class at 9:00.

Student unrest. Hmmm. Most unusual. Huston College existed in a time warp. Oh, there had been, he heard, a certain amount of unrest in the 60s. Nothing, however, like what he had experienced at The Ohio State University, where he had finished his doctorate the previous year. They had actually briefly closed the whole University down, shortly after the Kent State students were killed that May of '70, and before it closed down, everywhere he went the national guard stood at the ready with their guns. A heady time, in a way, in which one had to decide whether to cut classes and join the students protesting the Vietnam war, or not. Many of his own students–all graduate students taught Freshman English--refused to come to class so that they could protest and seemed to expect this not to impinge on their grades. He had to explain to them that he admired their taking a stand, but that there was a cost. But if Huston students objected to the Vietnam war, nothing seemed to remain now of the kind of objections to it that still fueled unrest in many other universities.

Even though moving from Ohio to Pennsylvania was like moving to the other side of the world, David was, nevertheless, rather enjoying his first year at Huston. It may not be the best known small school in the country, but it did boast some distinguished graduates, the poet, Graham Torme, the present senator from this very state, the former head of the Humanities Council. The grounds were beautiful, the buildings gothic, the outside world remote. Sometimes, he admitted to himself, he felt that he was living outside of time, which was slowly passing him by, but on the whole he was happy to be where he was. At least he had a job! And he was not in Vietnam fighting a useless, unwinnable war.

The coffee tasted unusually bad, David thought. Come to think of it, Susie Marsh, the young secretary who brewed the coffee each morning, had not been in the office as usual when he picked up his mail. Nor had Nora Stern, the pleasant, rotund senior secretary, been there. Part of April Fool's day? An absence of staff? Or were they hiding, brewing up something worse than the bad coffee?

And where was Erica Berne? Erica always looked in on David with an ingratiating smile and a sugary "Good morning" on her way to the adjoining office where he was sure she spent every possible free moment with her ear to the wall, hoping to pick up some incriminating bit of conversation with which she might undermine David with their fellow colleagues in the English Department. It was not that Erica bore David any more ill will than she bore any of them, though he fancied she was particularly bothered by the young; it was simply that as the most recent addition to the department at Huston College David was blessed with the unhappy vulnerabilities which accompanied moving into the least desirable office, the one situated next door to Erica's.

The chattering of students as they moved down the hall filtered into his office. When the bell rang, releasing yet others, David quickly glanced through the notes he had prepared the previous night, thrust his notebook and a slim volume of Samuel Beckett's *Endgame* into his briefcase, and walked briskly back to the main office. He needed to check with Susie on the time of the faculty meeting which he vaguely remembered was to be held this afternoon.

"Have you heard?" Susie inquired, as David and Jim Strand entered the main office door, almost colliding with each other and with her.

"Heard what?" David asked, with a queer sense of anxiety that Susie's excitement entailed bad news.

"Dr. Berne's fiancé has been murdered!"

"I know, April Fool," Jim guffawed as he moved to the boxes to pick up his mail.

"You mean it, don't you?" David asked, even as Susie began babbling the details.

"I wouldn't joke about that!" Susie continued. "Her fiancé, Dr. Berne's, was stabbed to death in London, stabbed and robbed." Susie's eyes glittered as if she could see the incident. "She heard about it last night and called Nora this morning to say she wouldn't be in. Nora went to her house and found her in a state of hysteria when she got there. She's going to stay with her until arrangements can be made."

David was so shocked that he barely heard the bell ring and rushed out, calling back that he would return for more information after his class. Although he had every reason to dislike Erica—she had made nothing but trouble for him since his arrival on campus the previous fall—the death seemed unnecessarily cruel. Unbelievably so, in fact.

It had been so hard to conceive of anyone courting Erica to begin with. In some ways the prissy associate professor was merely the traditional old maid, ageless, though probably in her fifties, not unpretty, but angular and sour, though often covering her disappointment in life with a syrupy friendliness. David had not been taken in by her overtures of friendship—her warm offers to help were fairly transparent—but he had grown to resent and almost to fear the acid remarks about him which trickled back from his colleagues, Nora, and even Wilfred Black, his department chair. Despite Black's laugh of dismissal over Erica's labeling of David and Jim as the "fraternity boys," Black took Erica far too seriously for David's sense of well-being.

David's class was chatting while waiting for him, and he noted with pleasure that Jill Lake was sitting next to the seat that was reserved for him at the head of the seminar table. Jill's blue-green eyes were fastened on her book, but she looked up and smiled as he entered the room. The smile was enigmatic, faintly amused, as if she knew something of which he was unaware, but it was less mocking than inviting.

David knew that his students were clearly out of romantic bounds, and Jill was his advisee to boot. He had heard many stories about the good old days when professors routinely dumped their wives of many years for their students without repercussions or threats to their careers. This behavior was apparently rampant in the French Department in the 60s where several of the professors did indeed have young wives, having disposed of the older ones with seemingly little conscience. There was also the famous story of the history professor, who had come to his class with a pair of tickets to a football game in his fly and asked who wanted to go with him. But such behavior was no longer tolerated in the 70s, and David knew it shouldn't be. It didn't take the women's movement to know that grading the person you romanced was a huge conflict of interest. Still, one could dream. And for some reason, the feeling of safety from involvement only tended to enhance David's attraction for the elegantly lovely girl.

"April is the cruelest month/Breeding lilacs out of the dead land, mixing/memory and desire, stirring dull roots with spring rain," David almost sang to get the attention of the class. "Who can tell me where that is from on this cruel April day?" he inquired.

A chorus of 3 students responded, "Eliot's 'The Waste Land.'"

"Excellent and now, on to Samuel Beckett's waste land. Let us look at his own favorite play in his canon, *Endgame*."

Mary Gill was not, it seems, ready for a discussion of the Irish novelist and playwright's drama. "Have you heard about Professor Berne's fiancé's murder?" Mary flashed a half smile, not bothering to hide her pleasure at the tragic news; Erica had been a source of torment to her since the beginning of the semester when Mary had signed up as a new graduate student for the professor's course in Bibliograpy and Historiography.

The class of fifteen graduate and upper-level undergraduates buzzed in reaction. Some had heard, others hadn't, but all were shocked. Despite Erica's unpopularity with the students nobody, with the exception of Mary, felt much glee at the news. They had noted more signs of humanity than usual since Professor Berne's engagement during the previous semester and were hoping for an even greater relaxation of her taut personality as a result of the now never-to-be-completed marriage.

"That's it," Melvin Stuart's voice boomed out over the others. "It was a miracle anyone wanted her in the first place, and God knows no one else will ever carry her off on a white charger now. We've had it!"

David felt compelled to squelch the gossip and continue the class, which he somehow got through, though he also thought Erica's only chance of marriage had probably been removed to the detriment of them all. But as Jill read the part of Clov with just the right hostile subservience to Stanley Green's extravagant Hamm, David began to enjoy the class and felt quickened with hope. He truly enjoyed his students and they were catching on under what he considered his expert, yes, he thought, expert guidance.

Beckett's world might be bleak, but it was also exhilarating.

"The main difference between *Endgame* and *Waiting for Godot*," Maurice Martin pontificated, "is that nothing happens in *Godot*. But here, Clov leaves. Something finally happens."

"Mr. Martin, I beg to differ with you on two counts," David said. "Although it may seem to you that nothing happens in *Waiting for Godot*, one may think of it another way. Nothing *happens*! We will need to think about what that means at some length. And as for Clov leaving? Are you sure that he does? Turn to page 82 and you will discover that Hamm thinks Clov has left, but the stage directions say that he actually hovers at the door, his eyes on Hamm until the end. And if Clov doesn't leave, what is the significance? We'll also take up that question tomorrow."

———※———

Erica usually sat next to Wilfred Black at faculty meetings, but her seat this afternoon was conspicuously empty. Black was still finishing up some work in his office which adjoined the conference room where the meetings were held, and so the room buzzed with talk of Erica and her loss.

"Does anyone know who called with the terrible news?" Leslie Podmonk inquired.

"Probably his family; I think his mother is still alive," Jim suggested. "Hey, where is the funeral? We'd better find out where to send flowers and all that garbage. Should we do it as a department?"

Susie, who was summoned and instructed to contact Nora to find out the particulars, was still chirping with excitement. "Nora told me last week that she was over at Erica's, I mean Dr. Berne's house—they're pretty friendly–and that Dr. Berne showed her all sorts of expensive gifts she had received from the guy. There was apparently a piece of glass art that Nora said blew her away, probably cost him a fortune. When Nora touched it, Erica apparently had a fit. And there was a letter saying he would be here in time for all the preparations."

"The poor chap is probably well out of it," Jim quipped, as Susie retreated to call Nora. "Bad enough to get hooked for the first time at that stage of life, but can you imagine what life with Erica would be like. Better to be stabbed to death than slowly jabbed to death by her tongue over the years." The fact that his remark was close to everyone's honest response made it all the more shocking. But with his blond hair and blue-eyed innocent expression, Jim was used to getting away with outrageous statements.

"Don't you think that's a little tasteless?" Leslie Podmonk asked. Although Erica did not spare Leslie her sharp tongue, the older woman overlooked her sharpness and kept up a rather possessive friendship with her. She specialized in the nineteenth century and clearly felt that her field was superior to Erica's medieval focus. Their friendship was based on a rivalry that they both seemed to enjoy.

Jim had commented to David last week, when David had told him of Erica's designation of them as the 'fraternity boys,' that Erica and Leslie were doubtless the gay girls and didn't even know it, poor things. "It's a classic case of doubling," Jim had informed David.

"What's doubling?"

"It's when you relate to another person as if he or she is a part of yourself. Maybe the darker part that you repress. Leslie looks in the mirror and sees Erica. She wants to possess her. She wants to be her. And in a sense, she is. Sometime I'm going to write a novel about them. I've become more and more interested in the figure of the double and may even ask Black if I can offer a course in it next year, if I'm still here that is."

"Erica may be Leslie's double," David agreed, "but Erica is way too repressed to be gay." Now, with the news of Paul's death, David thought that perhaps she was too repressed for marriage as well—perhaps the murder was a blessing: she could live on dreams of what could have been rather than face the hard reality of what might have proved impossible.

Just as Susie returned to say that nobody answered at Dr. Berne's apartment, Nora came bustling in. "I just put her on a plane to New York. She kept showing me all the gifts he's sent for the last month and crying and crying. I managed to get her bag packed and got her to the airport. And I called the dean's wife to tell her. I know she'd been looking at houses with Erica and thought she'd want to know."

"Did you get the address?" asked Jeffry Platz, the enigmatic, middle-aged, eighteenth century specialist who, according to the students, thought he was Samuel Johnson.

"No, I didn't think to get the address there; stupid me. Of course we should send flowers. I'll call over to the Baptist church. I think that's where she met him and someone might know him and know his family's address in New York."

Jim noticed that Margaret Lambert, who taught journalism courses in the department, seemed more upset than anybody else. She was certainly not a special friend of Erica's. Perhaps, Jim thought, the fact that she was quite pregnant made her more vulnerable to the death that was in their midst.

"Poor Erica," Margaret commented, taking a handkerchief out of her purse and dabbing at her eyes. And so near her wedding date."

Black emerged from his office, the student representatives arrived, and the meeting began. Black made a few remarks about Erica and hoped all would be particularly kind. Jim scribbled a note-- "For a brilliant man, he's sure got a blind spot over that dame"–and passed it quietly to David, who nodded slightly in agreement. Of course Erica did add something special to the department's stature. She had published steadily over the years on things medieval, and if the students sometimes complained about her classes, they did seem to respect her scholarship. Black had more student complaints about her than he cared to think about, but he attempted to handle them rather than confronting her and really coming to grips with the situation.

Black himself had apparently never married and David speculated that he might have a soft spot for Erica who, if not exactly flirtatious with Black, seemed for some reason to have significant power over him. It was hard to tell why, but Black, for whatever reasons, remained Erica's protector.

The meeting was brief. As it broke up, Nora stopped in to say she had been unable to locate anyone at the church who knew the whereabouts of Paul's family, although they had heard about the death. It had not, after all, been the place where the two had met. The minister, in fact, had made inquiries among Erica's acquaintances for the details so that the church community could send flowers to the funeral but without any success. They would simply have to send flowers to her apartment upon her return.

The murder, David thought, as he exited the meeting with Jim, had certainly removed any fear of April Fool's Day pranks. Fate had played its own hand.

CHAPTER II

Erica sat on the airplane in a daze. Nora had been helpful but terribly annoying. As if her sympathy could really help. As if anything could. She had no idea whatsoever how she could possibly go on with her life. Paul had been her best friend, her lover, her comfort, and her hope.

She tried to make the time pass by looking through a magazine that was in the pocket of the seat in front of her. Pictures of beautiful women showing off their slim legs in luxurious resorts. Disgusting. Erica closed her eyes and thought of the first time she had met Paul. She had been sitting and reading in a small park near her apartment. He had joined her on the bench and had pulled a book out of his pocket to read. She noticed that it was a mystery novel by one of her favorites, Elizabeth George. Had she started the conversation or had he? She wasn't sure. But soon they were chatting about their favorite detective series and he had suggested that they continue their discussion over a cup of coffee.

She didn't see why not. He was a good looking man, distinguished she thought, probably a bit older than she was, but the gray hair and slightly gray beard and mustache had their appeal. She laughed inside to think that at her age she was actually being picked up. They had ambled to a nearby coffee shop and continued to enjoy their conversation.

"A teacher of medieval literature? I haven't read much beyond Chaucer," he confessed, "but I can only imagine how fascinating that period must be. I always regretted," he confessed, "that I never did graduate work after college. Rather fell into my work for a company in Europe and have spent my life traveling. Sales. Must seem pretty mundane to you."

But it didn't seem mundane, Erica recalled. She had been very interested in hearing about those travels and her heart beat rather quickly when he said how sorry he was that he had never settled down, married, had the family that he had once dreamed of. A family was, of course, out of the question at their age, but marriage. She had long given up on marriage, but she couldn't help thinking about it, even at their first meeting. She loved the way Paul listened. It was refreshing after the continual friction she felt in her life at the college to spend time with a person who showed her not only respect but also interest. Yes, she had said, she would be happy to have dinner with him the following Friday after he returned from a short trip he was about to take.

Erica looked out the window and saw only clouds below. Where was she heading? What would she, could she do?

CHAPTER III

"This lousy beer tastes like nector," Jim beamed as he finished his second, lit a cigarette, and poured himself another from the pitcher. Jim and David had taken to sharing a pitcher on Friday afternoons to celebrate the end of the week at Fritz's, a local bar frequented by students and some of the faculty.

"What's the matter, David? You look really depressed."

"The long expected letter from The University of Chicago Press arrived today with the bad news," David confessed, finding it painful to talk about it. "Their readers liked the Kafka manuscript but not enough to make them publish it. They suggest it would work better as a series of articles."

"Well, don't give up, for Christ's sake; that's only your second try. Send it to a few more publishers before you get morose."

"I will, but it takes those bloody presses six months to turn you down and I was just hoping this would be it."

"Well, what the hell. Send it around to a few at the same time. It's unlikely that they'll ever know, and if you get more than one acceptance you can always tell the other ones they kept it too long."

"I don't know. I'd feel uneasy. The whole thing is a little weird anyway. After all, my field is Modern Drama. Why I got hooked on Franz Kafka in the first place beats me. Of course, Beckett and Pinter read Kafka and he's certainly present in their plays, but I probably should have written about that connection. The Godot guys don't know why they are waiting for Godot. Or even who he is. Joseph K. doesn't know what he is accused of or why he deserves the death penalty. Or maybe I should have revised my dissertation on Harold Pinter. There isn't that much out there on him. But everyone has something to say about old Kafka. I'm beginning to feel like Joseph K, lost in the labyrinthine publishing world of academia."

"Don't worry so much, David. I haven't even written a book, and my dissertation on *Measure for Measure* doesn't seem worth revising to me. At least you have a manuscript to send around."

The Two men sat and drank for a while. Jim thought about how he was going to escape the kind of pressure David was under to publish while David thought about how hard it was for young scholars to survive these days in academia and how much work and luck he needed over the next few years to make it.

"I'm not sure about this academic gig we're in," Jim almost muttered into his beer. "I find the students, especially the under-grads, can hardly read Shakespeare. I have to hold their hands. Just to get them interested, I have to point out how violent his plays are. I have to get them up on their feet performing scenes just to make sure they actually read the words rather than those Cliff Notes or whatever books about the plays."

"I know, I know," David agreed. "But I think your students like that performing part of your classes. They've asked me to add it to my drama classes. I have them read out loud, but maybe it's time to have them memorize scenes. Sounds like it works."

"Yah, it works. But sometimes I see some of our esteemed colleagues looking into the window of my classroom with disdain. Lots of eye-rolling over my methods. Like we're just playing around with plays. And with the god Shakespeare as well. I know we're lucky to have jobs at all, but sometimes I think this place is just too outside of time to even exist."

Dimly, through the noise of the juke box, David detected Jill's familiar voice in the next booth and he felt himself turning red under Jim's stare. "Hey, Romeo, who's back there? You been holding out on me?" Jim asked, pretending to raise himself up to see over the booth but stopping when he saw how uncomfortable he was making David feel. "Okay, Okay, later, but now I know why you haven't dug the last two girls I produced for you. You got something going on the side?"

"Change the subject," David ordered in a whisper.

"Hey, look," Jim laughed, waving to someone out the window.

"Oh my God, that finishes a great day," David moaned as he saw Erica Berne passing by. She had returned from New York and was back at school, generally rebuffing offers of sympathy with a hostile defensiveness. "Just gives her more ammunition. Is she spying on us? "

"Fuck her," Jim laughed. I thought her little tragedy had almost turned her human there for a day or two, but she just gave one of my best students a D on her midterm in Historiography and Bibliography and the poor kid doesn't know how to cope with her."

"I'm not sure I do either," David confessed. "I don't understand why people don't stand up to her more or why Black lets her get away with so much shit. Like even you, Jim. Did you intervene for your student? Look over her paper? "

"I did actually try to have a word with the good lady. Thought if I approached it from the 'How can I help Mary do better' angle that she might not jump me, but she cut me off with the big news that this isn't a high school and Mary is a big girl. Actually, Mary's just a little bit of a thing, but Erica didn't leave me much room to pursue the topic."

Jill and her friend Gwen passed by the booth on their way out and stopped to say hello. "Have you read my paper yet?" Jill inquired. "I'm afraid you may not agree with my conclusions." Her eyes held a faintly amused look and she seemed to challenge him with her smile.

"No," David lied, not quite knowing why. The paper had been exceptional and he had been forced, despite some preconceived ideas of his own, to agree quite fully with her conclusions. "Sorry, I'll get to it this weekend. This is Professor Strand, by the way, Miss Lake and Miss Thomas. You'll probably both be in Dr. Strand's Shakespeare course one of these days."

"Oh, we know Professor Strand," Jill laughed.

"Would you girls care to sit down with a couple of tired professors for a beer?" Jim asked, embarrassing David, who felt they could really get into trouble if they were seen drinking beer with their students.

"Sorry, we have to dash," Jill said.

"Another time we'd be delighted," Gwen assured them, and the girls were gone.

"Now which one is it brings the blush to the forehead of our young scholar?" Jim teased, "the diminutive, but deliciously delicate Miss Lake or the buxom and bonnie Miss Thomas?"

But David only laughed and they finished their beers and left. David felt vaguely disturbed by almost everything in his day.

"I must speak to Black," Erica muttered to herself as she entered the Barnes & Noble bookstore on the corner. She had forty papers to correct this weekend and felt entitled to a reward. Disgusting fraternization with the students! Her throat ached with fury, but she continued her muttering. "He'll probably refuse to speak to them about it, but if he won't, I will. I'll put an end to it. They may not have been sitting at the same table, but you could hardly tell which were the faculty, which the students."

Erica's eyes traveled down the aisle and settled on Jill Lake, who was chatting with her friend while they browsed. She could hear the fat one saying --well maybe not fat, but obscenely overdeveloped--"You were blushing, Jill. Now which one could it be? The dashing, but cynical professor of the age of rebirth or the prematurely graying master of modern drama?"

"They're both probably gay," Jill retorted, looking busily for a book on the shelf.

"I somehow don't think so. Why wouldn't you sit down and have a drink with them, Jill? "

"Did she hear us?" Jill hissed, suddenly noticing Professor Berne at the end of the aisle, looking at the section on mysteries.

"I don't think so, and what if she did. We weren't mentioning names."

Erica's eyes stung with tears, which she daren't shed before these repulsive girls. Paul would have saved her from all these sordid encounters. Young, empty-headed girls, obscenely interested in their professors who drank in student haunts, doubtless with the sole purpose of titillating them, arousing hopes, God knows even... if Paul had lived she would have been able to...

Erica hastily picked a mystery from the shelf just as Gwen and Jill moved past her. When she got in line, she elbowed her way past the girls, paid the cashier, and left abruptly, walking out into the cruel sunlight, vaguely nauseated by the smells of spring. The beautiful day excluded and mocked her, but she managed to hold back her tears until she reached the car. And she managed to guide the car the few short blocks to her apartment despite being almost blinded with the rage which she could not manage to dispel.

Once home, she poured herself a double bourbon on the rocks and threw herself into her favorite chair. Life was far worse than it was before she met Paul, she thought. He had clearly made her the center of *his* life. Long letters from France, Germany, Italy, Switzerland... Details about his hotels, his sales, the slight sightseeing that he managed to get in. Always the wish that she were there with him. And that first gift, a lovely leather purse from Florence. Every time she looked at it now, she began to cry. She had put it away rather than use it. Just too painful.

After downing half of her drink, Erica produced *The Wrong Victim* from its bag and did her best to lose herself in its pages.

—«(◊)»—

Jill left Gwen at the corner and walked the six, long blocks to her apartment. She was angry and she didn't know why. The song of the birds was piercingly gay and the warm breeze was gently prodding, but she didn't enjoy her walk.

Climbing the one flight of stairs to her tiny apartment, Jill unlocked the door, threw her books on her desk and herself on her sofa-bed. She lay flat on her back, scowling at the ceiling and tried to figure out why she felt so enraged. Her apartment, small though it was, really only one room, a corner of which was a slightly separate kitchen, usually offered her comfort. After four years of enduring dormitory life at the University of Pennsylvania, she had felt it essential to have a place of her own, a luxury she could ill afford on her graduate stipend. But as she rose from her bed and began to pace the floor, Jill felt her apartment was more of a cage than a haven.

Why was she so angry? She absently went to the refrigerator and took out an apple. Kicking off her shoes, she curled up on her comfortable, overstuffed chair, munched on the apple, and tried to sort out her feelings.

Why hadn't she accepted Professor Strand's invitation and joined the two professors for a beer? Why was she always so damned prissy about everything? She knew David wasn't gay. Maybe it wasn't just her interest in him that made her sense that he was taken with her. Maybe there really was something developing between them that was quite distinct from what a teacher-student relationship should be.

Her first semester at Huston had been almost as unhappy as her undergraduate years. Not that those years were terrible, but

Jill had not fit in well. The classes weren't all bad. In fact she had pretty much fallen in love with her history professor, but everyone knew that he was married. He had become just a bitter-sweet fantasy, though his lectures were truly fascinating. But there had been a distinctly anti-intellectual atmosphere in her dormitory and it had taken her a long time to make the few friends who had made life there endurable. Everyone's main concern had been with dates, and she was uncomfortable with the excessive drinking and the casual sex that were the dormitory way of life. It wasn't that she had any trouble getting dates, but almost none of them took. Once they found out that she wasn't interested in alcohol or a quick lay and that she didn't pretend to think their jokes were funny, the parade of young men gave up rather quickly; and the few who persisted were, for one reason or another, not what she was looking for. Oh, she did have a brief romance her sophomore year during a summer stint as a camp counselor, but Joe hadn't kept in touch when they parted ways and she was way over her disappointment, wondering now what she really had seen in him.

David was the man! She had been disappointed in her courses the first semester, but now that she was taking his seminar and a good course in the eighteenth century with Professor Platz, she began to feel that her work at Huston was worthwhile. Of course there was the blasted course she was taking with Professor Berne—she absolutely dreaded going to that class and the work was as senseless as it was arduous, but she was really excited by her work with David. She understood the way he thought, and he was not in the least dogmatic. On the contrary, he managed to make her feel that the points she made in class were significant. Maybe he was a little too old for her, but maybe not. This was his first year teaching—everyone knew that. Everyone knew too, she assured herself, that women were more mature than men. What were a few years?

Why, then, had she been so quick to say no? Would there be other opportunities to get to know David on a social level? Was she, so to speak, wishing to play with fire? Perhaps it was Professor Berne who was bothering her. Running into her in the bookstore, just when Gwen was questioning her about her feelings, was extremely unsettling.

Jill pitched the apple core into the basket. Yes, that was it. Professor Berne enraged her. It was as if the older woman was hovering over any possible relationship she might develop with David Stein, hovering and ready to pounce. Jill couldn't help it if Berne's chance for happiness had been stolen from her.

Having pinned down the reason for her angst, Jill felt somewhat better. She went to her desk, gathered her books, and got down to work. I have youth on my side, she thought. Hey Erica, don't mess with me.

Margaret stopped at the grocery store on her way home. What was she craving, she asked herself, as she pushed the shopping cart down the aisle. Apples. Really? Yes. Probably she should crave something wicked, marsh mellows or chocolate. Oh, well, apples it is she said, picking up a bag of them.

As she continued up and down the aisles, buying quite a bit just in case the baby came early, she thought back about the faculty meeting. Was she really crying for Erica, she wondered. Erica had not been as nasty about her as she was rumored to be about David and Jim, but Margaret had heard from Leslie that Erica had disdain for journalism and didn't think it should be part of an English Department's offerings.

Oh, well, Erica was old school for sure, not only in terms of disdaining anything the least unconventional, but also in terms of preferring older people to the young. On second thought, Erica didn't seem to be drawn to older people either. She didn't know if she was really feeling sorry for Erica's loss or sorry for herself and the rest of the faculty and students who would have to bear the results of that loss.

Margaret finished her shopping, felt the movement in her stomach with true joy, and hastened to her car. After depositing the groceries in the back seat, she struggled her bulk into the front, noticing that there was barely room enough to drive. "It will all be okay, sweet one," she whispered to her unborn child. With a little luck, Conrad would be home ahead of her and help her up with the packages.

Chapter IV

Nora had something on her mind. Susie could tell. "I think I'll stop by Erica's office–she seems out-of-shape," Nora said, taking a piece of paper out of her typewriter and putting it away.

"You're too nice, Nora," Susie laughed. "I'll take my break when you get back, but not with Erica thanks."

"Listen Susie," Nora almost whispered, even though everyone was teaching or in their offices and the two women were alone in the main office, "if you promise not to say a word..."

"Promise, cross my heart," Susie beamed, eager to break up her day with some good gossip. "I know, you're going to tell me Erica has a new boy friend and is living with him in sin, lest any accidents befall him before the appointed hour."

"Now, Susie," Nora scolded, waddling over to the door. She turned back and added, "It's about what we were talking about the other day. I'll be right back and I'll think about telling you, but it's serious and you have to mean it about the promise."

"I do," Susie smiled. She decided not to joke further since she really wanted to get any tidbit of gossip to liven up her rather dull routine.

Tapping softly on Erica's office door, Nora entered, received a nod from Erica, and lowered her bulk onto a chair. "Anything I can do for you, dear?" Nora inquired sympathetically.

"What could you possibly do for me?" Erica asked, suggesting to Nora that her case was beyond anyone's help.

"I just know how hard things must be for you and wondered if I could be of any help."

"Not unless you can bring Paul back," Erica snapped. Then she noticed Nora's kind eyes and felt she had gone too far. For days now though, she had felt those over-kind eyes on her and Nora made her feel uncomfortable. Making a huge effort, however, Erica completed the expected ritual of Nora's visits to her office. Erica never drank the coffee in the main office. She made her own, which sat on a small table next to her desk. Now she offered Nora a cup of coffee complete with Sweet and Low. Erica's own trim figure was not automatic—she watched her diet with care, but it amused her to supply the Sweet and Low for Nora, who took the inevitable Milky Way out of her bulky purse to help keep the pounds on her bulky person.

"Thanks," Nora said, only slightly offended by Erica's hostility which she was used to and which held a weird kind of fascination for her.

"The students are getting more wretched every year," Erica complained, flipping over the bibliographies which were sitting on her desk. "You would think they could spell and copy correctly. They don't seem to have any idea of how to use the library. Look at this!" She held up a paper by two fingers as if it were contaminated. "Miss Jill Lake, clearly too entranced with that fraternity boy, David Stein, to pick a viable topic. The plays and novels of one Samuel Beckett, a singularly overrated writer and not even dead for that matter."

Nora's plump face had turned pink. "Shhh… David's office is right next door–he doesn't teach this hour so he's probably there now." She raised the coffee to her lips and took a large gulp. "The coffee tastes off," she complained, "absolutely…"

"I don't care a hoot in hell if he hears," Erica chuckled. "Wilfred must have lost his mind when he hired him. Do you know where I saw him on Friday? Him and his side-kick Jim? At Fritz's, drinking, literally hanging out with the students. I was passing by and happened to look in the window. I plan to talk to Wilfred about it, and if he won't act I'll have to talk to David myself."

Erica paused as Nora suddenly turned extremely white and almost fell off her chair.

"Why Nora, whatever is the matter?"

"I don't know, Erica. I feel…" Nora stood up and before Erica could come to her aid she slumped down to the floor, writhing in pain.

"Help! Help! Someone. David! Come in here this instant. Don't be so slow," Erica screeched in the hallway.

David had heard Erica's shrill, complaining voice naming Jill and himself through the wall and had tried his best to ignore it. When he heard the thunderous crash which was Nora, he ran out into the hallway. But by the time Erica had clutched at him and dragged him into her office, Nora was clearly dead.

CHAPTER V

Jill had come to see David about her next paper. She had done well enough on her first one, and she admitted to herself that the appointment was something of an excuse for further contact. But she had found Samuel Beckett more to her taste than Harold Pinter whose plays frightened her; and she couldn't seem to get a handle on them or even find a topic on which to write.

When she knocked tentatively on his office door, David's voice boomed, "Come in." As she entered, Jill saw that David's feet were up on the desk, but he hurriedly dropped them to the floor when he saw who it was: Jill could have sworn that he actually blushed. His unease somehow made her feel less nervous, and when he actually rose and indicated a chair, she half expected him to push it and her in as if they were at a restaurant, although there was no place to push her in to.

"Oh, Miss Lake," he began, "and what can I do for you?"

"It's our next paper, Dr. Stein. I can't seem to get oriented or to find a topic I can dig into. I thought you might be able to suggest something."

"I see," David smiled, suddenly feeling ten feet tall and enormously wise. "What strikes you most about Pinter's plays?"

"They scare me to death," Jill laughed. "Even though they're funny. I didn't even want to finish *The Birthday Party* and since Nora was murdered I'm just so on edge that I'm afraid even to look at them too closely."

"I can understand that," David replied. "But actually, some of Pinter's plays have quite promising outcomes. You just have to go beneath the surface a bit. Subtext. I'll tell you what, you might try one of his later plays, *The Homecoming*. It's more difficult than *The Birthday Party*, but it's also more challenging in interesting ways. Or maybe try writing a paper on his latest one, *Old Times*. The main character in that play really works something important out for herself, at least I think she does. That might be just the ticket, given what's going on here."

Jill smiled but David seemed to have come to the end of the conversation. He stared into space for what seemed an endless amount of time. Maybe this was an authentic Pinter pause: he had been discussing the British playwright's silences with them, so maybe he was just offering her an example. And she was supposed to figure out what was under it? What was it he called it–the subtext?

"Okay, I'll give it a whirl," Jill said, getting up and heading for the door. But she turned back. "I understand you were there when it happened," she said, "Nora's death I mean, when she died." She didn't mean to pry but sensed some need in David to talk about it.

"I was too late," David answered. "She was already dead when I got to Dr. Berne's office."

"I gather from the papers and from Susie that the police think it was Dr. Berne who was meant to die, not Nora."

"That's right," David agreed. "The poison was found in Erica's,

I mean in Dr. Berne's Sweet and Low packets; Dr. Berne just happened not to have been drinking coffee at all that day–she had been having trouble sleeping."

"The awful thing," Jill said, "is that I can hardly think of anyone who wouldn't want to do it–including myself–not to Nora, of course, but to Dr. Berne. I suppose I shouldn't talk to you about it, but you are my adviser and that woman has been making my life miserable this semester. She gave me a C- on my Bibliography on Beckett, which you seemed to find perfectly acceptable in my last paper and her comments…"

"Miss Lake, Erica Berne resents pretty girls." David bit his lip knowing he shouldn't discuss Erica's prejudices with a student– but instead of stopping he found himself continuing to denigrate Erica. "Your youth, your loveliness, and your intelligence are more than Dr. Berne can tolerate," David blurted out, enchanted by the way Jill's long, brown hair flowed down her back, entranced by the way the earring that dangled from her left ear jingled in the sunlight that poured in through the window.

"Who do you think did it, Dr. Stein?" Jill asked, blushing slightly under David's gaze.

"I don't know," David said. "I have some ideas, of course, but despite the general hostility that Dr. Berne seems to provoke, I can't imagine anyone capable of murdering her."

"Will she come back?"

"Oh, I'm sure she will. She was quite hysterical yesterday, and I don't blame her. Of course the killer may seek another opportunity, but the police plan to keep her under their wing for some time. I'm sure she'll be very careful, and I imagine she'll collect herself and return." After what seemed to Jill like another Pinter pause he continued. "Who do the students suspect?"

Jill came back to the chair and sat down again. "You won't repeat anything if I tell you?" she inquired. "Greer Purlieu has had an even worse time with Dr. Berne than I have and he gets pretty stoned sometimes—some people think he simply had it with her and poisoned the Sweet and Low. He knows she has it because she's had him on the carpet several times in her office and he commented to a group of us weeks ago that all the saccharine she dumps in her coffee hasn't done much to sweeten her up."

David leaned forward slightly in his chair. "Maybe, maybe. Interesting," he said. "Though seems a bit pat, perhaps. The police think Nora knew something that might have helped." He wondered if he should go on. They certainly seemed to have strayed far from Pinter's menacing plays to what felt like the menace in their midst. Maybe he was sharing far more than he should with Jill. He reached for his pipe, leaned back in his chair, and without even realizing what he was doing, he put one leg back up on his desk, then the other.

"What do you mean?"

"Well, it seems she had some fat piece of gossip she was going to tell Susie after her coffee break, and Susie thought what with Nora being so sympathetic and concerned about Erica that maybe she knew someone really had it in for her, that ... "

"You mean she knew who her own killer was?"

"Possibly," David replied. "Susie is beside herself that she didn't detain Nora for the gossip before she left. She seems to think she might have prevented the whole thing in some way."

Jill suddenly felt tears come to her eyes and had no idea why. It was so sudden and David was so taken aback that he bit on his pipe for almost a minute before he realized his position, removed his feet from the desk, fumbled in his pocket for a handkerchief, and gave it to her.

"What's the matter, Jill?" he asked. Through her tears Jill couldn't help noting that David had dropped the formal Miss Lake.

"I'm frightened," she said. "I'm frightened of Pinter's plays, I'm frightened of Erica Berne, and I'm scared of her would-be murderer!" Her sobs were coming faster though they were mixed with laughter as she realized her own ridiculousness. "I don't even know if I can finish the term," she sobbed, burying her head in David's handkerchief, completely bewildered by her own outburst.

Oh hell, David thought, rising from his chair. He tentatively, then firmly drew Jill into his arms. Erica is at home, the door is closed, and the girl is scared, he rationalized, his heart beating at an alarming rate.

"Now, now," he muttered into her hair, "there's nothing to be scared of. I'll protect you." As he soothed her and her sobs diminished, Jill slowly became aware that she was in the arms of the man whose arms she had never dared dream she would be in, and just when she was afraid that he was only being a kind and protective adviser, David lifted her tear-streaked face and kissed her slowly and deliberately on her lips.

"To hell with Erica Berne," he smiled into her face, "I'm glad I did that even if I get fired, and I'll protect you from Erica, from her would-be murderer, and even from Harold Pinter if need be, so don't worry."

Jill sniffled happily, resting her head on his chest and feeling almost safe. She couldn't quite get the words out though that were only half formulated in her own mind, words that contained knowledge of the killer that she couldn't articulate, even to herself.

———◦《◉》◦———

For the next few days the offices were swarming with police. The faculty and staff were questioned at great length and all students who had any classes with Professor Berne also had their turn. For some reason, fewer parents removed students from the college than had been anticipated. Perhaps this was because the end of the semester was approaching and the newspapers had made it clear that a specific victim had been intended; the crime had been carefully planned and had misfired by the merest mischance. They asserted that the police had several clues and would probably be making an arrest within days. The intended victim was being properly guarded. There was surely not a psychopath at large in pursuit of young women or men.

Despite such assurances, the tension was palpable. All English classes had been canceled for the rest of the week, and no student who had ever been in one of Professor Berne's classes was permitted to leave town.

David made a brief appearance at the inquest where he described his efforts to help Nora. The verdict of murder was easily established, but the identity of the murderer remained unknown. Questioned later at great length by a Detective Norman Halloway who was in charge of the case, David observed that a young man in uniform sat in the corner taking copious notes. Halloway was middle-aged, balding, seemingly laid back, and certainly not threatening in any way.

Yes, David confessed, he had heard some of the conversation between Nora and Dr. Berne through the wall of his office; the walls were thin and Professor Berne had a particularly sharp, piercing voice. Yes, Professor Berne had been complaining about his behavior. Yes, she had complained about him before. No, he did not wish her dead. No, he did not feel threatened by her behavior toward him. *That, of course, was a lie. David was frankly almost sorry that the murderer had missed the mark. He didn't exactly wish Erica dead, but it seemed bitterly cruel that a woman like Nora should have died in her place—and irrational though it seemed, David blamed Erica.*

"Were there any people who might bear a grudge against Dr. Berne?" Halloway asked, giving David a penetrating look that made him uncomfortable.

"There were many people" David replied, "who might bear a grudge against Erica, myself included, but I hardly think anyone would wish to kill her. I'm sure you know that the woman has recently suffered the loss of her fiancé --people understand her rather acid behavior and feel sorry for her." *Another lie. David didn't think that anyone who had felt sorry for Erica had done so for long. His sympathy surely hadn't lasted long. How sorry could you feel for a lioness about to spring at your throat?*

Halloway allowed a long silence before he continued questioning the young man. It was as if he were reading David's thoughts. "In your estimation, did the professor grade unfairly?" he inquired.

"Yes, in my estimation she probably graded unfairly. But so many students have suffered in this area that I can't possibly point the finger."

"I understand," Halloway continued his interrogation, "that you and Jim Strand are close friends and that Jim has been known to make particularly gross remarks about Professor Berne." *I wonder if he'll give up his buddy, and if not, how he'll handle this one. He sure is a cool character.*

"Oh, everybody knows that Jim says outrageous things, but he behaves perfectly normally. I can certainly vouch for Jim," David assured the detective.

Yes, there had been some gossip about Leslie Podmonk and her jealousies, but there didn't seem to be much motive there since Professor Berne's fiancé was out of the way and the two women had doubtless resumed their friendship. No, he didn't know that Erica had refused to have anything further to do with Professor Podmonk. *This was indeed news and David wondered where Detective Halloway had picked up that piece of gossip and what was behind it; being uncomfortable with the whole conversation, he decided not to ask.*

No, there was no possibility in his mind that Nora had been the intended victim. She was a thoroughly pleasant woman with no enemies, either student or faculty that he knew of. No, nor administrators. She was efficient, friendly. Yes, Jim Strand had made the rather tasteless remark that he couldn't stand a sloppy killer--*now who told that one—doubtless Leslie—they all had been present when Jim made the remark*-- but no one ever took his remarks seriously and David had to confess that given a choice many people could probably have better spared Erica than Nora, though of course it wasn't a question of choice. *Why did he feel so threatened? Halloway was pleasant enough, rather fatherly, didn't seem to suspect him, was talking to him as if they were fellow investigators hunting down the clues.* Yes, anyone could have slipped into Professor Berne's office and replaced the Sweet and Low in her packets with cyanide. No one was in the habit of keeping offices locked during the day at least, and most people knew Erica kept her packets in her desk drawer. No, he hadn't seen anyone going into her office other than Erica herself.

"Tell me Professor Stein," David heard Halloway ask, "what exactly is your relationship to Jill Lake?" *There it was. No one, absolutely no one knew how he felt about Jill, though Erica had apparently decided that Jill had a crush on him, and only he had overheard the conversation between Erica and Nora through the wall, so how could Halloway be onto this? Unless Erica had said something, unless... no, she wouldn't go so far as to suspect he meant to kill her over Jill; she hadn't even seen him with Jill in the bar!*

"She's a student of mine. Why do you ask?" David said as innocently as he could.

"Is that all there is to it?" Halloway asked with a slight smile.

"Yes. I've never had a date with Miss Lake: she's merely a graduate student and an advisee. I certainly consider her an intelligent and attractive young lady, but as my student she is definitely out of bounds to me even if I were interested in dating her," David lied.

"Very high road," Halloway suggested, smiling as if he knew David was lying.

As Detective Halloway asked questions about other members

of the faculty, David felt more and more uneasy. He took out his pipe and put it in his mouth. No, Wilfred Black was the last person he would suspect; he sometimes took a special, protective stance toward Erica, but that was not to imply any hidden romance between the two; the idea was ludicrous. *It had been hard enough to imagine the unknown Paul's romance with Erica much less one with Wilfred Black.* Yes, a romance gone sour would doubtless be a good motive, but Black simply was not the type. No, he didn't know of any student that had a harder time with Erica than any others—and on and on until David was glad to be left alone. The mentioning of Jill had made him extremely nervous, and he wanted to mull over the possibilities and see what he could come up with.

Later, driving the short distance to his apartment, David thought to himself that he was more nervous about kissing Jill than he was about having a murderer at large on campus. He had nothing but scorn in the past for rumors about professors at Ohio State who had hit on their students. Discussing such gossip with other graduate students, he had agreed with the majority of them that such behavior was a gross misuse of power, worthy of expulsion even for those with tenure. One of his friends had even complained to him about a professor who was making unwanted advances toward her. He had advised her to report the professor to the chair. And now, here he was, the villain of the piece. Except… he was pretty sure the advances were not unwanted. And on some level, he was sure he could live with his guilt.

CHAPTER VI

All members of the Department of English, teachers, students, and secretaries alike, were at the funeral that Saturday morning, as well as several professors and secretaries from other departments who had known Nora only slightly. The sun shone brilliantly and the fresh, exhilarating breeze seemed terribly out of place.

Reverend Mellkin spoke in a soft voice about the fine qualities that Nora had possessed. Leslie Podmonk cried ostentatiously, and Erica, wan and grim, looking very much as if she would like to cry, shot disdainful looks at her. But few others shed tears. Greater than the sense of loss was a feeling of injustice, of the innocent struck down in the sunshine, of April gone awry, of lingering danger. Students, especially victims of Erica's, exchanged looks with each other during the service as if to say, Why Nora?

Jim managed to sit next to Susie, who was inconsolable. She had confided to him that she felt responsible for Nora's death. "If only I had persuaded her to reveal the information she promised to tell me before she went into Erica's office, maybe..." He had consoled her as best he could, but she was not rational on the subject and why should she be? She and Nora had been close, not just working together but going out for the occasional dinner. Jim wanted to put his arm around her, but of course he couldn't. He remembered how brazenly the head of the English Department at Harvard had dated his own secretary without suffering the least for what at this small college would be considered way out-of-bounds behavior. What, he asked himself, was he doing here anyway? On the other hand, if he were not here, how would he have come to know this charming if now distraught young lady?

Susie felt Jim's presence and found it somewhat comforting. It would seem very natural, she thought to herself, just to reach out and hold his hand. She, who had not herself gone to college as much as she would like to have done so, attracted now to this handsome young professor who must surely look down on her, his attentions clearly being more fatherly than anything else. He had tried to persuade her that there was no way she could have prevented Nora's death, but he was just being kind. She glanced up and looked at the assembled faculty, staff and students and was sure they blamed her as she blamed herself. A large tear moved slowly down her cheek and to her surprise, Jim slipped a handkerchief out of his pocket and handed it to her. She applied it to her face, not daring to look at him, but feeling his presence as a comfort. She hung onto his handkerchief, sensing the onslaught of more tears to come.

Jill Lake was inscrutable. She sat several rows in front of David and never once looked at him. David was also aware of Halloway and wondered if the detective was watching him. The thought that Halloway might have questioned Jill about her relationship with him was infuriating. As he looked around at the students and sensed how they must be feeling, David felt slightly guilty and was sure that Erica, who seemed to be staring at him, could read his thoughts.

Erica, however, was genuinely upset and as David suspected was holding back her tears. Despite her contempt for Nora's inability to control her obesity and her relish for gossip, the dead woman had been a friend, perhaps her only one, or at least the only one with whom she could talk freely. It was unfair. First Paul and now Nora. Erica knew only too well that most of the people at the funeral wished her dead instead of Nora. It didn't matter who was guilty. She felt their hate for her as a pressure, and she found herself gasping for air in a blind rage.

The people moved silently out of the chapel to their cars and drove the short distance to the cemetery, which was just outside the small town. Looking bright and tastelessly cheerful, Leslie Podmonk rode in David's car with David, Jim, and Jeffry Platz. She fairly bubbled with praise for the affair as if it were a graduation or a wedding. "Wasn't Reverend Mellkin splendid?" She gurgled. "He seemed to know Nora so well, all of her good qualities. And wasn't it a good turnout? I think there must have been a hundred people in the chapel!"

Jim cut in, "Yah, and ninety-nine of them were thinking that we were at the wrong funeral."

"Now, James," Leslie scolded, "you just don't understand Erica as I do. She isn't as bitter as she seems, and she has much more feeling than she displays."

Jeffry Platz sat stony faced. Everyone knew that he had not spoken to Erica or she to him for years, though nobody knew why; Jeffry's reserve was such that no one would dream of asking.

"Leslie, the police seem to think you and Erica are on the outs–at least Halloway asked me about it," David found himself saying, sorry the words had come out even as he said them.

"Nonsense, nonsense... wherever did he get such a notion? Halloway asked me about that too, and there is simply nothing to it. It's just that Erica has kept more to herself since Paul... since Paul's death, that's all. We are the best of friends and I seem to be the only one who understands her."

They rode quietly for a while. David wondered if Leslie might have been as jealous of Nora as she had been of Paul. Could they all be bitterly mistaken? Could she have poisoned the Sweet and Low, knowing full well that Erica was not drinking coffee that day, but that Nora would inevitably come to Erica's office for her coffee break? Or could she have been so angry at being excluded by Erica that she had wished to kill her? She certainly seemed overly cheerful considering the occasion. Wasn't there a tinge of hysteria in her banter? She had wanted to ride with Erica to the cemetery, but Detective Halloway himself had taken Erica with two of his men and had politely suggested that Leslie go with the others.

Erica sat back in the police car and closed her eyes. Halloway was being kind–no questions today... tomorrow would be fine if she felt up to it. No need to come to the station–he would drop by her home or the college if she planned to go in. Meanwhile she mustn't mind Sergeant Kheel keeping an eye on her–he would do his best not to be intrusive–only for her own protection.

Could there really be any protection for her, Erica wondered to herself. She was tired, so tired, truly spent. Riding along in the car, sitting between Halloway and Kheel, she felt almost safe. But if they alone in all the world did not wish her ill, how could they protect her? Paul… Paul…

She remembered the first time he had kissed her. After taking her out for a lovely dinner, he was walking her to her door. After she opened it with her key and turned to say goodnight, he had taken her in his arms, stared into her eyes and ever so slowly had kissed her first on each cheek and then very deliberately on the lips. She felt more warmth in that kiss, she remembered bitterly, than she had perhaps ever felt from anybody before. Her body shook slightly in the car as she remembered how the kiss seemed to awaken a dormant sexuality that she had not even been aware she still could feel. And now…

————)«(0)»(————

Susie had accepted Professor Black's offer of a ride to the cemetery gratefully. "The service helped a bit," she snuffled, wiping the tears from her eyes. "I think somehow everyone felt close because we all liked Nora so much."

Black patted her hand as he drove. "You mustn't take it so hard, Susie."

"But I might have stopped it. Nora was going to tell me something just before she went to Professor Berne's office. If only I had made her tell me then!"

"Well, well, it can't be helped now. Do you have any idea what it was?"

"Just some piece of gossip, I guess. But I kept wondering if it was about Professor Berne. If Nora was into something about her that might point to the murderer. And I have this eerie feeling that I know something that might help, if I could only think what it is."

"Best not to, Susie. Best not to. After all, Nora's knowing something, if she did indeed know anything, didn't help her, now did it?"

"No," Susie confessed. "No it didn't, did it?"

They rode in silence the rest of the way. Susie felt perplexed by Black's attitude. There had almost been a warning note in his voice, as if he wanted her not to think of what it was Nora might have known. Susie was not suspicious by nature, and she had always laughed when the faculty or Nora had kidded about Dr. Berne's mysterious power over Black. Surely he was just trying to calm her down. Or could Black have some reason for not wanting the truth to come out? Could all those jokes have any basis in reality?

A slight shiver ran down Susie's back despite the brightness of the day and the gentleness of the spring breeze. Black was pleasant to work for, clear in his directions, easy going, and very friendly, almost fatherly to her in a way. Hadn't he offered her a ride to the cemetery? Why did she suddenly feel uneasy with him?

Susie wiped her eyes and stopped sniveling. If she weren't careful, she thought, making an effort to smile at Black as he leaned over and patted her shoulder reassuringly, if she weren't careful, she would start seeing a killer behind every Huston bush.

David felt like an adolescent school boy. Jill had not looked at him once at the funeral, neither at the service nor at the cemetery. Even though he had kissed her and held her in his arms, he couldn't get himself to call her now. He sat by the telephone, but he didn't know what to say. Some comforter, some protector. He laughed at himself, fantasizing that she was sitting by her telephone waiting for it to ring. As it got later, he imagined her disappointment and then her anger at him and finally at herself for trusting him.

Why couldn't he call? Because he didn't know what to suggest? Huston was a small town; there was no place they could go to talk or just have a cup of coffee without someone spotting them. He could lose his job. At the very least they should wait until the semester was over and she had finished his course. She could then get a new adviser and the question of hitting on a student would go away. Although he guessed that she still would not be considered an appropriate object of his affections. And this murder business had to be resolved as well before they could really get together. She had been frightened. Perhaps that's why she hadn't resisted his arms. Somehow the puzzle must be solved; and since he was so close to the event, next door so to speak, it seemed to him he should be able to help piece the thing together.

Or was this all sheer rationalization? Was he afraid of a relationship with Jill? She clearly had him on some sort of pedestal. Could he keep her interest as their relationship developed? What relationship, for heaven's sake?

He was still, after all, recovering from his last relationship. Perhaps, he thought, that's why I feel so vulnerable. He had met

Laura the second year of his graduate studies at Ohio State in one of his classes. They had gotten to know each other well when they both were cast in a play that the Department of Theatre had produced, Irish playwright Brendan Behan's *The Hostage*. He found her irresistible in a funny role and admired her sense of confidence as she brought the house down with her singing at each performance. Slowly their friendship had turned into a romance and they became almost inseparable, attached as his friends there told him, at the hip.

He had, of course, dated several young women in the past but this was in many ways his first serious relationship, and it had not ended well. Laura began making excuses about not being able to study with him and she broke several dinner dates. Since he had no idea what he had done to offend her, and she insisted that he hadn't, he was extremely puzzled until he found out by accident that she was having a serious affair with one of his best friends. Terribly hurt, partly by her betrayal and lack of honesty and partly by the actions of somebody he had thought was a good friend, David had become much less trusting of women during the rest of his time in school. He had dated a bit, but he had never gotten deeply involved with anybody else.

Although he still felt rather vulnerable, Jill's admiration seemed truly sincere, he felt real chemistry between them, and if he had not been her professor, he would have asked her out immediately. He knew kissing her was an incredibly stupid way to behave, a true act of academic misconduct, but he had found the moment irresistible.

And what would his parents say? Well, that was really rushing the thing, as if perhaps he and Jill were going to be married next week after one kiss. Still, he couldn't help enjoying the fantasy of her sitting on the floor, leaning against his legs while he pulled his fingers through her hair. He knew, though, that if he brought Jill home, which he might eventually want to do, that they would be shocked. How could a nice Jewish boy bring home a Shikse? He knew they would like her when they got to know her, but they would have to get past her not being Jewish.

Maybe his father wouldn't care so much. When he was a kid, and his mother went to Boston once in a while to visit relatives, his dad would take him to a diner and they would both order bacon, lettuce, and tomato sandwiches. The bacon, strictly forbidden at home, was a treat, a secret between him and his father since they both knew his mother would be furious at this blatant ignoring of the rules. Perhaps it was because the bacon was forbidden that he found its flavor so exquisite. Years, later, however, it turned out that his mother knew just what they were up to and didn't seem to mind all that much.

But his mother, who had lost half her family in the holo-caust-- her father, stepmother, stepsisters—how could she accept Jill into the family? David had long given up most of his religious ways, no lighting of candles on the Sabbath, not even attendance at temple on the high holidays, yet he did love the traditions and respected his mother's orthodox ways. If things developed as he fantasized, then it would take some time, he thought, to get his mother to accept his choice. Or not. You never knew with these things, he guessed.

David sat on into the night in his sparsely but carefully

furnished apartment. Brown couch, two brown chairs, three lamps--only two of which were brown–one was orange and yellow, one rug, all sleekly modern, and one desk, incongruously traditional, a college graduation gift from his parents. What was needed, he thought, was the warmth of a woman to make them all work as they should together. He and Jill could lie on the greenish-brown rug in front of the fireplace, fire fiercely blazing if it were winter, sipping wine and... David stopped himself in mid-fantasy. He could see Jill smiling at him with a slightly mocking look in her eyes as if she disapproved. Was he conjuring up an advertisement for a furniture store rather than imagining a real-life romance?

Soon David's thoughts turned back to Nora and his earlier suspicions about Leslie Podmonk. Her gaiety today, punctuated with bits of hysteria, could be a gaiety of guilt. Perhaps he should talk to Halloway. Nobody seemed to have considered the possibility that Nora was the intended victim, not Erica. And with Leslie's jealousies she may even have wanted to kill them both. She certainly knew of their coffee klatches–not that everyone else didn't know too. Perhaps that was too easy a solution though. What about Jeffry Platz? David stood up and began to pace the floor. Automatically, he took his pipe out of his shirt pocket and put it into his mouth. What, he wondered, was going on between Jeffry and Erica? Was it just the adding up of hundreds of small irritations from Erica that had made him not even pretend to speak to her or was there something else that had happened... something that might make him angry enough to kill? He was a pleasant enough fellow, but extremely distant, not at all easy to know. As silent as Leslie was gabby.

Finding himself in the kitchen, David made himself a cup of tea, then returned to the living room, sat in its largest chair and ruminated. Surveying the walls, David wondered what Jill would think of his paintings. By all rights, they should be etchings, he supposed, if he were to lure her to his den. The paintings were his own, a hobby; he had never studied, and yet they were an important part of himself. Some were dark, with sweeping, abstract shapes, others brighter, their precise geometrical shapes peopled with tiny figures who capered acrobatically about them. Would she like them? Would she think him too egotistical for displaying his own work? Would she understand them? His dark side? His lighter flights of fancy?

Part of what had drawn him to Jill in the first place was her intuitive understanding of Samuel Beckett's plays. It was almost as if together they could speak in the playwright's language. It was interesting that Pinter was harder for her. David actually considered the younger playwright to be a feminist, and he was sure he could bring the class along to see this eventually. And Jill. But Jill was so shaken that she would need to take a big step to approach what she feared in his plays—too much perhaps like what she feared in her life.

Of course if he continued to sit by the telephone and never call, he would never know where things stood. It was too late to call now though. David rose, rinsed out his teacup in the kitchen, and went to bed.

Exhausted from the funeral and the numerous feelings that she had been trying to deal with for the past days, Jill lay on her bed, sleepless. Another letter from her father had arrived insisting that she return posthaste to the bosom of the family. If she did not come home immediately, he had written, he would sue the college. She couldn't help laughing. Her parents' concern over the unsolved murder was understandable; she was extremely anxious herself. But the hysteria with which her father had reacted to every minute danger in her life was reflected now in his obviously empty threat. What would he sue for? Allowing a murder to happen on campus? If it were up to him, neither Mike, her younger brother, nor she would have ever crossed a street alone, gone out on a date, or gone farther away from home than to the corner drugstore.

Although she had met almost every overprotective reaction and act of her father's with open rebellion, he had communicated his anxieties to Jill so fully that she often had to fight her own inclinations to give in as well as fighting his insistence that she do so. When she had been in high school and had enjoyed doing her homework late into the night and sometimes on into the early mornings, she had ignored her father's orders to go to bed. Now that she was on her own though, it was as if she had internalized those orders and found it a high priority to get at least seven hours of sleep. It would be so easy now, too, just to pack a bag, get on the early morning train, and go home where she could sleep in peace tomorrow night, not listening for unfamiliar sounds, not wondering why she felt so endangered or whom she had to fear.

Jill watched the shadows wavering on the ceiling. First of all, as she had told her parents on the phone, nobody who was taking any of Dr. Berne's classes was free to leave Huston at this point. Her mother, at least, had seemed to digest this fact, though her father had merely snorted. What she hadn't told them was that she not only had to stay; she wished to stay. David hadn't called her or seen her alone since the incident in his office, but Jill had thought of little else.

The episode seemed like a dream now. It reminded her of an incident when she was a freshman in college. After a series of inane dates, she had met a young man at a lecture on Virginia Woolf. He had been sitting next to her. They both enjoyed the talk and had a long conversation at a reception following it. He wasn't the best looking guy she had ever met, but they seemed to have a kind of chemistry together. Not only did they have much in common, both in their literary taste and in their feelings about college, but they also found the same things funny and found themselves laughing together. He asked her for her telephone number, which she willingly gave, and she felt happy and optimistic for the first time that year about the possibilities of a real relationship. He never called.

Now Jill found that she jumped every time the phone rang and was bitterly disappointed each time it turned out not to be David. She had avoided looking at him at the funeral, not wishing to pressure him in any way or hold him to what she had hoped was the promise of a relationship. But she couldn't possibly leave town while the prospect remained even a dim hope.

Would her parents like David if they ever did meet him? Her mother would doubtless take to him at once, but her father might find him a bit awkward, a bit too intellectual. Frankly jealous of any man in Jill's life, he sometimes signed his letters to her "Oedipus," aware of his own incestuous feelings, even if he had the wrong myth. Indeed, he had been against Jill going to graduate school. College was all right, that was expected, but he often joked about overeducated women and would clearly have preferred it if Jill had settled for a job near home and moved back in.

No way. Tomorrow was seminar day. She would see David in class.

Leslie Podmonk floated slowly, gracefully to the ceiling of her living room. The tiny bird in her clock chirped encouragement at her as she touched her head to the ceiling, then her back, her legs, lying on it as if it were a bed. Surveying the terrain below with amused indifference, Leslie saw her cat rubbing its grayness sensuously against the leg of her small coffee table; she winked at him, then turned to embrace the ceiling, pressing her breasts against its smoothness. The cat meowed his appreciation of her powers.

Floating in slow motion to the corner of the room, she slid down the wall, touching the floor lightly. Willing herself to continue the descent, she was able to control her body in such a way as to penetrate through the floor, moving first to the basement, and then, something she had not ventured before, even through the very foundations of her house into the earth below.

"The grave's a fine and private place,/But none I think do there embrace." She said the words of the poem aloud, tasting the earth that trickled into her mouth as she spoke. It was like nothing else she had ever tasted, a brandy both fiery and soothing for which she always had thirsted.

Now she must concentrate. "But none I think do there embrace." She must break the spell of these lines, create her own poem. But her rebirth would be in earth, not above. Moving slowly through the layers of dirt, she gathered momentum until her progress was breathtaking. With barely time to wave at the worms and the moles who were awestruck at her rapid speed, she found herself in what must have been a matter of hours but felt like a matter of minutes at his side.

He was waiting for her, as she had suspected he would be. The earth had smoothed her complexion, removed pounds, given her back her youth, which she offered him now as one who she well knew would always have preferred her. "Paul," she whispered in his ear, and the earth which enclosed them trembled in response.

Later, when she had returned to herself, Leslie thought back over the details of the funeral and tried to recapture the feeling of exhilaration that she had felt throughout the festivities. Erica had rejected her. Oh, she knew very well that even at the height of their friendship, Erica had really patronized her, doubtless out of envy. Erica was stuck in the Middle Ages and Leslie glowed in the romance of the 19th-century. She was also a better teacher and a superior intellect, and Erica knew it or sensed it. But since her engagement, Erica had removed herself completely. And quite unforgivably, Erica had never once allowed Leslie to meet Paul. Now let Erica taste defeat. No Nora. No Nora. No Nora. Not to talk with. Not to talk with. Yes, yes, some of the pleasure was returning. It was Erica, not she, who must feel empty.

The ringing of the telephone broke her reverie.

"Emma," she chirped. "I was just thinking about you."

"I was thinking about seeing the film at the Gramercy. You know, the one with Clint Eastwood. *Play Misty For Me.* And maybe dinner afterwards?" Emma suggested. Leslie had seen the film already and didn't much care for it, but it would be a distraction. And she was happy that Emma had thought of her.

"Sounds like a superb plan to me, Emma. Why don't you drive here and we'll go together." She hung up the phone, removed the pin she was wearing, and picked out another one, bright pink for the occasion. A blooming flower. Life, Leslie thought, offered much promise.

CHAPTER VII

Feeling weary after the funeral, Jeffry Platz nevertheless forced himself to correct twelve of his students' seventeen term papers on various aspects of eighteenth-century literature. His red pen moved meticulously but swiftly, correcting errors in spelling and grammar, noting mistakes in fact, weaknesses of interpretation, occasional flashes of insight. But despite the scrupulousness of his work, his mind was not on it. Nora had gone in to have her coffee with Erica. She had taken the poisoned packet of Sweet and Low; she had died… senselessly.

The doorbell rang, pulling him out of his reverie. It was Detective Halloway. Odd time for the fellow to arrive on his doorstep, but of course he had to let him in. "Won't you come in, Sir," he said to him. "Would you care for a cup of coffee?" Halloway always thought he could learn more about his suspects on their home ground. Therefore, he was not surprised to see a fine portrait of Samuel Johnson on Platz's living room wall above the fireplace. Some of the students he had questioned told him Platz thought he *was* Samuel Johnson.

Settled at a table in comfortable chairs with cups of coffee, Halloway began his interrogation. "Professor Platz," he began, "I understand from your colleagues and some of your students that you were not on the best of terms with Erica Berne. Some of them told me you actually don't speak to her. Would you care to tell me about that?" *Always best to be direct, get right to the point. Well, maybe not always, but this time, yes.*

"Yes," Jeffry confessed, "I am not on good terms with Erica. She is an obnoxious human being and nobody can tolerate her. I don't have any special grievance against her, but I'm not in the habit of pretending to be friends when I have no wish to be." *That was a lie, but it was none of Halloway's damned business what kind of grievance he had against the charming Ms. Berne.*

"Do you suppose Nora could have been the intended victim?" Halloway inquired.

"No, I can't imagine that. Nora was a pleasant person, whose greatest weakness as far as I could assess was a tendency to gossip, which was no more blameworthy really than her tendency to be overweight. I didn't know her well. No doubt you have heard by now that I make it a practice to keep my professional and personal lives separate." *Dear Erica had, of course, done her best to see to it that they were not separate, but never mind that.*

No, he had no idea who might have attempted to kill her. He did not know his colleagues well; as he had already stated, he was careful not to get personally involved at work. As far as he knew, everyone would have motives enough, but whether anyone was capable of acting on such motives was a question he could not answer. *Why didn't the man stop looking at him as if he were clearly the murderer? Did he know something? Had one of his dear fellow colleagues set him up as a suspicious character? Everyone knew that he hadn't talked to Erica for years. Perhaps it had been a mistake.*

Perhaps he should have kept up the kind of pretense of minimum civility that he kept up with the others. Why was his face flushed? He had better get himself in hand.

Halloway found the man to be quite a character, definitely right out of the 18th -century, just as the students had suggested. "Do you keep your distance with your students as well?" Halloway asked, not exactly sure how to get the man to open up.

The students? Yes, he did get to know a number of his students quite well—*careful now, Jeffry old man.* No, he couldn't think of any of them that complained about Erica anymore than any others. They all did, if allowed. He was not in the habit of encouraging such complaints though. That, you see, was what a departmental chairman was for. Jill Lake and Professor Stein? No, he hadn't heard that there was a relationship there. *How very interesting!* And Jill was a particularly sensitive, able student. What if there were such a relationship? How could it relate to the murder? *Relate, relate, how could it relate to the murder? Relate, relate...*

Erica jealous? Making trouble for them? I see. Seems unlikely to me. Stein seems to be a steady chap. I can't imagine that she could get at him to that extent—*can't imagine that she could get at him to that extent. Ha!* Yes, if he had any further information he would be happy to share it with the detective.

Halloway thanked him and left. He thought he detected a good deal of anxiety in the somewhat overly dignified professor. He would definitely have to look into this.

Jeffry felt he had handled himself well, on the whole. The information about Jill and David was certainly interesting. Ah, yes, the dangers of envy. How clearly Johnson had seen into the darkness of the human soul and into the dangers of envy... the vanity of it all. How startling still his understanding of how it could twist the mind, rob it of reason, cause one to repress, to project. Erica had doubtless found some way to make trouble for them if she knew about the romance. Infernal bitch!

Nora had gone in to have her coffee with Erica. She had taken the poisoned packet of Sweet and Low; she had died... for no reason.

Jeffry finished correcting his papers, prepared and ate his dinner, read for a while and then decided it was time. He went to the phone and dialed a number quickly. Bill's sleepy voice said, "Hello."

"I must see you."

"Are you crazy? It's 11:30. I have to get up at 6:00."

"Now!" Jeffry put the receiver down. He would come. He always did. And everything would be all right.

CHAPTER VIII

Sitting in his office reading the *Collegian*, David wondered how he could get to see Jill alone without being detected. Erica was back in her office although she had omitted her usual good morning remarks on her way to it. David was trying to get up the strength to go next door to offer his sympathies, but he didn't really have any, at least not for Erica; and even though it was probably the thing to do, he thought perhaps he wouldn't.

The lead article in the school paper was still about the murder. A professor in the chemistry department had reported the theft of several drugs, cyanide among them. They couldn't be sure, of course, that the theft had predated the murder because the missing drugs had been discovered by accident. No breaking or entering. Whoever had been in the room and the cabinet had either had a key or somehow procured one–none reported missing. Detective Halloway was now questioning all English majors who were taking or had taken chemistry. He had assured the reporter that they were making good progress on the case, but ...

Susie poked her head in the door. "Hi, Professor Stein. How are you doing this morning?"

"Fine, Susie, I was just going to stop in for coffee, only"–he pointed to the wall behind which he knew Erica sat and made a face.

Susie smiled. She knew that everyone felt odd about drinking the office coffee now. "Professor Berne doesn't feel well–I guess she shouldn't have come in this morning–she really isn't up to it." Susie lowered her voice to a whisper in case Dr. Berne could hear through the wall. "Sergeant Kheel was going to bring her car around to take her home, but she is so strung out that she won't let him out of her sight this morning, so they asked me if I would bring it round. You know for some dumb reason she never parks out front here, always up on the hill. I guess she thinks her car isn't safe from student drivers here. Anyhow, they have a temporary gal holding down Nora's work, so off I go."

"You're a good kid, Susie," David laughed. He returned to his paper.

Susie began to hustle. Erica had looked red-eyed and faint. She had better get the car around quickly. She was surprised Erica trusted her with her keys or with driving the car even the short distance from the hill to campus. Walking quickly, enjoying the warm breeze, she felt important, as if all eyes were upon her. She was helping the downtrodden... or was she helping the wicked witch? She was helping the downtrodden wicked witch. Laughing out loud, Susie spotted Erica's dark green Pontiac parked in its usual place on the hilltop and admired how well Erica kept it, how spotless, not like Susie's rattletrap. Locked. Probably Erica was the only one at Huston College who neither parked on campus nor left the car doors open.

Feeling slightly guilty even though she had permission to do so, Susie unlocked the door, climbed in behind the wheel, slipped on the seat belt, and turned the key in the ignition. It started easily, again not like her car which had to be coaxed into submission even in the spring. Susie started slowly guiding the car down the steep hill, thinking she hadn't far to go but not wanting to take any chances with Erica's car. In fact, she was probably going too fast. She pressed slightly on the brake to slow down, but the car was going faster now, not slower. "Damn, something is the matter with the brakes." She pressed her foot down hard, but the car kept going, gaining more momentum. Panicked, Susie saw that she was going too fast to turn in at the next street that led to campus. But if she kept going she would be on her way down a yet steeper hill and that one led to a busy street. She would be headed straight for traffic and would have no way to stop. "Oh, God, which is worse?" she moaned out loud, and then instinctively turned, knowing as she did so that she couldn't make it. Susie heard the screeching of wheels, saw the back of the parked car she was headed for, felt the terrible jolt and the sharp pain. Then darkness, soothing, as it closed in.

David heard the sirens as he finished reading the paper and prepared to collect his books for his class. It was a familiar enough sound near campus, but as the sirens came nearer he felt that it was time for what was beginning to seem like a daily disaster. Dropping his things, he rushed for the hallway and the door to the building, ran the short distance down the steps of the building to the gate of the campus and peered down the street. Followed now by dozens of curious students, David saw an ambulance and a police car pulling up next to a car which had apparently smashed into a parked car on the corner. Running down the street, David knew even before he arrived that it was Susie. He wondered if he might run fast enough to save her. Medics were carefully pulling her body out of the mangled car and placing it on a stretcher while police were keeping the gaping onlookers back.

The inert figure was transferred quickly, gently, and efficiently to the ambulance and spirited away before David could determine whether Susie was merely unconscious or whether she was dead. "Okay, okay, back to your classes, show's over, okay, okay, break it up, nothing left to see; the young lady's hurt, that's all, no, not dead, not dead… "

The students broke up and began to wander off. David was shaking. He walked back to the building and to the office… now he had to go next door. Knocking, he didn't wait to be invited in. Erica was sitting at her desk staring into space while Sergeant Kheel peered out the window to see what all the commotion was about.

"It's Susie," David blurted out. "She's had an accident in your car, Erica!"

"What!" Kheel responded in shock.

Erica turned alternately pale and bright red; then, with a note of abject despair, she cried out, "My car!"

———

David told his class about Susie's accident and then dismissed them. "Miss Lake, will you stop by the office at your convenience today. I'd like to go over some points about your paper with you. And you too, Mr. Clarke," he added as an afterthought, all too aware that the paper was a mere excuse to talk to Jill and not wishing to single her out in any way.

By the time he got back to Erica's office, Halloway had materialized, flanked by two officers, Jenson and Preston. They couldn't have been too far away. Erica sat stony-faced and Kheel was patting her on the shoulder awkwardly, apologizing to Halloway as if the accident had been his fault.

"Now let me get this straight, Kheel," Halloway was saying when David knocked and entered the now crowded office. "Professor Berne didn't feel well and wished to return to her home, correct?"

"And she wouldn't let me drive her in the police car," Kheel explained.

"And why, may I ask, didn't you get her car for her?"

Erica interrupted. "Because I wouldn't permit it. I didn't feel safe and I wanted him with me and I was too weak to walk to the car. I always park on the hill."

Halloway looked grave. "My men have had a look at the car. Someone tampered with the brakes."

Kheel, who had been looking uncomfortable, blurted out, "Christ, you mean this was another attempt on Dr. Berne and I muffed it!"

"Exactly," Halloway said, "or shall we say it certainly looks that way. I'm afraid your car has been totaled, Dr. Berne. Whose idea was it for Susie to get the car?"

"It was my idea," Wilfred Black said, entering the office without knocking. He had heard students discussing the accident in the hall and had come to investigate. The office was beginning to look something like a Marx Brothers movie at this point, and David wondered who would enter next. "Kheel came in and asked who was available to go for the car and I suggested Susie. Why? What exactly has happened?"

"Susie has had an accident in the car, Professor Black, only it doesn't seem to have been an accident. It appears to be another attempt on Dr. Berne's life," Halloway responded.

"Is Susie alright?" Black asked.

"We don't know the extent of the injuries. I'm waiting for a call from the hospital. She wasn't conscious apparently when they put her in the ambulance."

"Would it be alright if I went over to the hospital?" David asked, directing his question to Black and Halloway. "I dismissed my class and it might be nice if someone were there, especially if she has regained consciousness."

"If she does," Halloway muttered gloomily. "Yes, go ahead Stein, if it's okay with your boss. It's okay with me. Jenson, you go with him, he added, addressing one of the young men who had entered the office with him. But I'd like to talk to you later, Stein."

"Go ahead," Black said. "In fact, I'd like to come with you."

"I'd rather you stayed here for a bit, Professor Black," Halloway interceded. "I'm going to send Dr. Berne home now with Sergeant Kheel—I think she's gone through enough. But I would like to clear up a few things."

"Okay, go ahead David," Black said.

The phone rang in Erica's office. Kheel picked it up but handed it to his boss.

"Halloway here... I see. I'll be there shortly. Keep an eye on her." He put down the phone and they all waited anxiously for his report. "Susie's in a coma. She also has a broken collar bone and some broken ribs and bruises. She's stable, but… "

"If I had been driving it might have been worse," Erica exclaimed. "Susie is young. Her reflexes are excellent. And do you know what kind of care I take of my car? Do you have any idea of what a fine car that is… was?" The others looked at her with some amazement. Susie was in a coma and she was still worrying about her car? Halloway began to think he was caught in a sit-com instead of a murder investigation.

"We're going to get to the bottom of this and soon, Professor Berne," Halloway said soothingly. Kheel, take her home and stay with her. I'm going to get Sargent Jones to stay with you tonight, if that's all right, Professor Berne. She's a tough lady. No one will get by her."

"Yes, yes, but it's clear that there is no real protection," Erica complained bitterly. "And what about my car? Insurance never covers it, you know. It's unspeakable!" Nobody knew just where to look as they worried about Susie and Erica continued to focus on her car.

As David got ready to go to the hospital, he paused. Jill was waiting for him outside his office door. "Jill, I'm going down to the hospital to see if Susie wakes up. Do you want to ride along?"

"Yes," Jill replied. "I don't have a class until 1:00."

"Come along then." He rushed her out to the car, aware of Halloway standing in the doorway of Erica's office waving out Erica and Kheel. The detective gave Jill and David a penetrating glance.

"Go ahead, Jenson, get to the hospital before them. I don't want Susie to be alone with anyone, and that means anyone,"

Halloway ordered. "Preston, you wait for me outside," he added. "Okay, Professor Black. Shall we talk here?"

"Why don't you come back to my office, Detective," Black said pleasantly, proceeding to lead Halloway down the hallway. "Mrs. Garfelt, I'm afraid you're on your own for a while. Susie has had an accident and probably won't be in this week at least." *Or ever*, he thought, *or ever.*

"Oh, dear," Mrs. Garfelt said. "She was just going over some of the work with me. Well, I'll do the best I can. I'll try to figure things out. Was the accident serious?"

"We don't know how serious yet, I'm afraid. Oh, yes, and please have flowers sent to her at University Hospital from the faculty, and me, of course. And feel free to ask questions, Mrs. Garfelt. Detective Halloway and I will be in the office; you might bring in some coffee."

"Well now, Professor Black," Halloway began, sitting in the comfortable chair opposite Black's and next to a large window. "Things are looking rather worse here. What time does Professor Berne arrive in the morning?"

"Somewhere between 8:00 and 9:00, I believe. I come in at 8:00 myself, you see, and since my door is open, I usually see people come and check their boxes, pick up coffee, the school paper, you know." Mrs. Garfelt came in with two cups of coffee and left hastily, closing the door behind her.

"And did you notice what time she came in this morning?" Halloway queried, sipping the coffee tentatively.

"Well, now, I'm not really sure. I was a bit late myself this morning. Got here at about 8:30, and since I didn't see her arrive after that I can only assume it was sometime between 8:00 and 8:25. But couldn't you ask Sergeant Kheel?"

"Yes, yes of course," Halloway smiled. "I intend to. How many people, teachers or students, know where Professor Berne parks her car?"

"I suppose everyone knows," Black replied, leaning back in his chair which rocked slightly on its hinges. "It's one of the jokes, I'm afraid, about Erica. You know, everyone around here is rather hard on her, Halloway. I admit she is a bit eccentric. Wouldn't occur to any of the rest of us to park up on the hill, but it is quiet up there—no one much passes by—just fields—it's a bit out of the line of traffic as well. So I guess anyone could have slipped over and done something to the car."

"Even you, sir?"

"Why, am I under suspicion, Detective? That's rather refreshing. Usually I'm accused by my faculty and by complaining students of being too kind to Erica, and now you're suggesting I might have attempted to murder her?"

"I'm not suggesting anything," Halloway retorted affably enough. "But everyone is under suspicion until we have this thing solved."

There was a long pause while the men appraised one another. They were both slightly over fifty, able, acute, though Black was tall and agile, Halloway short and rather slow in his movements.

"Why didn't you come in until 8:30 this morning, sir?" Halloway inquired.

"Well, I thought I'd just stop on the hill, tamper with the brakes of Erica's car, and get here in time to put in almost a full day's work," Black quipped. "Actually, I just overslept… something which would be difficult to prove, I'm afraid."

"Why did you pick Susie to get the car for Dr. Berne?" There was a slight pause.

"She was the logical one. She was here."

"Why didn't you go yourself?"

"Never occurred to me."

"I see." Another pause. "Who do you think is trying to kill Professor Berne? Or shall I say, what thoughts or possibilities come to mind?"

"You asked me that before, you know," Black reminded the detective. "It's hard to say, Halloway. I try to stay out of the gossip, but I am aware of what goes on. Platz and Erica aren't on speaking terms. Nobody knows why. Leslie Podmonk is jealous and possessive of Erica. Strand and Stein think Erica's down on them. The students all complain… it's the fashion. She isn't all that bad, you know. Just a traditional teacher, a bit tough, sharp tongued. But if you stand up to her, she rather deflates."

"Deflates does she? Had any experience then, standing up to her?"

"Oh, just on teaching matters, you know. I find if I just hold firm, she usually backs down. That's all."

"If you think of anything, let me know." Halloway stood up to go.

"I will, I assure you." Black walked him out the door. "I expect once Susie's accident gets around we'll have to close down before the end of the semester. I'll be talking to the Dean about it."

"No one is to leave town, no one connected with the

department, teacher or student!"

"That'll be rough. I'm sure more parents will want their children home and safe."

"Soon, Professor Black. I assure you. It will be very soon."

Going into the main office, Halloway paused. "May I use the phone there, Mrs. Garfelt, is it?"

"Certainly, sir," she smiled, feeling very important in light of the present emergency.

"In fact you can use it for me. Would you dial Professor Berne's number please. I want a word with Sergeant Kheel."

A moment passed while Mrs. Garfelt located the list of faculty numbers and dialed. Apparently it was Kheel who answered. Mrs. Garfelt handed Halloway the phone.

"Kheel? Halloway here."

"Yes, sir."

"Go over your movements this morning."

"Well, sir, Kraft watched Dr. Berne's house last night, and when I arrived at 7:30 this morning she was just taking off for school. I offered to ride her over in the police car, but she said she preferred to ride over herself. She seemed to feel fit enough then. I stopped and picked up a donut on the way and still got to the college before she did. I guess it takes her several minutes to walk down from where she parks on the hill. I came direct."

"You shouldn't have stopped for the donut, Kheel. You should have stayed with her."

Contrite. "Yes, sir."

Halloway returned the phone to Mrs. Garfelt, thanked her and strolled out the door, down the steps and out the gate, where

Preston was waiting for him. He followed Halloway to the corner, where they saw that the police tow truck had removed the two damaged cars. It was as if nothing at all had happened. Students were walking about, backpacks on backs, and all was peaceful. Preston followed Halloway as he turned left and strolled up to the hill. "Certainly was away from the direction of life… not a person in sight," Halloway muttered, almost to himself. After examining the tire marks, some beer bottles, coke bottles, and bits of paper, they continued to look about briefly but without any luck.

"Rather an audacious thing for anyone to do," Preston volunteered. "Quiet spot, but still some traffic must go by."

"Right. Put a call out for information on all the local radio stations and channel 18. Request information from anyone passing by between 8:00 and 9:00 this morning who saw anyone tinkering with a car."

After taking a final look around, Halloway looked down at the campus, listened to the birds, and wondered at the peace. The two men walked back to campus, and as they reentered the building that housed the English Department, the detective gave further instructions to Preston. It would be tedious, but he would need to know the whereabouts that morning of every member of the English Department and every student of Dr. Bernes. Maintenance people too. With her delightful personality, perhaps Erica had offended some psychotic janitor. At least if any suspect's whereabouts could be established, the search for the killer could be narrowed down. It might help. Halloway explained that if Susie had awakened, he would have to go to the hospital and interview her. It would be a busy day.

Despite the sense of urgency he felt about Susie, David drove the mile and a half to the local hospital as slowly as possible. "Jill, I wanted to call you and I was afraid to," David blurted out. "I guess I just didn't know what to say."

Puzzled, Jill put the ball back in his park. "Well, here we are," she smiled.

"Yes," David smiled back. "But did you see the look I got from Halloway when he saw us leaving together? Aside from endangering my job and your graduate career, I will doubtless become a primary suspect for murder. 'Professor kills for coed!'"

Jill laughed, but she offered no help.

"I do have a motive," David bumbled on. "All of Erica's suspicions about me are completely true. '"Elderly professor in love with young coed attempts to murder colleague who is on to him.' Now I feel reckless though. Who shall be next?"

Astonished by this indirect but clear declaration of David's feelings, Jill could hardly believe her ears. She heard herself say, "I rather thought when you didn't call that you just felt sorry for me the other day."

"No," David beamed, sorry that her feelings had been hurt, but glad. "Mostly I feel sorry for myself because I haven't felt free to call you." David realized that it had taken a near catastrophe to bring him to this rather indirect expression of his feelings. He also realized that they were fast approaching the hospital and despite an exchange of concerns and feelings, they had made no further plans.

"This is a pretty ugly business with Susie," he said, dismayed at how fast they had arrived and pulling into a parking place a short walk from the hospital. They would only have a couple blocks for more private exchange.

Jill looked at David earnestly. "It's eerie, you know, Professor Stein."

"Hadn't you better call me David?"

"How can I?"

"We're not at school now." David took Jill's hand as naturally as if they had been long-time lovers.

"David, then. I talked to Susie just yesterday in the office when no one else was around and we both have this strange feeling that we know something important; but we don't know what we know."

"Was Black in his office when you were talking?" David asked anxiously. "He usually leaves the door open."

"The door was open, but I don't know whether he was there or not. Why?"

"I was just wondering if he could hear you."

"If he was there, yes. We weren't whispering."

"What else did you say?"

"Nothing much. Susie says that she and Nora gossiped a good deal and that she keeps thinking that they may both have known something dangerous. That's why I'm worried, David. First Nora and now Susie. I gather everyone is sure that this is another attempt on Professor Berne's life, but I wonder. And if it isn't, if Nora and Susie were the intended victims, then perhaps I'm next."

"I guess that's why I asked about Black," David confessed. "I thought perhaps Nora and Susie were onto whatever it is that Erica has over Black–or onto something. But it's absurd! It's the merest surmise. Black doesn't seem the murdering type, overly mild if anything."

"The weasel under the cocktail cabinet?" Jill smiled. She was referring to the remark David had made in class; Harold Pinter, it seems, had said this when someone asked him what his plays were about.

David looked away from Jill, overcome with affection for her and fear for her as well. They had arrived at the hospital door. "I don't know Jill. I don't see how Susie could be anyone's intended victim. You see no one knew she would be driving Erica's car this morning. No one knew Erica wouldn't feel well and no one could have known who would fetch her car for her. It's true that Black's the one who suggested Susie go for the car, but there's no way Black could have known Erica wouldn't be driving her own car–seems to me pretty clear that Erica was the intended victim."

David dropped Jill's hand abruptly when he saw several students in the hospital lobby who must have had the same idea that they had. He thought they looked at Jill and him with partly hidden smirks. Was he that transparent after all? But they all got into the elevator chatting. Melvin Stuart had checked; Susie was in room 232. Apparently she had come out of the coma about an hour ago, and it wasn't clear that they could go into see her yet.

When they arrived at the room, Jenson was on guard, his gun visible at his side. Susie looked extremely small and pathetic in the high bed. A nurse cautioned them–two at a time and only very briefly. David went in with Melvin, Jill afterwards with Mary Gill.

"What do you mean by wrecking Dr. Berne's car like that?" David teased, but Susie wasn't up to any humor.

"I bet she's furious," she whispered in a hoarse voice.

"Dr. Berne?" Melvin laughed. "She wasn't concerned over her car. Only over you, my dear."

"I'll bet," Susie smiled weakly. David cautioned Melvin that they had best leave.

"Anything we can get you?" he asked before they left. "You know we can't manage at school without you, so you'll have to get well quickly."

Susie closed her eyes and they left, nodding at the Sergeant as they departed.

———◦《◎》◦———

Jim Strand lurked in a hallway, waiting until all the visitors departed before entering Susie's room in the hospital. Her eyes were closed and he was about to leave her in peace, when she opened them and smiled.

"Professor Strand. How nice of you to visit."

"Susie, don't Professor Strand me. My name is Jim and you are not a student, so you don't have to do that. We are friends, aren't we?"

"Yes," Susie smiled. "I guess we are."

"Good guess. So what the hell, Susie? You could have been killed!"

"I know, Jim," she tried out the name and felt pretty

comfortable with it. "But it's just beginning to sink in. Dr. Berne could have been killed if she had gone to get her own car. It's all, what should I say, a little too exciting here these days."

"Erica Berne is indestructible. But I have to tell you, Susie, I could easily spare her, but I absolutely can't spare you. So no more of this."

Susie blushed. Jim had been extremely nice to her, lending her books, discussing them with her, even taking her out for coffee once. But he seemed very intense. She couldn't help but enjoy the way he was looking at her.

"I appreciate your coming to look in on me, Jim," she said, trying out his first name again and wondering if perhaps something was developing between them that was more than his just being nice to her. Maybe it wasn't just her secretarial services that he appreciated.

Jim came closer and took Susie's hand and she found herself blushing again. "I plan to keep tabs on you, Susie," he announced. "I'm not so sure that you are safe." Reluctantly letting go of her hand, Jim walked over to the door. "Get some rest," he said, and then he was gone.

⸻ ❋ ⸻

David didn't have another chance to talk to Jill on the way back to campus. Some of the students asked for a ride; they had been over-crowded coming in a small car. Jill sat in the back with Melvin and Mary. But on the way into the building, she managed to walk close enough to David to murmur under her breath, "Susie told me to be careful!"

CHAPTER IX

It had been raining on and off for two days; now that it had stopped there was still a sense of pervading dampness in the air. The campus was lush, brilliantly green, bursting with flowers. Jeffry Platz had finished teaching his last class of the day and decided not to keep his office hours. As far as he knew there were no students coming to see him and he wanted to make a few stops on the way home. He had parked behind the building, just under a large magnolia tree. Some of the petals, glistening with rain, had fallen onto his blue car. Pink, white, and blue, Jeffry noticed, smiling wryly as he patted some dew from his graying hair. Still plentiful, though, he thought, for his age.

He moved the car away from campus, deciding out of a strange sense of curiosity to drive by Erica's hill. No car there now, of course–it was deserted–nothing. Jeffry went a short distance, driving aimlessly; then he made a decision, turned left, returning to campus, but turned again several blocks east of it where he pulled into the Shell gas station on the right side of the street. A young man appeared from inside and filled up his tank.

"Guess we really needed that rain, rather refreshing," Jeffry commented to the young man.

The young man hissed under his breath. "They came here,

questioned me! I've got to talk to you."

"Tonight? My place?" Jeffry proposed.

"No way; they may be watching me. Or you for that matter. Or us," Bill replied.

"Then where?" Jeffry smiled pleasantly.

"At Greer's. I get off at 7:00. If I'm followed, I'll eat at the counter. If not, I'll join you in a booth. If you're followed, go to the counter and I'll buy a pack of cigarettes, leave, and call you at home."

"Don't you think you're being a bit melodramatic, Bill?" The older man inquired.

"Perhaps." And then in a normal voice, "Here is your change, sir."

Jeffry drove off. What had Erica said to the police about him? Probably nothing. Perfectly natural for them to question all students working in gas stations–logical–they would know about cars. Nothing to fret about. Erica wouldn't dare. Not after all these years. No, she wouldn't… she enjoyed having him under her thumb too much for that… unless… unless she was scared. Well, he would see what Bill had to say, take it slowly, carefully, as he always had. No need to panic. He would stop at the bank, perhaps forget his other errands and just go home and rest until dinner time, then drive out on route 47 and meet Bill… let's see, better leave at 6:30, nice evening for a bit of a drive. No, no need to panic.

—◉—

Bill went about his work mechanically, but he was deeply disturbed by the turn of events. How flattered he had been when

Jeffry had first taken notice of him in class, encouraged him and then befriended him. No teacher of his before had ever taken such an interest in his work or shown this kind of concern for him. He had felt quite carried away and was entirely in love, maybe for the first time in his life. He knew the distance in their ages probably precluded an affair. He was sure that Jeffry was gay from the outset even though there was no possibility of his coming out of the closet, especially so at this conservative university. And teacher/student relationships were absolutely forbidden. So when Jeffry had invited him over for dinner, he was totally unprepared for what ensued. Looking back now, he wondered how he could have been so innocent, so ready to get in over his head. Love? More like slavery. And there seemed no way out. And now this mess with Erica. Was it Jeffry he hated, or himself? But he was determined to find a way out of the whole mess.

⸻ ◈ ⸻

The two men sat in a booth talking quietly and earnestly, the younger one gulping his food down, the older one eating slowly, meticulously.

"All students who have taken any courses from Erica are being questioned. I told you just to keep cool."

"But they came to the station. I don't like that. My boss didn't like it. I'll lose my job…"

"I'll take care of you if anything happens. You know that."

"Most assuredly. And then what? You've already got me jumping whenever you call. Thanks, but no thanks, Jeffry. Just not enough of the Boswell in me, I fear."

Silence. Bill thought he was being so clever, Jeffry thought, indicating that he would not dedicate himself to Jeffry the way Boswell had dedicated himself to Samuel Johnson. He would not be his biographer. He would not worship.

Jeffry carefully cut another piece of roast beef and savored its flavor, then another. It fascinated Bill to see how he organized his eating, going from one item to the next.

"Exactly, and I mean exactly, what did they ask you? And how exactly did you respond? "

"Well, this one guy identified himself, I don't know, I forgot his name, and he showed me some identification stuff... informed me that he was investigating an attempted murder, but routine, everyone at school being questioned. He tried to sound casual. Quite friendly. Only I almost had a heart attack! That was how I responded, you see, by almost keeling over."

"And did you show it?"

"No, no, I was cool, you know, as if I got investigated for murder every day of the week, part of the job."

"Very funny. Then what?"

"Then he asked me where I was between the hours of 8:00 a.m and 9:00 a.m last Friday. So I knew where I was, of course, but I thoght, okay, Bill, cool, cool, so I said, 'Let me see now, I take classes at the college, and I was on my way there that day–I have a 9:00 o'clock class. I must have left the house about 8:30, pulled in about ten to 9:00 just before my class.'"

"'And did anyone see you arrive at the college'? the gentleman asked politely. I said, 'No, but you can check with Dr. Stein 'cause I take his seminar on Beckett and Pinter at 9:00 and I was there when he came in and told us about the accident. He let us go that day.' Then he asked if any other students had seen me, either on the way or coing in, and I said I couldn't remember seeing anyone in particular. Then he asked me a lot of questions about Dr. Berne and whether she brought her car here. Well, damn it, she does. So I said yes and that sometimes I took care of it if something went wrong. I told him I knew about cars—that makes me a really prime suspect, doesn't it—but I told him that she was a real fuss pot who thought she knew more about cars than I did. Told me just what to fix and how to fix it the last time I worked on her car and then wasn't satisfied and brought it back. I didn't tell him that I didn't do a damn thing to it, only told her I had, and she was finally satisfied. Thought I'd better not let him know how I feel about that bitch."

"I see. I like that story about not doing anything to it. Sometimes, my boy, you are a gem. I gather he never mentioned my name?"

"No. He asked me how I liked school and if I had any special trouble with Berne. I said I liked it fine, that I didn't have any more trouble with Dr. Berne than anyone did, that she wasn't a popular teacher but her course was required."

"You did very well, my boy, very well. Now that you see it was routine, you can calm down. There's no way they can prove you were anywhere near the hill between 8:00 and 9:00 on Friday, so just relax. But I do think we had best avoid one another for a time until everything cools down. I'll be in touch by phone of course, but even now we had better leave separately."

"I don't like it. Making the 9:00 o'clock class doesn't clear me of suspicion."

"There is nothing to like or not like. We will bide our time. We will simply bide our time. "

The two men talked on until they had finished their dinners and then Bill left. Jeffry had another cup of coffee and took out a cigar. On the one hand he felt safe and quite satisfied. On the other hand, however, he felt somewhat guilty about Bill and how deeply he had embroiled him in the complexities and difficulties of his existence. I'm getting old, he thought. Too old for the likes of Bill Brown. I don't even think he loves me anymore. Poor sod doesn't know how to break the news. Why was it always like this? Exciting at first. The conquest, love requited. Then some kind of surprise on the part of his young lovers when they discovered he wasn't a god. Ah well, ah well.

He couldn't help but question his chosen life-style. Why students? Why hadn't he ever found a contemporary, a partner with whom he could live with some stability? He suspected he knew the answer to his own question. He was the son of an absent father, one who was always off on business trips and had left his upbringing to his wife. And she, his mother? She had worshiped him, of course, an only son, an absent husband. Oh, dear, what would Freud say to that? He knew the answer to that one.

But despite her constant attentions, Jeffry's mother had been extremely controlling. She had kept track of his every move. He had to report in at ages where he should have been free to roam. She had to know everything that happened at school, exactly who his friends were, even what he was thinking. He sometimes felt quite enslaved. And now here he was, as controlling with his lovers as his mother had been with him. He thought to himself that he was a walking cliché. Rather late in life to change, though, he admitted to himself.

Until now, Jeffry's major weapon with Erica had been silence. He still remembered as vividly as if it were yesterday the after- noon—how many years ago was it now? – that she had come barging into his office without knocking and found him locked in an embrace with Richard Lance, one of his graduate students. The moment was still vivid in his mind, Richard turning from him in disgust—was it the disgust of exposure or disgust at Jeffry for permitting the situation to occur in the first place? Erica had turned bright red and had stood staring at him as if she expected an explanation or an apology. Despite the embarrassment of being caught by Erica in what he considered to be his private life, Jeffry had found himself enjoying her shock. Though he realized that her discovery would put him quite irretrievably in her power, he felt a strange power of his own welling forth and enjoyed meeting her stare with the utter defiance of silence. Finally, Erica had turned and left the office.

Jeffry had not spoken to the woman since that day. And as far as he knew, she had never spoken about the situation to anyone else, nor had she ever uttered another word to him. It was a strange game the two had played over the years, one which the rest of the faculty and students watched with interest but which only Jeffry and Erica understood. Only they knew the source of the silence (well, Bill knew something of it now, out of necessity), but only Erica and Jeffry grasped its full dynamics. The threat of exposing Jeffry made Erica feel that she had the advantage while

Jeffry's seeming indifference and sometimes his clear disdain just as often made her feel as if she were the one who was powerless; in some way she even felt she was at his mercy.

Most of the time Jeffry felt safe because he was quite sure that Erica enjoyed holding the threat of disclosure over his head more than she would enjoy using her power. Unfortunately, however, he could not be sure. Erica, on the other hand, was never sure that Jeffry would care if he were exposed–he seemed so proud of his conquests–she had watched closely over the years and was quite sure she knew exactly who the line of lovers had been. She sometimes even felt as if he were flaunting the affairs at her as if to prove his superior ability to be admired and loved. But Erica knew that Jeffry watched her relationship with Leslie Podmonk with interest and his barely hidden suspicion about the nature of that relationship was one of her major reasons for withdrawing from the friendship.

Jeffry ordered another cup of coffee and a Creme de Menthe. The waitress who took the order would never have suspected what thoughts were going through the head of this handsome, distinguished-looking gentleman, who seemed to be enjoying himself with never a care in the world. What he was thinking about now was the advent of Paul into the game between himself and Erica. Perhaps, he thought, Paul's arrival on the scene had introduced a sort of truce. Of course he felt sorry for the poor bastard who was actually agreeing to join his life with Erica's, but he had also felt less anxious and had even lost interest in the whole game of unspoken enmity. Bill had entered his life at about the same time and he had thought Erica too absorbed in her own romance to notice.

But Paul's death had been a catastrophe. After a brief period of withdrawal, Erica was back on the warpath, not just with him, of course, but certainly she gave special attention to their now ongoing game. It was as if she were watching him with a new intensity of vindictiveness. How dare he enjoy a relationship when she had none? And she really did have none. Jeffry was sure that he was responsible for Erica's break with Leslie. He understood her temptation and knew how she had fought it. He, too, had fought temptation. He may have lost, but her victory, it seemed to him, plus her loss of Paul, had made her dangerous in a new way. The game was clearly coming to a head. The masochistic playfulness had given way to a far more serious level of competition. No, it would seem there must be a winner and a loser. A pity.

Jeffry took a last sip of his coffee and asked for his bill. If there was to be a loser, he thought to himself, it would not be him. He would bide his time.

CHAPTER X

"For many a time I have been half in love with ease-ful death," she whispered into his ear, luxuriating as she did so in the taste of the earth. Then, as if by magic, they moved together through the earth that enclosed them, up, through the air, through the clouds—they too had a sweet taste—up through more clouds and finally, through a supreme effort of her will, out into space.

To be released at last from gravity, to float with such ease, and always together, in one rhythm. Leslie had never experienced such freedom. The stars flickered their admiration at the couple's daring arabesques, their startling pirouettes.

"No, Paul," she sighed as she saw him look down. "You must not regret the past. Erica no longer speaks of you, no longer thinks of you, no longer dreams of you. She has returned to the dryness of her life before you met. She is shriveled up. Indeed, my darling, she is all but dead."

A shooting star whizzed by, but they did not flinch, invulnerable in their lightness to all danger. "You must follow, you know," she sang as she felt him behind her, but then to her surprise he lifted her, carried her on through space.

"It was always you," he whispered in her ear as they hovered over earth and then together they sank down, through the earth, into its depths. And she felt so safe.

Afterwards, as Leslie searched the refrigerator for food, cheeses, cold meats, olives, wine, fruit, cake, she could not consume enough; she could not recapture the delicate taste of the clouds, the delicious taste of her flight, the richly comforting taste of the earth which they had shared. She ate and she drank, but she could not get full.

━━━━◆━━━━

Sitting down at her desk, Jill decided to read her mail before she got to work. She wasn't surprised to see a letter from her father, but she was amused to see that the same envelope contained notes as well from both her mother and her brother. For some reason, they preferred writing to the telephone. Well, it actually made her life easier than dealing with them on the phone.

April 23, 1972

My dear daughter,

The fact that you neglected to inform your mother and me in your last letter of the recent attempt at murder following the successful attempt before made it all the more surprising when we got a letter from President Irving assuring us that there was no reason to panic, that the murderer was still essentially after Professor Berne, and that all precautions were being taken. Precautions my foot!

This is the second time someone other than Berne has been killed or hurt and who will be next? Not you. I am sending your mother to pack you up and bring you home if you do not come of your own free will. Even she thinks it's time for you to come home. Even Michael thinks so. Although he is all for coming with your mother so he can capture the criminal single handedly.

I know that you said that nobody in Professor Berne's classes was free to leave, but just you let them try to stop you; they will have to deal with me.

I knew this graduate study business was a lot of rubbish, but anyway we will look forward to seeing you in the next two days. If you don't come, your mother will storm the citadel and carry you home if need be. This is your father speaking!

Love,
Dad

She read her mother's letter next. Then her brother's.

Dear Jill,

Your father, as you can well imagine, is hysterical. Don't you think perhaps this time he is right? I obviously can't drag you home, but he really does plan to send me to get you and we would all feel better having you here. I'm sure something could be arranged about finishing your work here. Think about it dear.

Love,
Mom

Dear Jill,

Mom and Dad are going bananas. Don't come home 'cause I want to come up with Mom to get you. I bet I could get to the bottom of this. You are probably next in line and that way we could watch, wait, and attack.

Mike

Jill decided that one letter would take care of the trio and addressed a letter to her mother.

Dear Mom, Dad, and Michael,

I appreciate your concern. You are all welcome to visit. I am safe and sound. I plan to stay. I am over 21.

Love and kisses,
Jill

————)(O)(————

Jill was taken aback. One short week after the accident, Erica Berne, now seemingly fully recovered, had returned to the classroom and her tyrannical ways. She had asked, no, ordered Jill to her office after class at a time when Jill usually got a bite to eat.

"You may sit there," Erica said, indicating the chair opposite her desk. "Don't worry, Miss Lake, I have not summoned you to my office to discuss your work." Professor Berne had dropped her tone from authoritarian to syrupy which only made Jill feel more anxious than before.

"I wish to offer you a bit of friendly advice, my dear," Erica fairly purred. "It's about Professor Stein."

Jill blushed and hated herself for being so vulnerable. What on earth was coming now? She waited, noticing that Erica was pink in the face herself, though hardly from blushing. Any strong emotion brought color to her face; it was a sure sign to the students of trouble ahead, or more trouble ahead than usual.

"Now you needn't deny that you have a crush on Professor Stein. I have eyes in my head and ears, and I have seen and heard more than enough to confirm my suspicions."

"May I ask you just what it is you have seen or heard?" Jill managed to ask, furious at the weakness of her voice and at herself for being so polite when she would like to have risen and left the office.

"No, my dear, no, you may not." A slight sharpness returned to Erica's tone, but she caught herself and resumed her pseudo-friendly manner. "I have no wish to prove anything or get you into any trouble. Actually, I only mean to warn you… for your own good."

"Warn me of what?" Jill managed to inquire in a firmer voice, even one with challenge in it.

"Professor Stein, my dear, is a dangerous man. No, don't laugh. I know he seems mild enough. But I have reason to suspect his motives. I do not know why, but he hates me, and I do not believe that you would wish to be involved with a murderer!"

"Really, Dr. Berne, that is absurd, and I would prefer not to discuss my private life," Jill asserted, having finally found her voice. Dr. Berne, she thought, looked like a bird, splotchy in the face, but eager to fly at Jill's face, at her eyes, and peck at them. How dare she discuss Jill's love life! It was a miracle, a sheer miracle that Dr. Berne had a love life at all. Jill's feeling of outrage was so strong that she was afraid to say anything further and simply sat uncomfortably in the chair waiting to be dismissed.

"Your young man," Erica continued, "is ambitious, very ambitious. He feels that I may stand in the way of his progress at Huston. And, of course, he is quite correct in that assessment. I find his work sophomoric, and I am far from convinced that the field he has chosen for specialization is worthy of the designation 'field.'"

"I don't see what any of this has to do with me," Jill said stiffly.

"Just be careful, my dear. Be very careful. Watch for any small ways in which Professor Stein may wish to take advantage of you. That is why we have rules about faculty/student relationships. The student should never be in the power, you see, of a professor, not in that way. If you come to learn too much about him, and you may, you are an intelligent girl, you may find yourself in danger. I know this all sounds slightly melodramatic, but it may not seem so later when you think back. If you do not wish to accept my warning, that is your affair. I merely urge you for your own sake

to be careful."

"Is that all, Dr. Berne?"

"Yes, you may go."

"Thank you," Jill muttered, ready to bite her tongue for the pleasantry even before she had finished saying it. Collecting herself and her books, she left with as much dignity as she could assemble. Glancing next door to see if David was in his office, she saw that the door was closed and no light showed under it. Jill rushed out of the building, unable to think who else she could talk to about the terrible interview.

<hr/>

David and Jim were having their lunch in the cafeteria. Some students had joined them and were talking all at once about the attempts on Erica Berne's life and the dire effect on the victims of those attempts. Greer Purlieu, the boy Jill had mentioned to Aaron as a suspect, had been cleared of suspicion along with several other students whose movements had been accounted for during the crucial hour between 8:00 and 9:00 when somebody had tampered with the brakes on Erica's car. Several of the students finished their lunches and moved out to the lawn to sunbathe or study or go to classes, but Melvin Stuart remained to chat with Jim and David about his theories.

"I didn't want to say anything in front of the others, but I think it may be Jasper," he confided to the two men. "Jasper has had a terrible time with Professor Berne—I mean really terrible. You see, I talk to him a lot and he's told me some of the things."

"Like what, Melvin, what?" Jim challenged, irritated that the pleasant old man who took care of the cleaning up so well should be accused by this young punk.

"Well, like she calls him in frequently and manages to find some bit of dust he's missed. And like last week she accused him of stealing something from one of her drawers."

"Of stealing what?" David inquired.

"It was a book. Only she wouldn't even tell him what the title was. She was so sure he had taken it that she told him she would have him fired if he didn't find it and return it."

"Why doesn't he complain to Black? Hardly seems any more justification for murder than any of us have who deal with the fair damsel on a daily basis," Jim retorted.

David didn't think Jim should talk that way with a student about Erica, though he remembered guiltily that he had said worse to Jill.

"Or," Jim continued when Melvin seemed to have come to the end of his case, "perhaps we are all guilty, guilty creatures sitting at a play, Karamazov brothers at heart, Joseph K. scrambling down hallways. Speaking of which, I must scramble down a few to my next class. See you all. Tell Jasper not to worry about the book. I have it!" And he was gone.

"Does he mean it?" Melvin asked, shocked somewhat by the professor's antics.

"No, Melvin, he doesn't mean it; that's just Professor Strand's way. You mustn't take him seriously." David noticed that Jill was approaching and asked her to join them. As she sat down and placed her tray on the table, Melvin got up to leave. "Excuse me, folks, got to get in a little library work. I'll stop by later about my paper, Dr. Stein. I still think someone should talk to Halloway about all this, but I don't want to get anybody innocent into trouble."

"I'm sure they have questioned your suspect, Melvin. I wouldn't worry about it too much."

Melvin walked off thinking his own thoughts, both about Jasper and about David Stein and Jill Lake. When he was out of earshot, Jill told David in detail about Erica's warning, but to her surprise David seemed to find the report on the interview extremely amusing.

"It wasn't funny. If you had heard her!"

"I can't help it, Jill. The picture of me as an ambitious murderer stomping down all who stand in my way and using you is just too much." He began laughing.

"She would be funny, David, if she weren't so malicious. She'd even be pathetic if she weren't so… I don't know. It was awful."

David wanted to pat her hand but couldn't. "I know, Jill. Once more it sounds to me as if these attempts on her life have sent her over the edge. And I'm furious at her for intimidating you. Jill, I know the semester is almost over, and that you have put a hell of a lot of time into that class, but I want you to drop it. And I'm going over right now to give Erica an extremely large piece of my mind."

"Oh, please don't, David. The course is required."

"I know. But she really does have it in for you now, and anyhow, just by sitting here together we're risking my job and your degree. But I still want us to sit here. You see, I'm beginning to understand what idiots we've all been about Erica. The reason she is where she is today is because nobody has stopped her. You're more important to me than my job, and as long as I know that I don't think she can hurt me. And you should be more important to yourself than getting through her course and taking her crap. Jill, you, handled her with splendid dignity. I'm going to tell her exactly where she can go, and now!"

"David, no! I know you want to help me, but I have a thing about passing that dumb course. I'm sure that if I just don't take her seriously I can get through the last three weeks. Then you can tell her anything that comes into your mind, and more, too, if you want."

"Come on, Jill. Finish up and let's go for a walk. Perhaps we should think about a three-way conversation with Black."

They left the cafeteria together. Jill loved David for wanting to rush to her rescue and half wanted to give in and be saved. But she had a strange desire to see the stupid course through. Or maybe she just didn't want to take advantage of her relationship with David to make things easier for herself. She was determined to handle Erica Berne herself.

CHAPTER XI

Jasper Mann finished making his rounds for the night. Everything was impeccably clean, he thought proudly. Even Erica Berne would have no complaints in the morning. At least she shouldn't– didn't really mean she wouldn't. Of course he had no idea what she meant about the stolen book, but he wasn't going to worry about that. No one was going to fire him after twenty-six years of service for some book he hadn't taken. Let her blather. The woman was a real nut, he thought. Ah, well, time to lock up and go home.

He whistled as he went down the dark hall, turning out the few remaining lights as he went. Ever since Nora's murder he had taken to whistling at night when he was in the building alone, alone that is except for an occasional professor or graduate student working late. He had never been bothered by the building before, but now he tended to jump when he heard a sound he couldn't account for. After all these years, too. It was a shame. He sighed with relief as he double-locked the front door and walked around the back of the building to his car, still whistling a note or two in the dim light of a street lamp.

Jim Strand heard the whistling and the double-locking of the front door. He had been sitting quietly in his darkened office waiting for Jasper to leave. He had even taken the precaution of parking on the hill, an ironical choice he thought, so that no one would know he was in the building.

When all was perfectly still, he pushed the button on the flashlight he had brought with him, picked up the small volume from his desk, let himself quietly out of his office, and made his way silently around the corner and down the hall to Erica's office. Using the various instruments on his pocket knife, he managed without any trouble to open Erica's locked office; with only slight difficulty he also managed the lock on her desk. And with unusual dexterity he again found the secret hiding place in the back of the bottom drawer in which he had first located the book. He dropped the book in, closed the false front, re-locked the drawer, stole out of the office, locked it, and found his way without the aid of his flashlight to the door of the building. The last time the double lock had presented some difficulties, but this time he negotiated his exit with ease, glanced furtively in all directions, and then walked casually out the gate and down to the corner where he began the ascent to his car.

After all, Jim thought to himself sardonically, I wouldn't want Jasper to get into any trouble. You've got style, Jim, old boy, real style. He almost laughed out loud remembering his words that afternoon at lunch to Melvin Stuart. "Tell Jasper not to worry. I have the book." He was laughing as he got into his car and still laughing when he pulled the car into the driveway of the apartment house he lived in a few short miles away.

The night was strangely still except for the chirping of crickets. He listened to them for a while, pondering what his next move ought to be. Whatever it was, he had better act soon.

CHAPTER XII

Erica Berne was sitting in the faculty smoking room on the second floor of the English building. She didn't smoke, considering it a filthy habit, but she liked one of its chairs and often corrected papers there. Hanging on the wall across from the entrance to the room was a reproduction of Picasso's portrait of Gertrude Stein. After glancing at the picture with disapproval–she felt Stein was looking down at *her* with disapproval--Erica began correcting the first paper in her pile. Soon Leslie bustled in with her own set. Erica didn't wish to talk with Leslie, who persisted in chatting away at her former friend's lowered head.

"Don't think that I don't know what you're going through, Erica. Why, I can just imagine what it must be like always to wonder who is walking behind you, to have a policeman or police lady for that matter guarding your every move. I think they could be doing a lot more than they are to get to the bottom of this too, don't you?"

"You needn't worry your head about me, Leslie, I'm really quite fine and quite capable of handling this."

"Oh? Then you don't find it frightening? Well, you are a brave one, Erica. If it were me someone wished to murder, I would be a nervous wreck. In fact, I'm nervous just thinking there is a killer about without fearing that he is stalking me."

"Are you?" Erica inquired.

"Yes, I am," Leslie retorted, refusing to be offended by Erica's tone. "I also have some theories on the subject and Detective Halloway doesn't seem very interested in them. Would you like to hear them?"

"Not particularly, Leslie. I'm trying to get some work done."

Leslie was quiet for a moment. Jeffry Platz, who rarely came into the faculty lounge, entered at that moment, nodded to Leslie, and picked up a copy of *Time Magazine* from the table.

"And how are you today, Jeffry?" Leslie asked in a kittenish voice, glad to have a listener if Erica was really determined to remain remote.

"Oh, fine, fine, Leslie, and you?" Jeffrey replied. He had actually come to the lounge to find out what the current gossip on the situation might be and proceeded to put the magazine down to give Leslie his attention.

"I was just telling Erica that I have an interesting theory about our campus killer, but she is meeting a self-imposed headline with her papers and doesn't care to hear it. Oh dear, did I say 'headline'? I meant 'deadline,' of course. There I go again. What would Dr. Freud say to that, I wonder?" Leslie giggled at herself and Jeffry made a few sounds of laughter to encourage her.

"And what is your theory, Leslie? I would be most interested in hearing it," Jeffry said. Erica got very busy with her red pen.

"I figure," Leslie began, "that whoever the murderer is, he or she, has two qualities. He or she is spiteful, he or she has a real grudge against Erica, and he or she is inept; he or she has very little skill in accomplishing his or her goals."

It was with some difficulty that Jeffry restrained his laughter. Erica was less able to control her reaction. "Excellently deduced, a truly profound theory, Leslie," she laughed. "People don't tend to kill if they have no grudge, you know, and we are all quite aware that this particular killer is inept. He or she, as you so admirably put it, has killed the wrong person once and injured another wrong person a second time. Is there any other word than inept? Stupid perhaps? Come now, you can do better than that!"

Leslie, seemingly oblivious to the cruelty of Erica's tone, was delighted that she had managed an audience of two and continued as if she had received words of encouragement.

"Now I happen to think that the murderer is a he, not a she. The reason why I have eliminated female suspects has largely to do with the tampering with Erica's auto. I can think of few women or even girls, liberated though they may be, who would know enough to tamper with a car or who would have the audacity to do so in plain view of whomever might pass in broad daylight on the hill. So, you see, that already reduces the suspects by very many, doesn't it?"

"Whoever, Leslie, for God's sake, whoever." Erica said.

"Whatever," Leslie retorted, unruffled, smiling at Jeffry, who was fascinated by the feline brawl unfolding before him.

"Well, now Leslie, that would certainly limit your suspects a good deal. And what man do you consider as the possible culprit?" Jeffry prodded.

"I think there are two possibilities. One is a student. The other is a man. I have heard the students gossiping, you see, and I happen to know that Hal Bridges has a particular grudge against Erica."

Erica looked up from her papers and sneered openly while Leslie elaborated on her theory.

"You see, Hal is very sensitive to begin with about being Black. I mean there just aren't many Blacks on this campus. I do believe I could count our Black majors on the fingers of this one hand."

"True enough," Jeffry conceded.

"But you see Hal feels that he is being persecuted by Erica because he is Black. Of course other students may feel persecuted by her as well, but we all do have students who feel unfairly treated, don't we?"

Jeffry realized that Leslie was half insulting Erica, half understating her unpopularity with the students, playing some sort of complicated game. How glad he was that he had maintained his silence all these years.

"Hal, on the other hand, thinks that he is a particular object of Erica's disfavor because of his color. And you must admit, Erica, that you have made remarks to me which indicate he just might have a point. Why, I remember…"

Erica, red-faced, interrupted Leslie with a tight-lipped smile. "You may interpret what I may have said to you in the past as you wish, Leslie. I do wish though that you would stop running off at the mouth! Do shut up! I am just as unprejudiced as you are, which may or may not mean I have no prejudices. And Hal Bridges is an indifferent student at best, whatever color he happens to be. I am sick to death of the Black students on this campus playing on their poor, victimized lives in order to get grades they don't deserve. I as much as told that to the young man, and if that has caused him to become a murderer then I certainly take no responsibility. But I think your theory is extremely farfetched. I hope your other one is more sensible."

Leslie and Jeffry both realized that despite Erica's admonition to Leslie to shut up that she was curious about her other theory. So was Jeffry.

"Oh, I don't know if it is all that sensible, Erica, but it is terribly romantic and I rather prefer it myself. You see I have hesitated to bring it up because I did not wish to hurt you further by mentioning Paul's name."

"What on earth does Paul have to do with anything?" Erica snapped, the color rushing back into her cheeks.

"Hasn't it ever occurred to you, Erica, that Paul's murderer may not have been just some thief on the street. After all, nobody was apprehended. We may be up against an enemy of Paul's, an enemy so clever, but so bitter that he was not satisfied just to kill Paul, carefully making it look like a robbery. Having achieved his goal, he simply boarded a plane, came to this country, and decided that you too must go. Indeed, he may be somebody who knew you both and bore a grudge against both of you."

"Ah, a grudge," Jeffry nodded, encouraging Leslie to go on.

"I don't mean to say that I could identify the killer. But it seems to me that he might be somebody from some other corner of Erica's and Paul's life, someone whom Erica either does or doesn't know who for some devious reason doesn't feel that he has completed his revenge until both parties are dead. Or perhaps there is no grudge. Perhaps Paul was involved in some shady business and our killer is afraid that he confided in Erica. She too, you see, must be silenced."

Erica rose to her feet and put her papers into a folder. "You are a fool, Leslie, an absolute, outrageous fool. If you weren't such a fool, I would almost think that you had tried to kill me yourself. But you are positively too asinine to have even approached the level of ineptitude of the killer!" Erica made her exit as if she were leaving the stage and expected a standing ovation.

As she walked down the hall, seething, she began to calm down and laughed quietly to herself. When she saw Jasper coming out of the men's room with some brooms and mops, she stopped him. "By the way, Jasper," she said to him quietly, "thank you for returning the book."

"I didn't return any book, Dr. Berne," the elderly man replied evenly.

"Well, if that's the way you wish to play it, it is quite okay with me, Jasper. I nevertheless think that was the sensible thing to do."

Jasper moved down the hall, throughly perplexed. Jeffry, who had stayed on talking with Leslie briefly, turned down the hall to his office wondering if Halloway was flinging about for motives as wildly as Leslie was. Leslie, however, remained behind and began to correct papers. She looked up at the portrait on the wall and smiled at the famous writer as if the two of them were in collusion with each other. Leslie was very pleased with herself.

Jill entered the student lounge, taking a few minutes to relax before her next class. Her friend Bill Brown was there, browsing through some magazines, but now he came over and sat next to Jill. "What up?" he inquired, making himself comfortable in the soft chair.

"Nothing good," Jill replied. "I find I'm beside myself and I can't concentrate on anything."

"All this murder stuff?" Bill asked.

"Yes, I guess. Everything, Bill." Jill felt the desire to confide in him that she had personal problems as well. She had come to know Bill rather well this semester since they had exactly the same courses, but she felt reluctant to discuss her feelings for her professor with him. He would doubtless be shocked that she was secretly seeing David. Perhaps not, though. Bill seemed a strange combination, serious and sensitive in his reactions to literature, but often clowning, refusing to take anything seriously.

"I'm in bad shape too," Bill confided.

"Two of a kind?" Jill smiled. Bill was fascinated by her smile. She seemed to find him really amusing, but he felt a slight mockery in it. Yet he didn't feel offended. Having pretty good instincts about people, Bill suspected that Jill's smile was more self-protective than patronizing.

"I wish I could talk to you, Jill."

"You can," Jill said quietly, thinking it ironic that he was about to confide in her just when she had thought of confiding in him.

"I don't know. What do you think of Jeffry Platz?"

"Platz? I like his course. I didn't expect to really; somehow I always thought the eighteenth century would be boring. But he makes it come alive. And he certainly seems to have a feeling for Johnson. Do you think he is old Sam reincarnated? Of course he's handsome as well, which doesn't exactly make him qualify, but he seems to have that sort of hard-won sanity that he keeps showing us in Sam." Jill paused, wondering why Bill was asking about their professor. "He strikes me as a lonely person," she added. "Why do you ask?"

"He's gay."

"Oh, how do you know?"

"Because I am."

"I see," Jill gulped. She wasn't sure she was up to this confession but was relieved that Bill was not the one to receive her own confession at this point.

Bill watched Jill closely for signs of shock, or judgment, or repulsion, but he saw none.

"What is it you're worrying about Bill? Are you with him?" Jill asked gently.

Bill's face contorted slightly. "I was terribly flattered at first. Oh, I knew he was gay almost from the first; I can tell, you know, all sorts of signs, and I'm not exactly a top student so I was really flattered that he took such an interest in me. *Brown's Life of Platz* was going to make *Boswell's Life of Johnson* second class, you see. But I'm in over my head, Jill, and I don't know what to do."

"What do you want to do?" Jill asked as calmly as she could.

"I want out."

"Then why don't you get out?"

"It's not so easy. I'm still taking his course. And there's other things. But I tell you, Jill, the man is eating my life. You would think a big, important scholar like that wouldn't bother with me for long, wouldn't you? But he won't let me breathe a breath without his okay."

"Then drop the course and to hell with it," Jill suggested.

"I can't. It's complicated."

Jill felt relieved when Melvin came into the student lounge. She wasn't at all sure that she wanted to hear about those complications. Her own life was complicated enough. She too was involved with a professor; she too felt somewhat out of her depth. But oh what a difference! David was not eating up her life. He was offering it to her.

"We'll talk more, Bill," Jill said. "Perhaps I can help."

Bill flushed, sorry he had brought the subject up. He stood to leave. "You won't mention this to anyone, Jill. I trust you," he whispered.

"Of course not, Bill."

He turned and left the lounge.

After greeting Melvin, Jill sat for a minute, wondering. What kind of hold did Jeffry Platz have over Bill? She remembered that Bill worked at a local gas station and wondered if Platz had used him to try to get rid of Erica Berne–after all, he would know just what to do to the car. The thought made her feel sick to her stomach. She liked Bill. Still, she had to admit that it was a possibility.

Something about the car and Bill didn't feel right. Jill retained her strong intuition that she herself was connected in some way with Nora's murder and the other attempts on Erica. Not only was Bill a good friend, but Jeffry Platz also seemed to think well of her. She was getting an A in his course and had been involved in several interesting and protracted conversations with him in his office. And hadn't Bill just confided in her, trusting her with information that could be destructive to him if it got into the wrong hands?

Maybe she was wrong. Maybe she was not in any danger. She could be suffering from the anxieties of her overprotected upbringing. Like her father, she could be sensing danger lurking behind every bush. In that case, what Bill may have wished to confide in her before Melvin came in was that he was not only involved with Platz but with murder as well.

Still feeling vaguely sick, Jill decided she must try to find another opportunity to talk with Bill alone. She was pretty sure though, from the manner of his retreat, that Bill had no intentions of confiding in her again.

CHAPTER XIII

Sometimes Jasper worked the day shift, sometimes the night. He had been on day shift this week–that's why Erica had seen him to thank him for some book he didn't know anything about– and this morning he arrived again at 7:00. All he really did in the early morning shift was to open the windows on nice days and air the place a bit, tidy up a little if needed, and wait for arrivals and the inevitable mess that accumulated during the day.

While he was opening Dr. Stein's window, he paused. Along with the chirping of a bird that had perched on the tree just outside the window, he thought he detected a ticking sound. Jasper was a veteran of the Korean war; in fact he often cornered Jim Strand and told him some of his favorite war stories. But ever since his experiences in combat he had been alert to danger and he sensed danger now. Moving very slowly, he stood in the middle of the small room and listened intently. The ticking was distinct and came from the direction of the left wall. Jasper moved ever so slowly toward the noise, and as he got closer he decided it was coming from the next office; that would be Dr. Berne's.

Uncertain of what to do, Jasper decided he might just call the campus police. Or maybe even Detective Halloway. But then if it wasn't what he thought it was, he believed he would look silly.

If he started jumping at every little noise, pretty soon they might not even want him around. He loved his job. Lots of the students liked to talk to him—for one thing he listened to them. There were things he knew about, things that went on around this building that he bet lots of other people would like to know. But he kept his mouth shut. He liked being around young people.

Then it occurred to him that maybe he could go outside and around the building and look in the window. That way he might just be able to see what was what. The shade would be drawn though as he hadn't yet been in old Erica's office and a good thing he hadn't, maybe. Was it his imagination or was the noise getting louder, the ticking noise? He felt pretty foolish standing with his ear to the wall, and the bird chirping outside the window seemed to be mocking him.

Well, better safe than dead, he thought. He picked up Stein's phone and dialed the campus police. "This may sound crazy to you guys," he said guiltily once he reached them, "but I think there may be a bomb in the English building. This is Jasper Mann and I hear some really strange ticking in one of the offices."

When two of the campus police came over, they decided that Jasper was probably wrong, but in the light of previous trouble there they called Halloway, who came over immediately with a bomb squad. In no time at all the men had broken into the window from outside and had dismantled a bomb attached to the door which, despite its homemade, crude quality, would have nicely blown Erica Berne into several pieces had she entered her office as usual that morning.

Jasper didn't feel so foolish after all.

CHAPTER XIV

In order to deal with the latest attempt on Erica Berne's life, the students developed a series of sick jokes which were circulating among students and faculty. The least Erica Berne could do, according to one of the jokes, was commit suicide since her killer might cause untold havoc in his bungling attempts to destroy her. Or, the killer gets an A+ for his concept, a B- for his efforts, and an F for his failure to achieve his goals. Jim Strand was still muttering as well about the sloppy methods of the killer. If Nora had not been killed, and Susie were not back at her desk, still bruised enough to remind everybody of her near miss, then the ineptitude of Erica's would-be killer might be a source of real enjoyment. Instead, everyone still felt anxious and endangered. And just to complicate matters, Leslie Podmonk's theories about the murder had become current gossip and an enraged Hal Bridges was talking about a possible law suit.

Once again Inspector Halloway was a familiar figure on campus and once more a series of interviews became necessary, this time to establish everybody's movements during the hours between 5:00 p.m. on Thursday when Erica left her office and 7:00 a.m. on Friday when Jasper Mann had detected the ticking noise. The only person who seemed clearly off the hook at this point was Jasper himself, whose caution and luck in hearing the bomb had actually not saved Erica's life but his own.

Leslie Podmonk confided her new idea that the murderer was an outsider to Inspector Halloway. "This latest incident with the bomb," she explained, "gives full validity to my theory that I have been developing for some time. The faculty, you see," she explained to Halloway, "are well aware that Jasper airs out our offices before we arrive in the morning. And when Jasper is on night shift, then Mary Fern does the same. So you see, only an outsider or a student would have thought to kill Erica with the bomb."

"You don't think," Halloway queried, "that an insider might have been so focused on killing Erica that he might have been sure the professor would be killed by the bomb?"

"No," Leslie replied. "None of us are stupid enough to have overlooked the possibility that Jasper or Mary, not Erica, would be the victim. On the other hand," she continued, "Hall Bridges is a likely suspect. Not too bright and definitely a victim of Erica's prejudices."

"I thought you and Erica were good friends," Halloway said, looking dubious.

"Yes, of course, we are the best of friends," Leslie lied, although she thought the rift would not last. "I'm only talking about Erica's prejudices because of the serious nature of previous events and in order to be helpful. If you don't wish me to go on, I'll be happy to end this conversation," she added huffily.

It wasn't really Hal that was her main suspect anyway, Leslie explained. If she were Inspector Halloway she would ask Erica some very pointed questions about Paul's business activities. Had it occurred to the Inspector that there might be some connection between the seemingly motiveless murder of Paul in London–well not motiveless, robbery perhaps–and the attempts on Erica's life. Couldn't Paul have confided some dangerous information to Erica which the murderer feared she might spill?

Leslie concluded the interview by thanking Halloway for taking her seriously and for his promise to follow up on her theory. "Yes, if I have any more ideas, I'll contact you immediately," she informed the detective. And out she flounced.

———)(◍)(———

Jill received a surprising call from her brother. He was being sent to collect her. Jill laughed, but he apparently meant it.

"I'll be there tomorrow. Pack. Or not," was his response and he quickly hung up. Oh well, Jill thought, it will be nice to see him anyway.

———)(◍)(———

Erica decided to take a book to the park and read. She would visit the bench where she had first met Paul. Perhaps she would be able to feel his presence and gain some comfort. As she walked down her street, she had a strange feeling that she was being followed. When she turned to look, nobody was in sight. She went on, crossing the street that led to the park. Now she could swear that she heard footsteps behind her. Again, she turned to look and only a few students were in sight. The students were walking toward her, not following her.

— 113 —

Walking down the path that led to the bench where she had been reading when Paul sat down next to her, she was glad for the solitude. No students lolling around sun worshiping. Too close to the end of the semester. They were probably studying for a change.

Erica began to read her book, an escapist thriller that she was truly enjoying. Then she looked up as she thought she heard something in the nearby bushes. She could have sworn that the bush looked different from the way it had looked when she sat down. Somebody was following her, hiding in doorways, hiding in bushes. Or was it the thriller she was reading? Was she imagining danger at every turn?

Returning to her book, she became absorbed. She didn't even see or hear Jim Strand when he quietly sat down next to her. "Hello, Erica," Jim said casually, as if they had arranged a meeting and were scheduled for a chat.

"You scared me, young man," Erica responded cooly. Seeing him there where Paul had sat was a terrible shock, but she managed to control her reaction. "What brings you out to my neck of the woods?" she asked as casually as she could.

"Oh, is this your neck of the woods, Erica? I didn't realize that," Jim said with a slight smile.

He's making fun of me, she thought, the wretched man. "Yes, I live just 3 short blocks from here. I often come here to read in the spring."

"It's quite a lovely spot," Jim replied. "I've only been to this park a few times, but I felt like a walk. Good book?"

"No, not a good book, Jim. Just escape, a thriller. I often read them just to get away from it all."

"Do you now?" Jim asked with what Erica thought was a sinister tone. Perhaps she *had* been followed. Perhaps Jim was following her. Maybe this meeting was not an accident at all.

"And how do you feel about your second year at Huston?" Erica inquired, trying to get onto a safe topic. "I notice you have quite a student following."

"Oh, Huston is a great place," Jim lied with ease. "The students are enthusiastic and there is actually plenty of time to write."

"And what is it you are working on?"

"I'm revising my dissertation on *Measure for Measure*. Hope to send it off in a few weeks," Jim replied, amusing himself with his second lie. He hadn't been writing at all this year.

"Wise thing to do. And what about your friend David Stein? Is he revising his dissertation as well?"

"Oh, David's way ahead of me, Erica. He's revised and sent it off. Hoping to hear something back soon." A third lie. David's manuscript had been rejected by Chicago. How many more lies could he tell, he wondered.

"Nice chatting with you, Jim," Erica said, becoming somewhat curt. "I hope you'll forgive me if I return to my book. Must find out who done it, you know."

Jim got the hint and stood up to leave. "Yes," he said. "We must all do that, don't you think?" He walked away, moving further into the park.

What on earth, Erica wondered, was that supposed to mean? Did Jim Strand fancy himself a detective who would find out who was trying to kill her? Laughable. But she was furious. How dare he sit down where Paul had sat? He had ruined the site for her. Polluted it! What an obnoxious man he was! She sat for a while longer, looking at the empty space next to her, yearning for Paul.

⸺《◉》⸺

Later in the day, Jim, David, and Jill went back to David's apartment in order to discuss the whole matter with some privacy. They were pretty sure that nobody had seen them heading for their meeting. It was Jill's first time there and she was fascinated with David's paintings. One in particular caught her eye–it was an abstract landscape filled with numerous tiny figures who were climbing, leaping, and swimming through it. She thought to herself that their tastes were quite similar. With a little fixing up, she could be quite comfortable here. When David offered her a beer, she wondered if he could read her thoughts and found herself blushing.

Jim was angry about the bomb. "Okay, you guys, Halloway doesn't seem to be making much progress, so let's us get down to business and wind this thing up. It's really beginning to disgust me."

"Fine with me, Jim," David said as he handed Jim a beer.

"I had a long talk with Halloway today," Jim continued, "and I don't think he's anyone's fool. On the other hand, I think we three might make a superb detecting team. After we solve this one, maybe we should leave the university life for one of crime. Crime detection that is."

"Well, at least we know that Jasper is clear," Jill said. "And as far as I'm concerned Hal Bridges is out of the question. I haven't any hard evidence, but I know Hal pretty well and he's about the last person in the world who would go after Erica in any underhanded way. He hates her guts, but he's perfectly open about it."

"Leslie may be wrong about Hal," David agreed, "but her other theory about a connection with Paul's murder may not be so farfetched. We all know that Jasper or Mary airs out the offices before we get there, at least most of the time. It would seem to let Platz, Black, and Leslie out. And after all, nobody knows much about Paul's business. I seem to recall that he was a salesman of some kind, working in gifts, but I suppose that could be a front for some heavy underworld peddling. I think it would be rather amusing to find that Erica was actually a budding drug dealer about to be wed to a drug thug."

"Not to worry," Jill said. "I just got a call from my baby brother. My parents have apparently lost their minds and have sent him to fetch me, even loaning him their car. He apparently thinks he can solve this business. Since my world has gone crazy, apparently theirs has too. I don't know what I can do with him, between needing to study and this whole business. He arrives, I gather, tomorrow."

"Great," Jim laughed. "We can use a spy from the outside world."

The thought of her brother as a spy made Jill laugh despite herself.

"Of course," Jim said, "it's possible that Jasper was the one who was supposed to die. Have you noticed which three people have been the victims of the murderer's antics? Two secretaries and a janitor? Maybe we have a clever killer who wants us to think

Erica is the victim but who is systematically wiping out the staff so that none of us can function. An anti-English Department nut or a clever fiend working indirectly to undermine the working of the department. No doubt should he accomplish that goal, French would be next. Then on to science and tomorrow the whole damned ivory tower." Everyone laughed half-heartedly but a sense of bafflement remained.

"Seriously, Jim," Jill said, still not used to calling either David or Jim by their first names. "David and I suspect that Nora and Susie may have actually been meant to die, and Susie seems to think I am in danger as well. Only nothing connects. I mean, if I'm in danger, your theory breaks down. Unless," she laughed, "first the staff, then the students must go."

"All kidding aside, Jim," David added, handing him another beer, "Jill and I think Nora and Susie were possibly intended to die. But the snag is that Susie was a last minute choice to get the car when Erica didn't feel well. Susie says Black has been behaving rather oddly lately and he may even be the best candidate just because it was he who suggested Susie get Erica's car.

But how would he know Erica was going to be sick and need somebody to get her car?"

"Maybe they're in it together," Jim mused. "But all kidding aside, let's take Leslie's theory that Paul was in money rackets, drugs, or some such. Erica, true blue, and up tight, learned of it all, told Black, her old flame, and together they plotted Paul's death, and..."

"Be serious, Jim," David admonished. "Jill has to leave soon. Why is Leslie so anxious to persuade us all that Paul was a crook? I thought you told me Leslie was terribly jealous of Paul. Wouldn't that make her eager to defame him in everybody's eyes and get even with Erica who hasn't been interested in maintaining their friendship? Maybe we should take a long, hard look at Leslie."

"Maybe," Jim conceded, "but I have a little trouble seeing old Leslie out there with tools working on the car."

"Oh, you men," Jill laughed. "Lots of us female types know about cars these days. Of course, I don't happen to be one of them, but… "

Jim was feeling the effects of the beer now and was warming to the conversation. "We're forgetting silent Platz. If anything Jeffry seems more communicative than ususal these days. Have you thought about that? Maybe a sign of guilt?"

"In other words," David noted, "everybody is guilty. Nice place to work! Maybe, what you suggested, Jim, is a good idea. The three of us *should* leave at the end of the year and open a detective agency. We can specialize in college killings. Although I guess we need to solve this one first if we're going to have any credentials."

"Maybe we should include high school killings," Jim added. "And I think we should rescue Susie from this place when we start the agency. She could start out as a secretary but I'm sure once we make our first million, we could find another secretary and let her be a partner."

"Ah ha! Don't think we're not onto you and Susie. I just wonder if Susie herself is on to you," David laughed. "She seems to be her old self again, finally."

"Yes," Jim replied. "but I do worry about her."

"Actually, Jill and I have decided to start seeing each other openly as soon as the semester ends. Only a couple of weeks to go. If we stay, I hope you do too, Jim. She is going to request you as her new adviser."

"Well, in that case, of course I'll stay," Jim smiled. "Only, David, don't you think we had better both be careful. I mean in any mystery story I've ever read, the least suspicious person has turned out to be the murderer. My vote is for Jill."

All three of them laughed. They decided to meet again and give it another go, maybe with Jill's brother and Susie present. After discussing the Supreme Court's unanimous ruling ordering the busing of students to achieve racial desegregation, which they thought a truly exciting development, the four of them nevertheless felt that they had merely been fumbling in the dark.

───≈)(O)(≈───

A bomb exploded; smoke pervaded the field and then dispersed. Bodies lay lifeless, limbs distorted. Erica sat in front of the television set and watched the succession of images without really seeing them. Noises came from the direction of the set, but she didn't really hear them. She was becoming inured to the dangers of her existence. This time, she would not even miss a day of school. She had told Halloway to leave her alone; she could take care of herself.

Images of war caught her attention momentarily. The set was steeped in blood which now lay in pools on the ground and on the corpses. Erica thought she could detect herself moving through the smoke, stepping over the bodies, looking for something, someone. Paul?

Set off. Lights out, first one, then the other. Into the bedroom, light on, robe off, slippers off. Out to the living room to check the door. Double locked. Back into the bedroom, light out, into bed.

Erica lay with her eyes open, wondering if she could sleep. She listened briefly to the crickets chirping and then sat up, rigid. She could have sworn she heard footsteps outside the window. Impossible. The window was almost closed, despite the spring night. Maybe, despite her instructions to him, Halloway had left a guard at the house and he was checking. Probably nothing though.

Her body slowly relaxed and she slipped back down deep under the covers. Indeed, she would have to go to school tomorrow. The apartment was beginning to get to her. Her bedroom was small and with the door shut, she felt closed in. Perhaps she would get up again and watch the rest of the film. She did not move.

Erica's thoughts flipped back to the time last month when she had been trapped in the elevator at school. The building only had three floors, but Erica usually took the faculty elevator in order to avoid the student rush on the staircases. She had barely begun the ascent when the elevator belched, jolted, stopped... obviously between floors.

Whenever she misbehaved as a small child, Erica's mother had locked her in her room, a routine that had left her more than slightly claustrophobic. She had been locked in for hours at a time, hours that were extended into more hours when Erica had pounded on the door to demand release. She was a regular Jane Eyre! Now, standing in the elevator, Erica had panicked just as she had as a child. After she found and pressed the emergency button, she heard a voice yell from somewhere, "Who's in there?"

"Dr. Berne," she had responded. "Get me out of here immediately!"

"Yes, Dr. Berne, of course. We'll get Jasper here right away. It won't be long. Just stay calm."

"I am calm," Erica had barked.

Erica knew that they would find Jasper or somebody else quickly. She knew she would get out. Her mother had always eventually relented. But she was having trouble breathing.

"Help is on its way, Dr. Berne," the voice had yelled at her. But the minutes ticked by and Erica felt faint. What if the elevator fell? She was frantic.

Then she heard tinkering noises. Jasper had come. There was some more tinkering, another jolt, and the elevator had returned her to the first floor; the doors opened. "You certainly took enough time," she snapped at Jasper. "Go and dismiss my class, please. It's room 342."

Too shaken to teach, Erica had gone to the faculty lounge and had simply sat for hours. Margaret Lambert had come in with some papers to correct. She was very pretty and very pregnant. Erica could remember staring at her rounded body, wondering what it felt like to have another person growing inside you. She had thought to herself that it must be terrible. It must be like being caught in an elevator for months. You couldn't escape. You couldn't divest yourself of that other life. How could Margaret sit there so calmly, so smugly, with such a terrible burden to carry. How could the poor woman sleep at night?

Reminding herself, as she lay in bed, that she was neither pregnant nor caught in an elevator, Erica ordered herself to stop tossing and go to sleep. But the minutes ticked by and she was unable to divest herself of the panic that was effecting her breathing. It was worse, she realized, as she lay there in a sweat with a growing sense of agony, than being caught in an elevator. It was her own skin, her own body that encased her and there was no way out. She lay there far into the night, aware of the weight of her body on the sheets. She was irrevocably trapped.

———————

Jill was working on her bed, her books and papers spread out around her. She knew this was a dangerous place to work; she would inevitably fall asleep. But she didn't feel eager about the paper. While trying to make sense of the imagery in Harold Pinter's *The Homecoming*, her mind kept coming back to the situation at school. It all seemed terribly unreal. Despite her excitement about the growth of her relationship with David, she felt that her life had taken on a nightmarish quality and she couldn't quite wake up.

Something about the Pinter play kept nagging at her too, something that she felt related to the nature of the events at school. Even though Pinter's plays were enigmatic, to say the least, she had discovered with David's help that one could approach the mystery. The first time she read *The Homecoming*, before they discussed it in class, she had been truly shocked. She had even said in class that she thought Pinter had just gone too far. He had depicted this family of animals, well maybe people, but jungle types, and when the one intellectual person, the son who is a professor, brings his wife home to visit, they keep her and send him back to America. And the son doesn't even fight to keep her!

She was further shocked when David seemed to be teasing her about her reaction. He announced that he himself identified with the family, the butcher, the pimp, the chauffeur, and the demolition worker by day, boxer by night. When some of the students said that they found the family despicable, he replied, "Careful there, you're talking about my family!"

It was the professor, he suggested, who might be the villain of the piece. The first actor who played the part, he added, had thought of him as an Eichmann, the Nazi World War II criminal who had insisted, when protected from the public by being put in a glass booth, that he had just followed orders. "I want you to think about how the professor differs from the rest of the family. And I don't mean that he is an intellectual. Pinter is playing around with your expectations."

A lively discussion had ensued. Many of the students thought that the professor's wife, who accepted the family's invitation that she stay with the family, was a whore. But David had questioned that interpretation as well by telling them that Pinter had said the play was about love and that the characters were not evil but desperate. He had referred them to the Book of Ruth in the bible. The wife's name was Ruth.

Jill didn't feel ready to write a paper on the play. Clearly Pinter was indeed playing around with expectations and appearances, presenting a reality as difficult to unravel as this murder at Huston College. Who were the good guys, who the bad?

Jill remembered that the day they heard about Paul's death, David's class had been discussing Samuel Beckett's play, *Endgame*. Some of the students had mistakenly thought that Hamm's helpmate, and possibly his adopted son, had left at the end, gone out into a world that might well be empty of all life. But in reality, the stage directions indicated that Clov remained. The audience knew he was there. Only the blind Hamm was left in the dark.

Jill rose from the bed and turned on the radio. She heard the voice of Leonard Cohen singing some of her favorite songs. She enjoyed the darkness of many of his lyrics, his rather raspy voice. After all, wasn't she in the dark?

Flopping back down on the bed, she kept wondering why she felt like a victim herself? And if she was in danger, why? Was she a whore because she was having a flirtation with her professor? The answer seemed to come from the radio as Cohen sang, "There ain't no cure/ there ain't no cure/ there ain't no cure for love." Who had killed Nora and why? She rose again, turned off the radio, and collapsed back onto the bed.

Pushing the papers and books aside, Jill reached for the light switch, turned it off, and fell back exhausted on her pillow. Her sleep, though, was restless. She was running on campus to meet David, running as fast as she could; it was terribly important to be on time. And somebody was chasing her, somebody who wanted to kill her, to drown her, to smother the life out of her... and she was losing her breath, straining, in slow motion now, and then she felt herself falling and it was pitch dark.

Now she was deep in the forest and someone was stealthily moving toward her. Was it David? Was it the killer? She could hear the beating of her own heart, but she slithered down into the weeds, holding her breath, praying that the danger would pass. How long could she bear to hide here? Which way was the noise coming from? Behind her? To the left? Should she call for help?

Lying there, trying not to make a sound, Jill realized that she was dreaming, but she couldn't wake up. All she could do was will herself to change the dream slightly. The danger was not so close. She could get up, she could move... walk, slowly, slowly silently... but she was lost. Which way to go now? Back toward the light or on toward the dark, giant trees ahead? She found herself moving toward the trees, closer, closer...

The sweat was oozing from her body as Jill finally managed to wake up. She lay there for what seemed like hours. Forcing herself to keep her eyes open, listening for unknown sounds in her apartment, afraid to go back to sleep, to return to her dream, afraid to stay awake, afraid to see the face which she knew was behind the tree.

⟞⟝⟞⟝

The next day, tired and anxious after her restless night, Jill was tempted to skip Dr. Berne's class, but she managed to drag herself there. Dr. Berne was discoursing in her usual ultra-boring fashion about some abstruse sources for obscure articles, when she noticed that Jill was nodding off. Jill hadn't meant to be rude, but feeling almost drugged in the slightly hot classroom, she was having a terrible time keeping her eyes open.

"Miss Lake," Erica shot out "am I to understand that you are too bored to stay awake in my class? Is the scholarly life a bit too much for you, my dear?"

Jill was now thoroughly awake. Enraged, but cool, she rose to her feet and found herself walking to the front of the room. "Professor Berne," she heard herself say, "I find your class uncommonly dull and almost totally worthless. I also find your tone with me insulting and unprofessional. I am dropping this course, and I have no intention of taking it as long as you are its teacher." Jill left the room abruptly, leaving Erica and the class stunned.

Marching, rather than walking into the main office, Jill asked Susie if Dr. Black was busy. Susie, who had returned to work only the day before, still seemed shaky to Jill, but she was able to show her into Black's office. "Good luck," she whispered to Jill. "You'll have to tell me what's cooking later." Jill nodded, Susie exited, closing the door behind her and Black offered Jill a seat. Taking a deep breath, Jill repeated to Black the words she had just spoken in the classroom. She was beginning to enjoy herself thoroughly and was delighted to see the shock on the chairman's face. He was making noises about some alternative possibility being found, the great irregularity of it all, and what would Professor Berne say.

"I don't in the least care what Dr. Berne says," Jill announced. "I refuse to be treated in such a fashion. I'm not asking for special consideration. I'm issuing a complaint." Before Dr. Black could reply, Jill made a fast exit, winked at Susie, and almost skipped down the hall to David's office to tell him the news. She wasn't sure of the implications of what she had done or what it all meant, but she did know that in some very profound and important way she was now free.

CHAPTER XV

Margaret Lambert was walking to Welkin Hall, the art building. She had given her journalism class an assignment that involved the use of art in their reporting and she needed to check on a few of the paintings there. She could feel the baby kicking inside and put her hand tenderly on her stomach. Humming softly to the unborn child, she felt it would not be long before she would hold him or her in her arms while she sang. She hoped she could finish the semester before the arrival, but just in case she had the final papers due early so she could try to finish grading in time.

Jill Lake passed by, headed to the cafeteria where she thought she might find David. "Jill," Margaret called to the girl, who turned back to see what she wanted. "Where are you rushing off to?"

"Hi, Dr. Lambert," Jill said, still somewhat flushed from her experience in Dr. Berne's class. Just going for a bite to eat."

"Well, slow down and walk with me a bit. I'm headed for Welkin. It's on your way."

"Sure," Jill said, slowing down to walk with the professor.

"I need to know the latest, Jill. I don't seem to be in the main stream here but I'm as anxious as the rest of you to see this murder thing settled. Catch me up," she smiled.

"Not much new," Jill replied. "Some of the students who were under suspicion have been cleared since they had alibis for the Susie incident. I knew they were innocent anyhow, but now the police know too. Susie is much better, but she's still fragile."

"Well that's good, I guess," Margaret responded. "But must we all suspect each other?"

"I think you're the only one nobody has yet suspected," Jill said. "But I can imagine that in your condition it must be pretty awful to be in a place filled with suspicion and danger. I feel in danger myself and have absolutely no idea why."

"I hope not, Jill. I mean I hope you're not in danger. But I must say if one more awful thing happens on this campus, I may fold my tents. I don't want my baby feeling all this angst even before entering the world."

"I can well understand. My parents are having fits because I won't come home, but I do want to finish the semester if I possibly can." Jill paused to consider, but she was so full of her experience with Erica that she thought she might explode. "Dr. Lambert, I just did something that may have upset Dr. Berne more than the attempts on her life."

"You? But what on earth do you mean, Jill?"

"I told her that her class was boring and that I was dropping it."

"You what?"

"And I did it in front of the rest of the class. She was picking on me in front of them and I just had it. And believe it or not, I'm not one bit sorry."

"I see." Margaret knew all the students would have dreamed of doing the same thing, but she was a bit amazed at Jill. "You must be the student heroine. I bet they all would have liked to join you but didn't have the guts. Are you sure you want to major in literature, Jill? I think you'd be a good journalist. I'd be happy to have you in any of my courses."

"Even after what I've told you?" Jill inquired, surprised that the professor wasn't scolding her.

"Even after what you've told me," Margaret confessed. I know the faculty and students think of me as quiet and retiring and to some extent they're right. But I've worked in the field, Jill, and let me assure you that one has to take chances and behave a bit, what shall I say, a bit out of the range of the polite if you're going to get a real story. I've heard that you are a fine student and I doubt very much if this somewhat outrageous action of yours will interfere with your progress here. At least I hope it won't."

"Thanks so much for understanding," Jill said. "It just happened and though I stopped into Professor Black's office to tell him about it–I told him I was issuing a complaint because of what she said to me first–I'm still a bit rattled from the whole experience. I guess I haven't digested it yet. And I know it puts Professor Black in an awkward position with Dr. Berne. I can only imagine what she'll have to say to him."

"Well, that's his problem, Jill," Margaret said reassuringly. If I were you, I'd go have a huge, fattening lunch, treat yourself to a big piece of chocolate cake, or a huge apple--that's my craving at the moment–and enjoy the beautiful day. And do let me know what develops if you have a chance. Here's my stop."

As the professor entered the art building, Jill called after her, "Thanks so much. You've made me feel much better." And she did feel much better, much better. What a lovely woman. Too bad I'm not interested in journalism, Jill thought. She beats Berne and Podmonk as a person any day of the week. It would be nice to have a sympathetic woman professor. Ah well. She must find David.

Entering the cafeteria, Jill spied David at a table in the back, eating and reading the newspaper. Without even considering how it would look, Jill sat down next to him and poked her finger into the paper.

"Well, hello there," David said, startled as he lowered his newspaper. He looked around, wondering why Jill was openly approaching him as he ate.

"I did it!" Jill blurted out.

"Did what?"

"Dropped the course. She was at me again, in front of the entire class so I gave her a piece of her own medicine. I went up front, announced that the course was boring and that I was dropping it. And then I went to Black's office and issued a complaint. And told him what I did."

Breathless, Jill waited for a reply.

"Well," David said, "as my family would say, *Mazel tov*! That means congratulations. Let's get out of here before anybody else joins us or reports us or whatever. Unless you need to eat lunch, that is," David added.

"Too excited to eat. Let's go. You go first and I'll join you outside in a few minutes."

When they had rejoined each other outside, David suggested that they take a walk down at the lake. It wasn't usually crowded there during the day, and perhaps they would even be alone. The lake was a favorite spot on campus for late night strolling, surrounded as it was by trees and rocks. David had told her that it very much resembled Mirror Lake, a pond as this one really was, that he frequented when he was a student at Ohio State.

"I'll meet you there in a few minutes," Jill said. David sauntered off, whistling, and Jill sat on a nearby bench for a few minutes to let him get a head start. When she finally joined him at the edge of the water, she found him staring into it. "Narcissus?" she said in his ear. "You must be in love."

"You've got that right," David laughed, but with you, nymph that you may be."

Jill knew the myth about Narcissus falling in love with his own image and rejecting the nymph, Echo.

"I'm not much of an Echo," she retorted. I really, truly told her off, David."

"And I couldn't possibly reject you." David added. "So I can't be Narcissus."

Joining hands, the two walked almost all around the pond, enjoying the slight breeze, the blooming flowers, and even the squirrels that occasionally hastened across their path. It was as if anything went, as if all murders in the world had been solved, and as if their careers were growing with their infatuation with each other, which did not endanger them so much as help them grow. They knew they would have to come back to reality soon, but for now…

After looking carefully in both directions to be sure nobody was about, David pulled Jill into a long embrace. Her body collapsed into his as he kissed her, long and hard, over and over again.

"Oh David," she sighed. "I can't tell you how liberated I feel."

"You don't have to," David laughed. "I can feel it in your kiss."

After another long kiss, he whispered in her ear, "I do believe this is love, Jill, that I feel I mean. And I feel liberated too."

"Love," Jill sighed. "Yes, I do believe it is."

CHAPTER XVI

Wilfred Black thought of himself as a well-balanced, cool individual. Of course his job made certain demands on his emotions, but he had managed admirably over the years to keep a fairly even relationship with his faculty and to handle various problems which came his way. His method was to listen to everyone, give them some degree of support, but hold firm to a few principles which everyone knew could not be bent. Every four years for the past twelve there was an election for a new chairman, and every four years his faculty had voted for him yet again. He was grateful, both for the extra salary the position afforded him and for the continued vote of confidence.

Arriving home on this particular evening, Black felt disgruntled. Being the compulsive person that he was, he followed his regular routine. First he mixed himself a martini, which he sipped while he prepared his dinner: a small steak, boiled potatoes, peas, coffee, nothing fancy, but no T.V. dinners for him. Then as the steak broiled, he set the table, his mind churning with the recent events of the day, the week, even the month. He put a record of Mozart's *Don Giovanni* on—he was very particular about the sound—turned the steak, and sat down to listen, gazing at some of the objects of beauty with which he had carefully decorated the room. The faculty, whom he invited to small cocktail parties once or twice a year, were always surprised at the elegance of his bachelor taste, which was eclectic in nature: a lovely copy of a Monet landscape, a rather frivolous and playful Matisse etching, and several Japanese prints. They enjoyed entering his world of comfort and elegance, and he was happy to have them there, as long as the occasions were few.

Black, however, wasn't as comforted by his surroundings as he usually was. Too much excitement, he thought. Susie was behaving strangely. She looked at him as if he had something to hide. Maybe she actually thought he had been responsible for her disastrous ride in Erica's car, even though ever since he hired her he had treated her, he thought, in a truly fatherly fashion.

And then there was Erica. Always Erica! She had been making accusations about David Stein and Jill Lake, which was a crashing bore. David, of course, should know better than to show interest in one of his own students, but Black couldn't imagine that Erica's accusations were anything but the fantasies of a spinster who had just lost what was surely her last chance at a romance of her own. Once Erica got a hold of something of this nature, she could and no doubt would make everyone miserable.

Having finished his martini, Black decided to make himself another. An unusual bowing to temptation, but Jill Lake had truly put him in an impossible position and he felt he deserved another. He mixed the drink, checked the steak and sat down, thinking perhaps the second drink would relax him enough to see his way through what lay ahead. Jill was clearly not going to take any more of Erica's attacks: she wouldn't even let him reason with her about returning to Erica's class. To date, nobody had really tested him on the business of the course as an absolute requirement. He was always expecting it to happen, but now that it had he didn't know what to do. It would be ridiculous to hold up Jill's degree work–she was an excellent student–just because she wouldn't finish Erica's class. On the other hand, Erica would be furious, and if the other students discovered that he was letting Jill find some other way of fulfilling the requirement that would be the end of student enrollment in Erica's class. Erica would become an intolerable problem if that occurred. In fact he knew he was in serious trouble with her right now and he couldn't afford that. He simply couldn't.

Black went into his small kitchen and checked the steak again. Perhaps if he just waited, the whole problem would go away. The semester was almost over and Erica usually spent the summer on Cape Cod. But with the unresolved situation at school, he knew that she might remain and that she would surely push for a decision on the issue. He knew he couldn't let the faculty as a whole discuss something that was so loaded with the increasing conflicts between Erica and the students.

His telephone rang. It was Halloway.

"May I drop by briefly?" the detective inquired. "I have something important to discuss with you."

Not particularly hungry, and curious about what Halloway might want to discuss, Black encouraged him to come along, turned off the oven, and removed the steak. His dinner was ready, but now it could wait. He would offer Halloway a drink, but he was sure he wouldn't accept one, not when on duty. When the detective arrived, Black enjoyed his reaction to his apartment.

"Nice place you have here, Professor Black. No kids to mess it up either. I can't take a step in my house without tripping over a roller skate, a walking, talking, crawling doll, or one of the kids themselves."

"Care for a martini? I was just relaxing with one before dinner."

"No thanks, must make this fast and get home to the family for a change. But if you were about to eat, do go ahead. I'll just keep you company."

"I'm just relaxing with a drink; do sit down, Detective."

"Well, Professor Black," Halloway said, arranging himself in a modern chair which he sat into harder than he expected, "I'm making slow progress here, and I thought you might be of some further help. I think I'm onto the culprit, you see, but I haven't really any evidence to speak of, nor am I really clear on the motive. So I do need more information if I'm going to put together a case."

"I see," Black smiled. "Sounds like guess work, though, if you have the murderer without evidence or motive."

"That's the problem, Professor Black, that's just the problem. Though it's a bit more than guess work; it's based on hours of investigation by several of my force as well as by myself. And one of your faculty members has also made quite a contribution."

Black felt dismayed, but he managed to keep his usual calm exterior. Was Halloway playing a game with him? Was it he, Black, whom Halloway suspected and was he here on some sort of fishing expedition? If he had another suspect, who could it be? Black decided to be extremely careful, to listen as much as possible, and to say as little as possible.

"I wish I could level with you Professor, but I'm not at liberty to do so. I hope you won't mind just going along with me a bit and answering a few more questions."

"Of course not, shoot," Black replied, almost convincing himself as well as Halloway of his wish to cooperate.

"I feel a bit embarrassed asking you this, Professor, so I do hope you'll bear with me. We are trying to figure out Erica Berne's relationships with a number of people who may be involved in the case. We think we have a pretty good idea now on what the problem is between Jeffry Platz and Erica, but to be honest we don't understand your own relationship with the good lady."

"I see," Black mused, not offering any information.

"You're a smart man, Professor Black. I'm sure that very little goes by you that is going on in the department. You must know that every person that we've interviewed, student and faculty member alike, has told us in the strictest confidence that Erica Berne has something on you that prevents you from either getting rid of her or putting her in her place. At least, in the place that most of them think she deserves to be. I do recall that you mentioned to me that Erica is somewhat maligned here, that she is just a bit traditional as a teacher, etc., etc., etc. But what I'm getting from everybody else is the suggestion of a flaming affair in the past, I mean one between you and Erica; the going theory is that Erica is blackmailing you. I think it would clear the air considerably if you could tell me about it. You don't have to, of course. But if you decide you would like to, I can promise you that the information will remain something that is between you and me–unless, of course, it becomes necessary to air it in a court of law."

"Will you pardon me while I just check something?" Black inquired, not waiting for permission but retreating to the kitchen to think. Halloway sat expectantly, feeling somewhat uncomfortable in the chair he had selected. He wondered if the direct question had been a good idea after all but decided he probably had nothing to lose.

"You know," Black said, resuming his position in his favorite chair and taking a sip of his second martini. "I'd tell you, but I don't think you would believe me. I even think that I could trust you not to take the information any further. And I assure you that this is a matter that I have never discussed with a living soul in the past. My gossiping faculty have been very careful to keep their talk behind my back. Of course, I'm well aware that they think Erica has some special power over me, and in a sense they are right. But it's really trivial, Halloway. I don't see how it could help."

"Why don't you let me decide. If you really trust me Black, do go ahead," Halloway said gently.

"There was no flaming affair between Erica and me; of that I can assure you. But I was taken in by her when she first came here, Halloway. She was not nearly as unattractive then as she has become in the last years, and she was always rather supportive of me, quite flattering to be honest. I don't think she was interested in me as a man though she did flirt with me a bit. But I can sense these things, and I don't think she would have been flirtatious if she was really expecting me to make a pass at her. We did, though, spend some time together. Out to dinner, at her place, ate here, went to an occasional concert. I'm rather a solitary man, Halloway, no family to trip over as you have, and I found her companionable, even enjoyed her sharp tongue when it worked on others."

"I see," Halloway nodded encouragingly.

"Well, that's about it," Black explained.

"What's it?" Halloway asked, baffled. "I don't see how hanging out with Professor Berne would put you under her influence in any way."

"No, I suppose not. But what did happen is difficult to articulate. You see, we used to gossip quite a bit. I trusted her then, and I let my hair down somewhat. She would lead me into it subtly by saying something herself and before I knew it, since she was rather astute, even if her satire was a bit sharp, I would either agree with her or make some crack myself."

"Yes?"

"It's damned hard to know how it happened, but I guess you could call it a form of blackmail. I found later on that when I was about to make a decision about something, she would put her two cents in, and if I balked she would remind me very carefully of something she had said that I had agreed with or something that I had said, and without coming out and threatening me, she would insinuate that if I didn't do as she suggested, she would expose me."

"Expose you for what, for God's sake?"

"You see, I told you it was trivial and hard to believe. Just expose me as a gossip, I guess. I don't know, Halloway, it was really insidious. And as soon as I realized what was going on I gradually withdrew from the relationship. But I have a feeling , whether it's based on reality or not, that she could do me in. I suppose it has been very weak of me to care, but I do. My faculty picture me as a dispassionate, fair chairman and that's very important to me. I guess I would rather have the faculty wonder about her power over me than let her exercise that power."

"I see," Halloway said. "I see."

"What is it that you see, Detective? Motive for a murder? Is that what you need? I can't say that I would grieve to have Erica quietly removed from Huston College. I would breathe more easily and be more my own man. But I assure you that I manage quite nicely as it is, and I am not your man. Aside from anything else, if I did decide to do away with Erica, I assure you that I would not bungle the job."

"She's quite a gal, our Professor Berne, quite a gal," Halloway said.

"Yes, that she is."

"Well, I can only thank you and assure you that you can trust me not to blackmail you myself in the future, Professor Black. I know this was a difficult conversation and I appreciate your candor."

"Does it help you, Detective?"

"I actually think it might, but I have to sift the thing through. I may be in touch again shortly. Oh, by the way, Professor Black, I understand you were a married man yourself some years back."

"I see you have been doing some research, Halloway," Black commented cooly. "That is also one of my little secrets, and since I don't see how it could have any relevance to the present case, I would appreciate your keeping that information to yourself. Is there anything about the marriage that you wish to know? Such as, perhaps, did I kill my wife and any offspring? "

"Not unless you wish to tell me."

"No Detective. I think the present is complex enough, don't you?"

The men parted amicably, Black wondering if Halloway had believed him and Halloway wondering about the mysterious nature of man, and of women too for that matter.

As Black turned to his now far from inviting steak and began absently to eat his meal, his mind went back to the days of his marriage which had ended before he came to Huston College. He thought almost wistfully of his early relationship with Adele. He had hardly been able to believe that a woman with such beauty and vigor could be attracted to anybody as stodgy and pedantic as he knew he was.

At the beginning, however, the woman had actually seemed to worship him. They had been students together at Swarthmore College, and she had hung on his words as if they were sacred sayings. She leaned on him for ideas for her own papers and quoted him to their mutual friends as if he were the founder of a new philosophy. At first, he had hardly dared to ask her out. Possibly Adele herself had suggested their first date, a school play that he had mentioned some interest in seeing. He had been terrified. Adele had the kind of vivacity and good looks that kept her surrounded by men. She was flirtatious and almost ostentatiously sensual, as well as being bright in her own way. Yet she had wished to see the play with *him*!

And had he taken her hand on the way back to the dorm or had she taken his? In retrospect, it was probably she. From that time on the courtship had been rapid: and it was not until they had been married for a number of years that he realized how completely she had taken over and imprisoned the man whom she had supposedly so admired and worshiped. He was shy and retiring and liked to stay at home and work or read. She was gregarious and dragged him to party after party, often staying on into the late hours after he had left. He liked an occasional drink and conversation with a few close friends. She liked to invite every passing stranger to the house, giving parties at which she inevitably ended up drunk. The next mornings were difficult, to say the least.

The children had come along almost inadvertently. Had she planned them or just let them happen the same way she kept house, carelessly, if at all. What would the faculty at Huston think if they knew he had three sons, all grown up and in college? And why had he made such a point of keeping his past a secret?

Guilt, no doubt. Extricating himself from the marriage had led him to the brink of despair. For one thing, he loved Adele. But he knew perfectly well that she had indulged in a series of affairs. He was quite incapable of satisfying her and he knew that as well, which did not, however, prevent him from being furiously jealous and outraged at her behavior. And the children. He loved them as well. Hadn't he all but brought them up by himself? When she thought about it, Adele had been Mother Nature herself with the children, nurturing, loving, playful. Often, however, she didn't bother with them, and there he was, good old dependable

Wilfred. Oh, yes, Detective Halloway, I know about roller skates in the hall and all the rest of it. And I know that in her own way Adele loved me and the children did too. It was just that I was… overwhelmed.

"I'm moving out," he informed Adele one night when he had least expected to be able to get the words out. She was horrified. Claiming love, she begged him to explain and when he tried, she promised a complete reformation of character. She even rushed about the room, cleaning up the mess she knew he despised. "Tell me what you want changed or how I should change and I'll do it," she had promised, tears pouring forth as she clung to him.

So he had stayed for another year. And then, amid the chaos that had gradually and inevitably re-invaded their lives, despite his wife's best efforts, he had left, almost more to his surprise than to hers. The divorce had been ugly. Letters of recrimination. The children turned against him. A major part of his salary gone for child support and the house gone, of course, too. He suffered agonies of guilt and hours of loneliness.

But Adele had adjusted at last. She became a model and then a casting director. She moved the children to New York and managed everything surprisingly well. Indeed, she made far more money than he did at his new position at Huston. She still lectured him on the wickedness of his desertion at the few meetings that were unavoidable when he went to visit the boys, but his feelings of guilt gradually abated and on the whole he now felt well out of it.

The life he led now was his. His apartment was impeccable and designed entirely to his own taste. Elsie came in once a week and saw to it that not a particle of dust interfered with the serenity with which he surrounded himself. Black smiled to himself as he remembered only one unfortunate incident with his prized cleaning lady. She had, she confessed apologetically to him, broken his prized reproduction of a Lembruck statue of a kneeling woman that sat on his piano. "I broke your doll, I'm afraid," she confessed to him. "Head just broke right off." But he had managed the repairs so that one would need to inspect the statue closely to see its imperfections. He invited only those he chose to invite to the apartment. He spent his time as he wished. He was respected at the college and enjoyed his work.

And now Erica! When they had first met, her difference from Adele had been the attraction. She was not overly attractive, but she clearly expected nothing from him romantically. He rather enjoyed her sharp tongue, and he appreciated that she was understated, her actions far from the flamboyance from which he had escaped. Why, then, was it his fate to find himself once more in the power of a woman whom he had thought of only as an admirer? And why, despite the agony of the divorce and the break with the past, had the present become a nightmare from which he was finding it so very much harder to extricate himself?

After doing the dishes, he cleaned off the sink and table top and turned out the light in the kitchen. He returned to the living room and sat in his favorite chair doing nothing whatsoever... far into the night.

Leslie poured herself a glass of Chablis and sat before her fish tank, watching the lovely small animals as they sought escape; they almost seemed to look at her with accusing eyes. As the wine began to help her relax, she closed her eyes and her mind began to drift.

Making faces at the fish, they let the water carry them beyond their expectations. "There is a certain slant of light," Leslie whispered to Paul. "It is ours–now." As the light slanted down through the ocean depths, she took Paul by the hand and they let the current sweep them into its radiant confines.

"I don't care, you know, about your past," Leslie confided, serene in the light's warmth. "Erica is not to be trusted because at heart she is prissy and judgmental. She is rigid. She is so rigid," Leslie laughed in her delight, "that she is bound to explode."

The sharks approached the light, the starfish too, but even the minnows could not enter. They could not even hear the cathedral tunes which united Leslie with Paul forever, nor fathom the internal musings where the meanings were. As they slid along the light and tasted its music, Leslie admitted that there had been more excitement in the taste of earth and cloud. Still, the serenity of the light's golden glow lingered on the tips of their tongues and left them mysteriously satiated.

But when Leslie came back to herself, the fish, alas, were no longer at bay.

⸺⸺≫«(◦)»≪⸺⸺

"I won't tolerate it, Wilfred! I am telling you plainly and clearly that Jill Lake must not be allowed to drop my class. I will give her an F in the course, and I fully expect it to be recorded and counted. And if she does not return and apologize to me, then I expect you to suspend her from Huston College. I did not come in here to discuss the matter with you. I came in to tell you exactly what I expect you to do."

"And if I do not do exactly what you expect me to do, Erica?"

Erica smiled and answered Black's question with one of her own. "What else did you plan to do, Wilfred?"

"I asked you a question first, Erica."

"And now I'm asking you a question, Wilfred."

"I haven't decided how I'm going to handle the situation, Erica. When I do decide you will be among the first to know my decision."

"I expect to be, Wilfred. And I want you to know," she added, "that I don't like the tone you are taking with me. Not one little bit."

As Erica flounced out of Black's office and out of the main office as well, Susie, who had overheard some of the conversation, winked at Mrs. Garfelt and stuck her tongue out at the retreating figure. Wilfred Black, who had never ever in the past shown anything but the greatest deference for Erica before the secretaries, had come to the door and, unbeknownst to Susie, had seen her sticking her tongue out at Erica's retreating figure. "She does make you want to do that sometimes, doesn't she?" he laughed. And as Susie turned a bright pink, he retreated to his office and closed the door behind him.

Chapter XVII

Jill returned home from class to find her entire family camped on the doorsteps of her apartment building. Having only expected her brother, she was actually shocked to see her mother and father as well. Partly dismayed, but partly deeply touched, she found herself holding back tears as she embraced first her mother, and then her father, who held onto her tightly as if she were in immediate jeopardy. Mike offered his hand in a high five to ward off any hugs which would only have embarrassed him.

"Come in, come up," Jill said, leading her family up a flight of stairs to her apartment on the second floor. "You are absolutely nuts to have come, but I have to confess I'm delighted to see you," she said, encouraging her family to sit down on the couch and chairs, though Mike plopped himself down on her sofa-bed.

"How are you?" her father asked as if he expected her to pull a knife out of her side and collapse .

"Fine, Dad, fine. As pleased as I am to see you all, you know you're going to have to come back to pick me up in just 3 weeks when the semester ends."

"None of that young lady," Jill's father remonstrated. "We are not going home without you, and I'm sure you don't want us hanging around here for 3 weeks watching your every move."

"I'm actually happy to miss school for 3 weeks," Mike offered from his perch on the bed." I'm prepared to stay."

"Jill," her mother said. "Jill, Jill, Jill."

"I know, Mom," Jill replied, pulling her mother down onto the couch. "I love all of you too, but you're just going to have to accept that I can take care of myself. I'm being very careful. I accept no rides from strangers, and I'm always with people."

"You weren't with people just now when you came home. In fact, there was not a soul on the street except us, of course. Anybody could have come by in a car and snatched you."

"Dad," Jill said, trying desperately to remain patient. "It's not like that. Look , let me fix us all some coffee. Would you like a coke, Mike?"

"Yeah, sure," her brother replied. Jill prepared the drinks in the kitchen and served them from a tray.

"Actually, as long as you're here, there's somebody I'd kind of like you to meet, if he's willing."

Jill's mother's eyes lit up. "A boyfriend? That we can meet?"

"Now, Mom, don't jump to conclusions. He's not exactly a boyfriend. He's actually a professor of modern drama, a friend."

"Yeah," Mike laughed. "A friend. I'll bet."

"Michael, if Jill says he's a friend, he's a friend. And I would like to meet him before we take Jill home."

"Dad, I'm not going home yet. But maybe you'll feel better about that after you meet David. He's quite protective of me, so I think you'll like him."

"Jill, you are going to introduce us to a professor friend who protects you. Give me a break," Mike laughed again.

The telephone rang and Jill decided to answer. "David, you heard us talking about you. My folks are here. Yes, they came along with my brother. Do you want to stop by? Sure, we'll be right here. See you." Jill turned to Michael. "And you behave yourself, young man! No cracks while he's here."

"Moi?" Michael queried, all innocense.

"After David comes over, we'll find you guys a place to stay over if you want."

"No," Jill's mother replied. "We'll take you out for an early dinner and then head back. We all have obligations. I feel better knowing David is protecting you. I like him already."

Jill's father insisted that she go over all the events of the past weeks which she did patiently, pointing out as she went how distant she was from the victim whom the killer ineptly kept failing to eradicate. "I seem to have delivered the victim a more serious blow by dropping her class than the would-be murderer has managed with his or her failed attempts," she concluded just as the bell rang.

"He doesn't have a key?" her brother innocently inquired. Jill kicked him as she went to the door to let David in. After making introductions and David had plopped down next to Michael on the bed, her brother gave Jill a knowing look as if to say, he's comfy on the bed, eh?

"I know you're here to carry your daughter away to safety," David addressed Mr. and Mrs. Lake, "but I honestly think all will be well. The detective handling the case told me he's not far from making an arrest, and if it will make you feel any better, I don't plan to let Jill out of my sight." David pulled his pipe out of his pocket and put it in his mouth.

"Appreciate that, David, but from what Jill has told us, both the murder and the attempted murder took place in the open, so hard to be sure you can protect Jill."

"I think I can, Sir," David replied.

"Oh, call me Jacob, David. Not comfortable with Sir."

While the others continued discussing the dangers and lack thereof, Michael ambled over to the window that looked out onto the street, parted the curtain and looked out. He could hear the conversation, but he quietly took out a pen and a small notebook from his pocket and wrote something down. He then walked into the kitchen and helped himself to another coke. "Hey, Jill, could you come here for a minute," he called into the living room. When Jill came in he handed her a piece of paper with a number on it. "Don't ever say your brother didn't help solve this thing," he whispered to her. When she looked at him blankly, he continued in a very low voice. "I stood at the window while you guys were talking, and sleuth that I am, I saw a car drive by twice. Then it must have gone around the corner again because it drove by a third time. Then it stopped right behind what I gather must be your new boyfriend's car, and the person inside–couldn't see if it was a man or a woman–clearly took down the license number on David's car. At least I assume it's David's car because it wasn't there when we all came up. Now, how do you like them apples?"

"Thanks, Mike," Jill said softly. "I'm not crazy about them apples, but we better go in or they'll think something's wrong. I'll catch you later." The two returned to their seats and the conversation went on for a while. When Jill's parents invited David to join them all for dinner, Jill was pleased that they clearly liked him. But David excused himself, work to do, and bid his farewells. "Remember, I have my eye on her," were his parting words.

Before they went out for dinner, Jill's mother managed to have a private conversation with her daughter in the kitchen. Jill was washing the cups and glasses and Mrs. Lake was drying. "I see David has quite a bit of gray hair," Mrs. Lake said, a question in her voice.

"Oh Mom," Jill responded. "He's prematurely gray. He's closer to my age than you would imagine. He just finished his Ph.D. last year, for heaven's sake."

"Well, that's good, dear. But is Mike right?"

"Right about what, Mom?"

"Oh, you know, about David having or not having a key."

Jill knew exactly what her mother wanted to know. The "key" was code for her sleeping with David. Growing up, Jill's friends thought her mother was the most open and modern one they had come across. They would come over and tell her about their boyfriends and nothing they said ever shocked her. And she had made a point of telling Jill the facts of life rather early, which most of the other mothers never got around to with their children. She liked a drink or two before dinner and thought of herself as a really progressive type.

But as Jill got older, she began to realize that her mother was far more Victorian than anything else. Her rendition of the facts of life had been restricted to a bare minimum and Jill had to learn the rest from her friends over the years. Another way her Victorian nature emerged was through her attitude to ear piercing. All of

Jill's friends had pierced ears, but she had been so brainwashed by her mother that Jill would never have dreamed of piercing her own. Only loose women, her mother had explained, pierced their ears, mostly sluts and prostitutes. And sleeping with a man before marriage, out of the question. The man would never respect you enough to marry you if you did that. Clearly her mother wanted to know if Jill had succumbed.

"David," Jill assured her mother, "does not have a key. And I have not slept with him, so relax. He's my professor, for heaven's sake."

"Just checking, darling. I didn't think so. Mike's such a brat." They finished up and joined the others. Mike may be a brat, Jill thought to herself, but I kind of wish he were right.

"So, what do you think of David?" Jill asked her family over a delicious dinner at Jill's favorite Italian restaurant.

"What's with the pipe?" was her father's reply.

"He used to smoke it," Jill laughed, and he gave it up. But he still uses it as a… "

"Pacifier?" Mike introjected.

"Probably," Jill said. "Is that all?"

"Seems like a lovely young man," her mother added.

"Except," her father continued, he should not be seeing you while you're his student. Not only can he get into trouble, but it could be trouble for you. Ask me again when the semester's over and you're home and he has saved you from the murderer and I may have a different take."

"Fair enough," Jill said, sensing that her parents had liked him just fine.

After they had finally agreed to return home without her, Jill had gotten Mike aside long enough to thank him again for his detective work and assure him that after she looked into the license information he had given her, she would keep him abreast of any developments.

As soon as they departed, reluctantly accepting her promises to be extra careful and keep them posted, Jill went right to the phone and called David. It was getting dark out and her parents' anxieties had fueled her own. "David, they're gone. I know it's late and we both have work to do, but I need to talk to you. Thanks, I knew you'd come." Jill sank down into a chair and waited.

David must have flown over as it seemed only minutes before the bell rang again.

"David," Jill said, falling into his arms as he entered the door. "I think I may have made a mistake. I think maybe I should have gone with them."

"Now, now, I'm here," David said, caressing her head, holding her tightly to him. "I'm here. Nothing's going to happen to you. I promise." But when Jill told him about her brother's sleuthing, he became very thoughtful. "Jill, give me the license number and I'm going to have Halloway look into this. Don't worry, I'll ask him to keep it between us. Nobody in the department needs to know I was at your apartment. On the other hand," he added, "somebody was clearly very interested in the fact that I was here today and I'm going to get to the bottom of that."

"David, stay with me tonight. I'm really frightened. Move your car around the corner in case the stalker returns, but then come back." When David looked reluctant, she added, "Please!"

"My darling Jill, what makes you think if I stayed here with you that I could resist taking advantage of the situation. Don't we also need to keep you safe from me?"

"No," Jill replied firmly, tears now streaming down her face. "No. We don't need to keep you safe from me."

"You're sure? Your awfully vulnerable now, Jill."

"I'm sure. Move your car and come back. Hurry."

Chapter XVIII

Jill was working at her desk. She had given up doing a paper on Pinter's *The Homecoming*. She just couldn't figure out the figure of Pinter's somewhat whore-like heroine as Ruth, a biblical-style savior. Instead she was working on Pinter's *Old Times*. The paper was due tomorrow and she was still puzzled. She also wondered how she could possibly hold her head up and look everyone in the eye when she and her professor, for heaven's sake, were now lovers. And she was the guilty party. She was the Ruth! David, gentleman that he was, was perfectly willing to wait and was able to as well. But no, she couldn't. Somebody was stalking her and rather than face that mystery head-on she had given the stalker grist for his or her mill. She got up and walked over to the mirror. Yes, she thought, her guilt was there, clear for all to see, right on her face. How could David be objective about the paper she was now writing? He would have to give her an A.

On the other hand, she was actually glad, guilty though she felt, that she had precipitated the advancement of their relationship. Despite some first-time awkwardness, she was more in love than ever. David had been gentle, but he had also been passionate. And she had been also. Indeed, she surprised herself. It had been almost as if they both sensed that this was a life or death situation that they were in and they had better face it together. "To die, to die for thee. In sweetest liberty..." The song she had learned in school some years ago floated through her mind. In the 16th century, she had learned, to die sometimes meant to have sex, as if there were a kind of loss of self akin to death itself. Yes, but a kind of life too, she insisted to her image in the mirror.

David was going to call her as soon as he heard back from Halloway about the license number that Michael had written down. She smiled as she thought of how unlikely it was that her brother could really help with the investigation and yet he had. At least if they could get to the bottom of it, he had. Well, he had done something. Go Michael.

She would find a way to get through the next weeks. But now she must turn to the play and write the damned paper if she was going to feel she deserved the obligatory A. It was the play's final images that perplexed her. The heroine or central figure of the play had not said much. Her husband and their visitor, Kate's former roommate, had somewhat taken her over, speaking of her at times as if she weren't even there. But now at the end she seemed to be taking over, delivering a very long speech in which she removed herself from both husband and former roommate. What on earth did it mean when Kate recalled offering her husband dirt from a plant she had—an offer to rub it on him. He refused. "Ah," Jill said out loud as a possible interpretation dawned on her. Earth. She had offered him earth. She was the earth. He had rejected it. He had rejected her. Ah. As everything fell into place, Jill wrote and wrote until she had finished a first draft. Then it occurred to her that Kate had put herself in a terrible position. By rejecting her husband and former friend, she must now be alone. That was the Pinter who scared her. He brought Kate to the edge, the very edge. But when she thought about it some more, she decided it wasn't so awful after all. David had been right to suggest she work on this play. Kate was not alone! She had reclaimed herself. She had herself. Go Kate, she thought to herself as paragraphs tumbled out onto the typewriter. Go Kate!

David sat in his office, staring into space. He was suffering less from guilt, the day after the night before, than he was from worrying about being found out. He actually disapproved of his own behavior, but how could he resist the invitation. Well he could have, since he realized it came partly out of fright and he no doubt should have been stalwart and protective. But hell, he hadn't been. Should he contact Halloway with the license plate that Michael had delivered? Or would that just make Halloway sniff around his relationship with Jill more. Hey, he thought, nobody ever told me about the biggest danger of being a young professor; falling for one of your students.

He sat for a while longer and then looked up Halloway's number. When he was put through he explained as best he could. "Halloway, I know this sounds bad, but I was visiting at Jill Lake's house yesterday because her family was visiting and she wanted me to meet them. Her brother was looking out the window and saw somebody go around the block 3 times and then write down the license plate on my car. Michael, Jill's brother, wrote down the stalker's plates and I wondered how you would feel about looking them up. You see, I'm trying desperately to behave about Jill, but I might as well confess I've fallen for her and am desperately afraid for her safety. You will? Oh, that's a big relief. No, I understand. If you feel you need to keep what you find to yourself, sure. Just so Jill is protected. If you can keep me out of this, I sure would appreciate it. Yeah, young love. Thanks, Halloway, for being so understanding."

David felt immediate relief. No lectures from Halloway. He was more understanding, David thought, than he probably even should be. Everything about his life seemed so on the line. His job, his relationship with Jill if the thing blew up, the dangers that seemed to be lurking now for her, for her life perhaps. Did somebody else on campus feel as strongly about her as he did? Was he in danger from a rival for Jill's affection? The whole thing was becoming more complicated every day. He could hardly wait for semester's end, whatever happened with the killer. Meanwhile, he must prepare for class.

————))(((O))(((————

Halloway didn't have much trouble tracking down the license plate. And he was not in the least surprised. He wouldn't tell David Stein, though. He had to keep attempting to get evidence so he could make his arrest. If he couldn't get it any other way, he would, he realized, probably have to involve David after all, much as that went against the grain. But clearly Jill might now be in danger and he didn't want to take any chances. Soon. He must make a determination soon.

Michael called his sister. He knew his father would check the telephone bill and confront him if he spent too much time on the phone with her, but he wanted to know what, if anything, his sleuthing had produced and he was actually a bit worried about his sister. She picked up at the first ring.

"Mike, here," he said. "Just want to be up on the latest. Talk fast, as Dad will have a fit if I run up a big bill here."

"Oh, Mike. That's sweet of you. But nothing to report yet. My friend David has passed the license number you got onto the detective on the case so we may know something soon. But I have a big paper due tomorrow, so I can't talk long anyway."

"Dad and Mom are nut cases about you. I mean they've gone truly apeshit."

"I know, Mike. See if you can calm them down. I'll write after I finish my paper. The weather is beautiful and the campus is pretty calm. And believe me, I'm not going to take any chances."

"Okay then."

"And Mike, thanks again. Who knows, you may have solved the whole thing. You'll be a hero."

"Yeah, yeah. That'll be the day. Take care Jill."

"You too, and thanks again."

They hung up. Each one thought about the conversation for a while but decided that they were somewhat out of their depths. The license might be the answer. They could hope.

Jim Strand was 88% sure that he knew what was what or rather who did it. He had half a mind to call Halloway and discuss his theory with him. But it was only a theory. Perhaps he could find out a bit more before approaching the detective. He wondered, though, if Jill Lake might be at risk. If anything happened to her and he had withheld his theory, he would be guilty as hell himself. Maybe he should spin his theory to David. But David might not be able to control himself, and Jim felt that control was imperative if evidence was to be found. He decided to put any action off, at least for a few days. Could he perhaps trust Susie? He had to confess to himself that he felt very drawn to her. He must make an effort to get to know her better. Well, tomorrow perhaps. He would see.

Chapter XIX

There was really no way that Wilfred Black could avoid having a faculty meeting although such a meeting was the last thing in the world that he wished to have at this time. But aside from several business matters that really needed to be discussed, the rules called for a monthly meeting. May first had rolled around, and there were not many weeks before the end of the semester. What he feared was that Erica would make an issue of the Jill Lake situation and put him on the spot. He hadn't completely decided how he would resolve the matter, and he wasn't about to be pushed by Erica or other members of the faculty to do something he would regret.

Everybody was in attendance, Erica, Jeffry, Leslie, Jim, David, and Margaret, who looked as if she was about ready to deliver. It was amazing, Jim thought to himself, that she was making it to the end of the semester. Nice, though, to have some new life in the offing amidst all this business of death. Susie was present to take notes and Melvin Stuart was there as the graduate school representative while Lila Goth represented the undergraduates. Both students had gained a voice in the meetings because of unrest in the 60s, but they were not allowed to vote which remained a bone of contention. The group met in the faculty lounge, some sipping coffee and a few smoking. Gertrude Stein, captured by Picasso in his famous portrait, looked down upon the gathering with what to Jim seemed like a certain amount of disdain. But she was clearly, he thought, following the business with interest.

Black was moving swiftly and efficiently through the agenda and had just cleared his throat to ask if there was any more business before they parted when, to his dismay, Erica said that yes indeed there was more business and began to present her case.

"As you are all well aware, there are two required courses for all undergraduate English majors at Huston College as well as one required course for all graduate students." She continued as if she were giving a prepared speech that she had rehearsed, which was, in fact, the case. "All undergraduates must take a course in Introduction to English studies and one course in Shakespeare. And all graduate students must take a course in Bibliography and Historiography. The only exception to the latter rule, which as you all know is written into our *Rules for the Department of English Handbook*, is if a Ph.D. student enters with an M.A. and has already taken a course that we find acceptable. There are, of course, as well you all know, other requirements which are taken into consideration when planning an individual program depending on the emphasis of the program, but no student has graduated from Huston College since I have been here, and I might add that I have been here longer than any other person present in this room, without fulfilling the requirements that I have just reminded you all exist in our rule book.

"Now, you may not all have heard about the incident in my classroom last week with Jill Lake, but…"

Black interrupted Erica nervously. "I must ask you to hold off with this business, Erica. The situation which you are about to discuss is an unusual one and I think it may best be resolved by some meetings between the parties involved. I don't in the least think it need concern the entire faculty. The rules are clear," he went on, "but the circumstances are a bit special, and I am sure we can work something out to everybody's satisfaction, yours too, of course."

Everybody in the room hoped that this would end the discussion and the meeting. Although some of them, possibly Leslie and certainly Margaret, felt sorry enough for Erica to be surprised that Black was standing up to her at this point when he never had before. The others, still shaken by the attempts on Erica's life, did not sympathize enough to wish her any success with her goal, which was clearly to put Jill Lake in an impossible position.

"I'm sorry, Wilfred, but I can't agree with you," Erica retorted to Black's suggestion. "This does seem to me to be an issue which concerns the faculty and the students, who are more than adequately represented here, and I wish to state my position and demand a vote on the matter."

"Well, if you must, go ahead and state your position, but I don't see that there is anything to vote on, Erica."

"Miss Jill Lake has been an average student in my course this semester. She has completed her assignments, handed them in on time, and has certainly to date done passable work."

Black interrupted her again. "I don't think the achievements of a particular student should be discussed in front of other students, Dr. Berne." Everyone noticed his sudden use of Erica's last name.

Erica, now furious, continued as if she had not heard the reprimand. "Last Thursday, however, Miss Lake behaved in a very rude fashion in my class and fell asleep, quite ostentatiously so in fact."

There was a general discomfort in the room, each person shifting in his or her seat as if they were a chorus in a comic review. "I am sure," Erica continued, undaunted, "that for one reason or another each of us has had the experience of finding at least one of our students dozing off despite the pearls of wisdom that fall from our lips. What I find inexcusable is the rudeness of Miss Lake's behavior when I called her attention to her falling asleep and the nature of her exit from the classroom. Rather than apologizing, which I do think would have been suitable behavior, she informed me of the worthlessness of the course, said that she had no intention of returning to the classroom, and made a dramatic exit."

There was a full moment of silence while everybody digested Erica's version of the great rebellion, stories about which had been circulating among students and faculty since the event. What exactly did she want from them?

Melvin felt he had to say something. He was hesitant to do so, since he had not yet taken the course—indeed, he had been putting if off for as long as possible—but he took his duties as graduate representative seriously. Hence he raised his hand.

"Yes, Melvin," Black recognized him.

"I believe, Professor Berne, that your version of the episode, if I have been properly informed by students who were present in your class, is not complete." His voice was shaking slightly, but he went on. "Many of the students felt that your remarks to Miss Lake were rude and provocative. Apparently you said something personal about her social life and something negative about her scholarship. Actually Jill has received nothing less than an A this year until she took your course this semester."

David could hardly believe his ears. Go Melvin, he thought to himself. Jim and David exchanged looks.

"What the students may think or say is beside the point, Mr. Stuart," Erica snapped. I think I am a better judge than you or other students of the scholarship of one of my students. And if every time a professor made a slightly sarcastic remark when he or she is being treated rudely by a student, it provoked an exit such as Miss Lake's, then we would soon need to fold our tents and close the place down. This is not a popularity contest we are running at Huston, young man, it is a school."

"Professor Black," Jim Strand introjected, "I would like to make a motion at this time which I think, according to the rules of our formerly mentioned handbook, would be in order."

"Yes, Jim, what is your motion?" Black asked with some relief. He hoped Jim might save him from further embarrassment, but he still feared the worst.

"I move that all requirements, undergraduate and graduate alike, be dropped from the English Department curriculum and that each student's program be planned with his or her adviser and approved by his committee. I might add that I may lose a hell of a lot of students myself if this motion is passed and that I do think all students should take the three courses under question, except under exceptional circumstances; but the exceptional circumstances just outlined should not endanger the academic career of a student such as Jill Lake, and if the rules are not to be applied with flexibility and humanity, then I'm for changing the rules. I rest my case!"

"Do I hear a second to the motion?" Black inquired.

There was a long silence. David, who was anxious to second the motion in order to help Jill, was not sure that this was the best way to proceed.

"I would be happy to second the motion," Jeffry Platz announced, after some consideration. "I don't think the results would be world-shattering. We all would surely encourage most of our students to take the three courses under discussion. But the new rule might make for some flexibility where there seems to be none." Jeffry looked fully into Erica's eyes as he made the last statement, as if he were challenging her, after years of silence, to a duel.

Black, who was about to speak against the motion, for a multitude of reasons, still hoping he could settle the matter without all of the sub-textual confrontation which seemed to be at play, thought he might just listen to others and see which way the wind was blowing. He knew, however, what Erica expected of him. "Is there any more discussion?" Black asked. "Such a change is a major one and it may be best to let this rest until the fall, think it through, let our student representatives talk to the students about it, talk some more among ourselves, and then make a possibly less emotional decision."

"I would like to speak against the motion, Professor Black," Leslie Podmonk interjected. "If we permit our students to drop our classes the last two weeks of the semester, then we will be losing what small authority remains and our standards are quite sure to be lowered. I think Erica is to be commended for sticking with such a naturally unpopular course through the years and that she deserves our support. After all, the skills of scholarship taught in the course are essential even if they are not ones which students particularly enjoy learning. Anything tedious these days is considered out of date. Huston College, I'm happy to say, has remained more up to standard than many of its counterparts in the country, and I would not like us to bow to student pressures in this instance. I think it would just produce further rebellion."

Erica was having an enormous amount of trouble controlling herself. Everyone saw the redness coming to the surface of her cheeks and feared an explosion, but the room was quiet, uncomfortably so. Aside from her fury at Jeffry, who dared to treat her this way, dared to–well, he would certainly pay for it–and Black who was as weak as ever–but he too would pay–she resented being supported by that fool of a woman!

Having planned this meeting with great care, Erica felt it was not living up to her expectations in the least. She had expected David to be Jill's big supporter and so far he hadn't said a word. She had been looking forward to making a fool of him before the others. On the other hand, there was always some joy in losing for Erica. The role of the martyr was one she had played before and from its stance a great deal could be accomplished.

"I agree with Professor Black," David said. "I think the complexities and the personalities are such that the issue should be tabled until the fall. In fact I move to table."

"I second the motion," Jim chimed in.

"All those in favor of tabling the motion please raise their hands," Black said.

David, Jim, Jeffry and Margaret raised their hands.

"All opposed?"

Erica and Leslie raised their hands.

"Then we will take up the matter in the fall. And I am sure Erica, that you and Jill and I can come to an understanding on the present issue, which I think you must admit, is not simply a matter of requirements or lack of requirements. Meeting is adjourned."

Erica flounced out of the office with Leslie at her heels. David and Jim left, the students and Margaret close behind. Jeffry Platz sat for a moment thinking. Before he left, he and Black exchanged a long and searching look. Well, Black thought to himself as Jeffry rose and left him there by himself, that puts me exactly back where I was before. Nowhere.

Chapter XX

Jeffry Platz returned to his office and began methodically to pack his briefcase. There was a knock at the door.

"Come in."

"Close the door, please," he said as Bill entered.

Bill closed the door to the office and sat down on a comfortable, overstuffed chair that Jeffry usually sat in when he had time at school to read.

"Do sit and make yourself comfortable," he snapped at Bill, continuing to select books and papers that he wished to take home for the weekend.

"I just heard about the meeting," Bill muttered.

"News travels fast. And so?"

"And so, I gather you lined up against Erica. I thought she was such a dangerous enemy who held your future in her hands. I thought you had to watch your every step lest she give you away. I thought you were her slave." The last was said with particular bitterness.

"I'm tired, Bill," the older man finally spoke. "I don't think I much care anymore."

"Oh, that's fine for you, now. But isn't it a little belated? What about me? They still suspect me of attempting to kill Susie and probably of Killing Nora as well. If Erica gets going on you, they'll find out about us—I know they will, and then what? Oh, it's very nice that you don't care any more. You don't care about anyone but yourself. And you sure as hell don't give a shit about me. You've just used me."

Jeffry saw the tears in Bill's eyes. "I'm sorry, Bill. I do care about you. I don't think there is any way you will be implicated. We've been very careful."

Bill's words had unsettled him. He felt the boy's rage, his hate for him, his desperation. Jeffry had known for some time that Bill wanted to end the relationship and he had been unable to face that fact or to let him go. Instead, he had found more and more ways of embroiling Bill deeply in his life and his needs. "It's ironical, isn't it, Bill," he said gently. "I've been Erica's slave, and I've done my best to make you mine."

"Well, if you consider yourself so goddamned liberated that you can side with Jill Lake against Erica, then for Christ's sake, why don't you let me go." Bill was sobbing quietly now and Jeffry wanted to reach out to him, to take him in his arms; but he didn't. All his relationships had ended this way. First the young boys had admired him, been truly infatuated with him. He had enjoyed guiding them, helping them develop their minds, initiating them into the mysteries of the body, allowing them to lean on him. Then they had grown restless, disrespectful, disillusioned, hostile. He had thought to avoid this with Bill. He had thought in some way to wind their lives together in a more lasting way for which he hungered. Now he saw that this was not possible. But he also felt beyond the despair which had always lingered at the edge of his existence, ready to engulf him.

"Okay, Bill. Let's call it quits. I hereby declare you a free man. You had best stop now or someone will hear you."

But Bill could not stop the sobbing. All he could manage, as he buried his head in the handkerchief that Jeffry provided, was to muffle the sound.

———— ◦((◦))◦ ————

Jill was getting daily telephone calls now from her father. She knew how it pained him to spend money on the telephone, which he despised, but he wasn't satisfied with her letters coming only every few days and wanted updates on her every movement. Each time he called, she reassured him that all was quiet, no more murders, no more attempts on anyone's lives, nothing to worry about. No, she was not in trouble for seeing her professor socially since nobody except her own family knew about that and David was, she lied, a complete gentleman. Actually, he was, she thought. It was she who had behaved like a brazen hussy if the truth be told. But of course her Dad need not know about that! And then the next day her father would call again.

She and David had decided that his staying over in her apartment was far too dangerous and had agreed to wait until the semester ended, but neither one seemed to be able to adhere to the plan. He had stayed over twice since her parents left, carefully parking blocks away from her street. Apparently, they couldn't help themselves.

"You know," David had told her, "locked in her arms, kissing every inch of her arm until he finally reached her neck and then her lips.

"Know what?" She had asked, breathless, thinking perhaps that he was going to profess his undying love.

"That you should publish the paper on *Old Times*."

Jill laughed and laughed, unable to stop, pulling out of his embrace. "Well that's a romantic thought," she finally managed to say. "I think we need to sort out the teaching from the loving, my darling," she added, convulsed again with laughter.

"Yes, yes," he joined her in the laughing, even though it was directed at him. But as if she had not gotten her point through to him, he continued: "I mean you should *submit* it for publication. You have a fresh theory. And that would be a real achievement, publishing a paper before you even graduate."

Jill sat up in bed. "Graduate? That's years away, David. Could we possibly talk about this later? I'm glad you approve. But I don't want to think about Harold Pinter. He's coming between us, the old rogue."

"Sorry, just wanted you to know what I thought," David said, and began to work his way with kisses up her other arm until all thought of Harold Pinter was totally eradicated.

———— ◦《◦》◦ ————

Jim and David had planned a second sleuthing meeting, but this time they included Susie as well as Jill in their plan. Dinner was on them, they informed the ladies, the goal to discover hidden knowledge that Jill and especially Susie might not know they harbored. Susie, who was as drawn to Jim as he now seemed to be to her, was delighted to accept and the four of them were headed in Jim's car to one of his favorite outlying restaurants, Gus's Steak House.

Jim was asking Susie how she liked a book he had foisted upon her the previous week. David, who often teased Jim about corrupting Susie, was amused. She had come to her position in the Department of English an innocent, conventional soul, but as Jim led her through the mazes of Dostoevsky, Kierkegaard, and Vonnegut, among others, she was gaining rapidly in sophistication.

"What we have in mind tonight, Susie," David proclaimed, "aside, that is, from eating a huge and delicious meal, is putting you and Jill into a double trance and finding out what all this dangerous information is that you think you have. Then, when you tell us, we'll wake you up and go straight to Halloway, killer in hand."

"I wish I could tell you what you want to know," Susie said, becoming serious. "I think about it all the time. I've gone over and over the days before Nora was killed, and I know something is there that I'm missing."

"Maybe," Jill suggested, "what you have gone over means something and you just don't know what it is. Maybe going over it with us will help. I have exactly the same feeling you have, but I just don't know what it is that I... know."

"Yeah, yeah," Jim laughed. "You both know what you know but you don't know what you know." The others joined in, though their laughter was tinged with the fear that all of them felt about the whole situation.

Jim pulled up at Gus's, parked, and let everyone out. It was so dark inside that it took a while for their eyes to adjust, but they were led to a pleasant, candle-lit table in the corner, nicely decorated with flowers and far enough away from the piano player so that they could hear each other.

"Umm," Jill leaned over to smell the two perfect yellow roses in their delicate vase. "My favorite." David made a note in his mind to remember that, and when they sat down he secretly took her hand under the table. After they ordered their dinners and were sipping their drinks, Jim plunged in. "Now young ladies. We are not plying you with dinner and drink for naught. Who is to begin?"

"Before we start, Jim," Jill said, "I would love to hear more about the meeting. I mean, I know you shouldn't tell me, but Melvin gave me his version and I would like a more balanced account. He gets rather carried away."

"I'm sure Melvin had it pretty straight, Jill," David said. "The only surprise was Jeffry Platz. He has avoided Erica and any confrontation with her for the entire year I've been here; it was really odd for him to be the one to second Jim's motion to drop all requirements. Erica was beside herself. Neither of her "men" actually behaved. Black wasn't really strong on the subject, but he almost stood up to her. Something odd is going on, and we both voted to table so we could sort it out."

"We had a majority, schnook," Jim scolded. "If you had voted with Jeffry and me on dropping all requirements, we would have had her cooked."

"It was an awkward situation for me, Jim." David paused to think of how to put it, since neither Jim nor Susie knew about the developments in his relationship with Jill. "I don't want to give Erica any more provocation to attack me or Jill, especially Jill. I just want to cool it with her until the semester is over."

"Okay, okay," Jim responded. "But now it's down to business. You may start, Susie, since we have had one go-round with Jill. Maybe if you come up with something, it will resonate with her too."

"What do you want me to do?" Susie asked innocently.

"Go over the things you have been thinking to yourself about Nora and you but do so out loud."

"Nora was a terrible gossip, you know. Well I am too I guess. It just takes my mind off the daily drudge of typing. Or rather it used to. Mrs. Garfelt isn't much into the personalities around here."

Jim put on a serious expression. "You are going into a trance. You are feeling sleepy, sleepy, you will remember all, all, all."

"I feel so foolish."

"Not foolish. Sleepy."

"Oh, very well. Whenever Professor Black left the office we usually gossiped about him. I mean he is a rather mysterious figure. And I'm sure he must have come in on us talking several times. And since he's been acting so strangely lately, almost warning me at Nora's funeral not to try to remember whatever it is that I think is important, I can't help but wonder. The reason we speculated so much about him is because nobody knows much about his past. Nora was almost sure that he had previously had something going with Dr. Berne. Dr. B talks to him much differently than she does to the rest of us mortals, so Nora figured that even if the relationship was dead, she was nicer to him because of memories. Nora even considered the possibility that Erica had jilted him and he had never married because of her. And then when Paul came into the picture, he was jealous as hell, at least according to Nora."

"Ah, I see." David interjected. "We may conclude that our esteemed chairman, enraged by overhearing you two cats speculating about his passion for the lovely Erica, plotted and planned how to get rid of first Nora, then you, Susie. And if Erica had taken the poison, so what. After all, hadn't she jilted him?"

"Shut up for a moment, David," Jim said. "Continue, Susie. You have only just begun. There is much more, much more."

"Well, Nora was very curious about Paul, and she couldn't get much out of Erica. She talked to me a lot about that. She did seem to think that Paul did a lot of national and international traveling regarding some line of gifts which he sold to retail stores. And Erica did receive lots of gifts from him. We talked about those a lot. I know Dr. Podmonk has a theory about Paul's work being criminal in some way, so I've been trying to think what I know about that, from Nora, I mean."

"You are being systematic, Susie. Stream of consciousness is what is needed here—no theories if you please. Just what did you and Nora talk about and what did you hear? That and nothing more. We will supply the theory when you give us the information," Jim remonstrated.

"I don't know, David," Jill laughed.

"Don't know what?" David asked.

"Whether I want Jim to be my adviser next year. If he gets to have all the ideas, I might just feel belittled and then who knows what I might do."

Jim looked chagrined. "Sorry Jill. Didn't mean to sound like a superior male. It's just that thinking hasn't gotten Susie anywhere and I'm trying to get her to relax and just give us stuff."

"I know, Jim. Just couldn't resist. Especially since I plan to solve the murder myself, with the help of my brother of course."

"She probably will, too," David added.

"I'm really trying," Susie insisted. Their meal was now served and the rest of Susie's memories of conversations were punctuated by bites of rare steak, baked potato with sour cream, and french beans. "We didn't talk much about Professor Podmonk because I guess she just doesn't seem that interesting. I imagine Erica talked about her some with Nora, who did tell me about their conversations. Professor Berne has no use for Leslie, thinks she's silly and empty-headed, and I guess she's embarrassed by Professor Podmonk's admiration of her. Of course, you know they used to be thick as thieves. I saw them together a lot, always friendly and talking. I guess Paul came between them in some way."

"Oh, I would say so," Jim commented, his mouth stuffed with a rather large bite of potato.

"I do remember," Susie continued," that Erica came in on us once in the lady's room when we were talking about Paul. I'm afraid she may have heard Nora say that Paul was almost too good to be true. We felt terrible. Then Nora thanked her for the wedding invitation, which was rather embarrassing because, of course, I wasn't invited."

"You're doing splendidly, Susie. Want a bit more wine? Very good for enhancing the trance!"

"No thanks. Now, let's see. We talked some about you and Jill, Dr. Stein."

"Away from the office, it's David, Susie. And what pray tell did you and Nora have to say about us? We didn't even connect until after Nora was killed. Were you a couple of fortune tellers?"

Susie laughed. "Oh we knew. Just had to look at you looking at Jill or at Jill not looking at you. Nora would be very happy that you did get together. She had it all planned."

"And here we thought we were free individuals," David teased. "But that Nora was a good women."

"I hope you'll be careful though. I know Erica would be happy to burn you alive if she found out what was going on. And even Professor Black has to keep proper behavior in the Department."

"Did you do any talking about David and Jill when Erica might have heard you?" Jim inquired, leaning forward expectantly in his chair.

"No, I don't think so. But I really can't remember who heard what where. We rarely gossiped when anybody was around, except Professor Black. We were so used to his leaving his door open that we often forgot he was there."

"And?" Jim encouraged Susie.

"Well, about the only other thing I can remember is that Nora told me Leslie had become pretty bitter about Paul. I guess she overheard Leslie talking to Professor Black, making insinuations about Erica's teaching. Nora couldn't hear the conversation too well, but she got the impression that Leslie was trying to get Erica into trouble in some way and that Paul came into the picture."

"You may wake up now, Susie," Jim mused. "You will forget everything you have said. you understand, everything."

Susie laughed at Jim and accepted more wine. "Wish I could remember more, but that's about it."

"Your turn, Jill. Or would you like to order some dessert

first?" Jim asked. They decided against dessert in favor of brandy and chatted about other things until it arrived.

"Now the magic potion!" Jim announced. "You cannot resist. You will tell me all you know."

"I thought I really had," Jill smiled.

"Frankly, I don't understand why you should be involved or what this sense of danger is all about," David put in.

"It has something to do with you, David. I mean the feeling I have connects in some way with the day Gwen Thomas and I ran into you and Jim at Fritz's. But I don't know why."

"Okay, Miss Lake. We will have a total recall of that fateful meeting. What were you two ladies talking about? Where had you been? Where were you going? No censorship. You may proceed," Jim commanded.

"We had been talking about school work, believe it or not. And I was embarrassed, Jim, when you asked us to join you because I just wasn't prepared for it, I guess," Jill acknowledged. "Gwen teased me about it in the bookstore, I remember. We went there because I had to pick up some books and to browse. Then, just when Gwen was teasing me, we ran into Erica, and I was afraid she had overheard us. Gwen said she hadn't, and anyhow we didn't actually refer to you by name. I remember that Erica was in the mystery section which struck me as being odd, but I was too upset to figure that one out. I guess lots of people read mysteries: I've never cared for them much myself, and somehow they don't seem to go with Professor Berne's personality."

"Hasten on, Jill. You are doing admirably," Jim said with encouragement.

"That's about all. We were at the cashier's and Erica elbowed her way right in front of us to pay for her book and left. She had that red-faced look about her–I guess she was upset about us. I seem to be upsetting her in every way lately. I don't think she can stand other people being happy, especially if they're young."

"Did you notice what books or book she had selected?" Jim inquired, a funny note in his voice.

"I don't think so. Oh, yes, something about victims, I think. *The Next Victim, The Last Victim*, something like that."

"I see."

"What did you do then?" David asked.

"We parted, and I went back to my apartment, had dinner, watched some television, did some studying, did some wondering about David and went to bed."

"Sounds pretty innocuous," Susie said.

"And it was something in that day that subsequently felt dangerous to you? "

"That's right," Jill responded, "and now I feel sillier than ever about it." Then Jill remembered something else she thought she should share with them, although she was reluctant to do so. "There is something else."

"Ah?" David queried.

"It's about Bill Brown," Jill continued.

"What about Bill?"

"Bill wanted to talk to me about something. In the student lounge. But just as he was about to, somebody else came in and he left in a hurry. I personally don't think Bill would hurt a fly, but he did seem super upset and rumors are flying, of course, about the fact that he works at the gas station that Erica goes to. Maybe he knows something about all this. I could try to get him to talk to me if you want."

David had again taken Jill's hand under the table and as if he knew, the piano player started playing the Simon and Garfunkel song, "Bridge Over Troubled Water." "Like a bridge over troubled water, I will lay me down," he sang as Jill clung to that hand.

Jim claimed their attention. "The trance has worked. I am just amazed at how I missed important details myself. Unfortunately, without evidence there is little I can do. But I have an idea or two and will report my findings to you at our next meeting."

Not just Jill and Susie, but David as well expressed their dismay so that people at other tables looked over to see what was wrong. "You can't do this," Susie complained. "If you think you know who did it, you have to tell us. We've cooperated. We've trusted you. Now you can trust us!"

"Are you serious, Jim? Do you think any of this helped?" David asked.

"Yes, I do. But I think if I told you what I thought, none of you could carry it off. I'll tell you what. Give me a day or two and if all is not resolved, I'll share all."

"Oh, Jim," Jill moaned. "You've only managed to make me feel spookier than ever. I'll never sleep tonight."

But despite their clamoring, Jim Strand held firm. They talked of other things for a while before Jim took them home and went about planning his next move. It was time to contact Halloway.

Chapter XXI

Too late. Those who knew the murderer's identity would feel guilt for the rest of their lives. They should have acted sooner, they later agreed, evidence or no evidence. And now, on this Friday morning, there was another dead body.

Jeffry Platz was found dead in his office by Jasper when he entered to air it out early in the morning the last day of the semester. His extremely sharp letter-opener from Italy had been removed from its elegant leather holder and used as weapon. Since exam week had now ended and some of the students who had finished their exams had already departed, Halloway agreed that even Erica's students could now leave. Others, urged by their now distraught parents, quickly packed their bags and were on their way. Except Bill Brown, who actually was from the town and needed to keep his job at the gas station.

Jill called her father with the news before he could read it in the papers and assured him that she would be ready and packed when her brother came for her on Monday. If her father wanted to send Michael now, he could stay the weekend with her and be on guard. But Jill was deeply troubled at the thought of returning home, mystery unsolved. And Jeffry Platz, of all people. Nobody knew him very well, but he had been highly respected. It felt like the death of a century, his. He had opened up the 18th century for so many of them and nobody could imagine another professor taking his place. Like Nora, and Susie too for that matter, Jeffry didn't have an enemy in the world. It seems, though, that he did.

And the murderer was becoming more violent. When Jasper entered the professor's office, he found Platz face down on the floor with a knife sticking out of his back. Literally stabbed in the back. Everybody noted the irony although without any laughter whatsoever.

Poor Jasper. He was beginning to feel his age, he thought, distraught that after all the basically quiet years he had been at Huston, it was now turning into a war zone. By the afternoon, this murder made the front page of almost every major paper in the country. "Murder rampant at Huston College," was the typical headline. The Dean had come over to Black's office and carried on about how this would be the ruin of Huston. No parents would want their children at a college at which a murderer had roamed free for more than a month. The President of Huston was on the radio assuring whoever would listen that an arrest was imminent and that everything possible was being done to take care of the situation. But personally, he said to the Dean and to Black in separate telephone calls, he doubted if Huston would recover from the terrible publicity. The Board of the College had already met several times over the issue of the murderer, but now the President arranged another meeting to keep them informed of developments.

Jill's father called her that afternoon and said that Michael would be on his way as soon as he returned from school and to expect him before dinner. Black called a meeting of the faculty and any students not yet departed. Halloway was present, as well as Sergeant Kheel.

Jim Strand, looking somewhat disheveled, was talking to Halloway before the meeting started and though David sat nearby, he couldn't manage to hear their conversation. Jill sat next to her friend Bill, who had left his work to attend the meeting and seemed more upset than anyone else in the room. Margaret, who was very near term, was not present. Erica sat in the only seat left, next to Leslie, although she seemed reluctant to be that close to her old friend.

Black called the meeting to order. "This has become a true nightmare," he began. We can't say that Professor Berne was the intended victim this time. All we can say is that there is a murderer in our midst and that there now seems no rhyme or reason for his actions. I say his, because I, for one, can't imagine a woman strong enough to manage to get Jeffry Platz in a position to stab him in the back. We all will miss Professor Platz. He was a remarkable teacher and a fine citizen of this department. Detective Halloway has assured me that we are near closure and that nobody should panic. I will now turn the meeting over to him.

Halloway rose slowly from his seat and spoke quietly and calmly. "I think Professor Black has summed up the situation. I have little to add. I am really here with Sergeant Kheel to ask all of you where you were late yesterday afternoon and evening and to see if any of you saw anything unusual or noticed anybody near Professor Platz's office. Rather than have you speak out loud to the group, I'd like to talk with you one by one in

Professor Black's office while the rest of you wait here. We'll work as quickly as possible. And thank you in advance for your cooperation."

Jim asked if he could go first and disappeared into Black's office with Halloway and Kheel while the others waited in the outer office where they had met. When he came out of the meeting, and others entered the office one by one, Jim made a motion to David and Jill to come out into the hallway, which they did. "David, keep Jill by your side," he advised his friend. Jill, don't take any chances. I mean it, be careful. I have to go now, but I'll be in touch. Halloway says he knows who took down your license number at Jill's place, David. That should help."

Both David and Jill tried to detain Jim, almost literally, as Jill grabbed his arm, but Jim managed to get away from them both and disappeared out the door. They had no choice but to reenter and wait their turns for an interview. Bill, who was sitting next to Jill, leaned over and whispered to her: "I was having an affair with Platz. That's what I almost told you. It was over. If they find out, they'll suspect me. They already do because Erica brings her car to that station where I work. Any advice?"

Jill was truly dismayed. All this information came at her like a flood. She looked at Bill and thought carefully about how to respond. Jim had just warned her to be careful. She couldn't help but think it possible that Bill was the murderer. After all, he was a disappointed lover, a student who like the others would have been all too glad to see Erica dead, and one who had the means to fix Erica's car, or rather unfix it as the case may be. She had better protect herself. On the other hand, she just couldn't see Bill as a murderer. And if he were, why would he now confess the affair to her? He trusted her. She must trust him.

She whispered back :"Bill, you must be beside yourself. I'm so sorry. Your secret is safe with me, and I'm sure all will be well." Bill smiled at her, but she thought she saw tears welling in his eyes and could only wonder. If he had broken up with Jeffry Platz, would he be this distraught over his death? Yes, he could be, she thought. Would there be no end to this terrible puzzle?

When it was Jill's turn for an interview she found herself saying very little. She had not seen anybody near Professor Platz's office and she didn't know of any enemies he had. He was distant and didn't really get into the politics of the department at all. She was sorry she couldn't be of more help. When she left, she was glad she had not said anything about Bill. It was none of their business.

Since David hadn't yet had his interview, she thought it would be suspicious if she waited for him, so Jill headed home to wait for her brother's arrival. True, Jim had said to stay near David, but nothing could happen to her in the daytime, she thought. It was another gorgeous day, and as she left the college she saw birds flying in formation, swooping now this way, now that, changing their formations as they switched directions. She had read some-where that birds flew in such formations to protect themselves from various disasters and wondered if perhaps she should have waited for David after all.

Arriving at her building, she looked around surreptitiously just to be sure she hadn't been followed, climbed the stairs to her apartment, and let herself in. She got her suitcase down from the closet and slowly began to pack. Part of her wanted Michael to arrive and immediately deliver her from the dread that she felt escalating. Another part wanted to stay and be with David. How could she leave with so much unresolved?

Chapter XXII

Jill had arranged to meet Susie for a farewell dinner at a small Greek restaurant not far from campus. Mike would come along, of course. She had left the campus in a hurry, so she planned to stop by and be sure she had no mail in her box as she probably wouldn't go in again over the weekend. And on Monday, Mike would drive her home. A hair-raising prospect, since he hadn't been driving for that long, but if her father thought he was ready, he must be.

A piercing ring of the bell. "Mike, you must have flown," Jill said as her brother gave her an awkward hug and dropped a small overnight bag on her bed.

"Where am I going to sleep?" he inquired.

"We'll put two chairs together," Jill suggested.

"Actually, I brought my sleeping bag. You're still safe, I see."

"Still safe, but I'm sure Dad told you there was another murder. One that actually doesn't make any sense as this was clearly not another attempt on Erica Berne. Have to admit, I'm glad you're here and I'm glad to be going home Monday. Well, sort of glad."

"Ah, the guy?" Michael inquired.

"Yes, if you must know, the guy. But I'm sure we'll get together somehow. Anyhow, unpack if you want. There are hangers in the closet. We're meeting my friend Susie for supper near campus. You can drive if you want."

"No thanks, Jill. I'm pooped. Why don't you just bring me back something. But I'll drop you off if you need a lift."

"No need. I can use the walk. There are cokes in the fridge if you get thirsty and maybe a few crackers in the cupboard over the sink. I'll bring you back something yummy."

"Don't worry about me."

"Mike, I do appreciate you're coming early to collect me. Be back in a couple hours."

"Not to worry. I'll probably take a nap."

Jill grabbed her purse, checked herself in the mirror, put a comb through her hair and left. After she had been gone for a short time, the telephone rang. Mike answered. He listened and said little. "You're sure?" he did ask. "You better be right. I'll be there right away. Yes, I have the directions." He grabbed his car keys and left the apartment.

———————◦((◦))◦———————

Everybody except Wilfred Black had finally left and Susie was collecting her belongings to leave for the day. She knew things were somehow coming to a head. With Jim as well. He seemed to know what he was about and he really did appear to be interested in her. Of course she knew it would probably never be serious. She hadn't been able to go to college, as much as she wanted to do so. Just couldn't see going into the kind of debt she would have to have incurred, although she was saving every penny she could in hopes of some day going back to school. But Jim was so well read and so intelligent. The dinner the other night had been fun and he did continue giving her those books to read. Sometimes she even felt that she saw things in the books that went right by him. No fool me, she thought to herself, thinking perhaps that after all Jim might be a possibility in her life.

Susie stopped in to say goodnight to Black. She had arranged to have a farewell bite with Jill, but she decided to go home and shower before meeting her at the library at 6:00. Walking down the hallway to the outside door, she saw that Leslie Podmonk was still working in her office, which was unusual. Leslie usually left at about 4:00. But the meeting had gone rather late.

⸺ ⦅◊⦆ ⸺

Jill strolled down the sidewalk. She was early on purpose so that she wouldn't need to hurry. It helped calm her to be outside. She saw students loading their cars with luggage as she sauntered on, some of whom she knew. Several times she stopped to say goodbye. It was unsettling to see the school year ending this way with nothing really settled.

When she arrived at the English Department building, she walked down the hall and into the main office where the faculty and graduate students' boxes were. Margaret Lambert was checking her box. "Hi, Dr. Lambert," Jill said, pulling a message out of her own box.

"Hi Jill," the very pregnant woman answered. Dr. Lambert was rather more informal with students than the other professors, who tended to call them by their last names. "I'm glad to see you are fine and no doubt getting ready to leave this mess," the professor said amiably.

"Thanks," Jill replied. "I imagine it has been very stressful for you with the baby and all."

"That's putting it mildly," Dr. Lambert replied. "If the semester hadn't ended I was going to end anyway. It could be any time now."

"Are you coming back next year?" Jill inquired. "I mean with the baby and all."

"You know, Jill, I had planned to come back. But only if this mess is cleared up. I'm not going to put myself in any danger any longer. Of course I have no idea what the whole thing's about, but the killing of Jeffry seems so random. What about you, Jill? Will you return?"

"I think so. But I have very protective parents, so they may not be willing to pay for me here anymore. They've been working on me to come home since the whole thing started."

"I can sympathize with them. I don't want my baby in any danger either," she laughed. "Well, whatever you decide, Jill, lots of luck."

"You too," Jill responded. "All best with the baby."

They parted, Margaret to her car, Jill to the student lounge to read her message. Melvin and Hal were playing chess in the corner, but Jill settled in a comfortable chair. The note was from David. He had even typed it. She guessed that her teasing him about his handwriting had led him to become formal. "Meet me at the lake at 6:00. I have something important to tell you." He had sealed the note in an envelope but of course still had not dared to sign it "love." Just "David." He had probably feared prying eyes with what was going on. What would she do? She was supposed to meet Susie at 6:00 at the library and it was 5:30. She knew David had gone home because she had returned to the English Department and stopped at his office after she had been interviewed by Halloway; his office had been dark and locked.

Jill decided to go down the hall and call him at the public phone. There was no answer. Well, then, she would call Susie and arrange to meet her a bit later. But Susie wasn't home. Jill shuffled back down the hall to the student lounge to wait. Melvin Stuart and Hal Bridges were still playing chess in the corner and she decided to watch their game while she waited for a bit to call Susie again.

"Hi, Jill, you're back? what's doing?" Melvin asked, Hal muttering a "hello" while he pondered his next move.

"Nothing much. Just getting ready to leave for the summer. Who's winning here?"

"Just getting underway," Hal said. "But this guy doesn't have a chance. Just watch my action, Jill."

Jill couldn't concentrate on the game, and when she was sure she had given Susie enough time to get home, she went down the hall to call her again. The phone rang and rang, but there was still no answer. Maybe Susie was doing some local shopping and hadn't gone home. She would just have to be a bit late at the library. Maybe David would join them for dinner. He could tell her whatever was so important on the way to the library.

Jill returned to the lounge, watched the game a bit more, browsed through a copy of *Time Magazine* and decided it was time to head for the lake. She felt relaxed and strangely happy.

She wondered if David had something particularly romantic on his mind. They could talk privately there. She wished she hadn't arranged to meet Susie.

It had been unusually hot for May, but there was a pleasant breeze now that Jill enjoyed as she walked along the path to the wooded area. It was extremely quiet. Well, of course, most of the students had left for home. They would be able to talk in peace.

Jill glanced at her watch. She was a few minutes early. There was nobody in sight. She sat down on a stone bench next to the pond to wait, putting her purse down beside her. Absently, she picked up a stone and sent it skipping across the water, watched the ripples it made, and wondered what David would have to say to her.

A figure moved out from behind a large tree and approached Jill softly. "May I join you, Miss Lake?" Erica Berne asked politely.

Shocked at the appearance of the older woman who seemed to materialize from nowhere, Jill was speechless. "You see," Erica announced as she sat down next to Jill, "I wrote you that little note, Miss Lake. The one from your David. So he won't be along after all because he has no idea that you are here. It was in answer to yours."

"In answer to my what? I haven't written you a note," Jill responded.

"That, my dear, is a blatant lie. I wasn't at all sure after the scene you made in my classroom that you would want to speak to me. But when I got your note I realized it was very important that we have a little conversation. I do hope you will forgive my methods."

There was something about the way that Erica Berne spoke and looked at her that terrified Jill. She had the urge to get up and run, but she wasn't even able to move her lips. Finally, in a voice that sounded much firmer than she had expected, Jill managed to say, "I have an appointment with Susie Marsh, Dr. Berne. I was just meeting Professor Stein to tell him so. I'm afraid I can't stay and talk just now."

"Susie can wait, Miss Lake. And your David will not be here to save you either. This is very important." Erica said. "You're the one," she continued, "who got Jasper to steal the book, aren't you?"

"What on earth are you talking about, Dr. Berne?" Jill gasped, thinking to herself that Erica had gone completely round the bend and that she was sitting here absolutely alone with a mad woman.

"I have a secret compartment in my desk at school where I keep my private possessions. But nobody has ever found the compartment before. Jasper Mann not only found it, but he also stole the book. I told him that if it were not returned, he would be fired. He returned it. But I must assume from your note that you put him up to it. And I would like to know who else you informed about the matter. David Stein, no doubt. And Susie? Who else?"

"You must believe me, Dr. Berne. I honestly don't know what you're talking about. What book do you mean?"

"Oh, yes, play dumb. The book, of course, that you saw me purchase at the bookstore when you and that other obscene girl were tittering at me, the one you sent me the note about."

Jill's head was spinning. "You mean the book you selected that day? *The Victim? The* mystery? Or was it *The Next Victim?*"

"That's very clever of you, Miss Lake, to pretend that you didn't notice the title and that it wasn't you who wrote me the note about it. You know perfectly well it was *The Wrong Victim,* and you know perfectly well that it was you who put Jasper up to stealing it from me. Now all I want to know is exactly with whom you have discussed the matter."

As the pieces came together for Jill she realized that she was in grave danger. The woman was mad, utterly mad. Jim must have put it all together the other night. Susie had recalled that Erica overheard Nora saying in the restroom that Paul was almost too good to be true. What an unfortunate turn of phrase. Nora's comment was no doubt innocent. She didn't mean that Paul didn't exist, only that he was unbelievably ideal. *There was no Paul!* That was the key. No man in his right mind, kindly or criminal, would want this woman. When she overheard Susie and Nora in the ladies' room gossiping about Paul, she must have imagined that they had stumbled on the truth.

She had killed Nora and tried to kill Susie to keep them from telling a truth they didn't even know! Something now about the book. Erica must think that Jill had put some importance on the title of the book. *The Wrong Victim.* Jill wished that she had remembered the title more exactly. Then she might have figured out a long time ago that Erica was setting herself up as the victim. Wrong indeed. She had set herself up as the victim while killing anyone else that she thought was endangering her fantasy. Even Jasper. Erica knew, of course, that he would clean her office before she came in and hopefully be the victim of the bomb she must have planted herself. And Professor Platz, though why Jill couldn't begin to surmise. And now Jill. And there was absolutely no one in sight. Jill opened her mouth to scream but nothing came out.

"I asked you a question, Miss Lake and I expect an answer. With whom have you discussed my Paul?"

"I have discussed the situation with several people," Jill lied. "I have discussed it with Professor Stein, with Susie, with Professor Black, with... Professor Strand. So you see there is no point in going any further with this. If anything happens to me, they will know."

"Nothing is going to happen to you, Miss Lake. Don't be absurd. I'm glad you are finally being truthful. For you see if you have already discussed the matter with so very many people, then everything is alright. There is no evidence. All speculation. And there is no motive. So there is absolutely no danger, not to anyone, my dear."

The sudden shift to "My dear," and its sugary tone only frightened Jill more. Erica obviously thought she could kill with impunity. She now believed that several people were aware of her as the killer but that she had been too clever for them. They couldn't touch her.

Jill thought desperately that she must keep Erica talking, anything to gain time. Maybe somebody would come down this way. Susie would be waiting at the library. She would ask questions. But oh, damn, she hadn't told a soul where she was going. Mike might eventually wonder why she had not returned with his dinner, but by then it would be too late.

"You killed Nora, didn't you Professor Berne?" Jill asked evenly.

"Nora was a busybody. Always butting into other people's lives. She dared to say something about Paul which I couldn't forgive."

Jill had been about to say, but there is no Paul, when she realized just how mad Erica Berne was. Paul was as real to her as if he were sitting on the next bench.

"And Susie?"

"That was easy. You see, Susie also believed anything that Nora said. And what Nora said was unforgivable. I know everything about cars, my dear. And I know Wilfred Black like the back of my hand. I knew that he would suggest Susie should get the car. And as you see, I was right."

"But Jasper? What on earth did Jasper do to deserve being blown up?"

"You are very astute. That was unnecessary. Just a precaution. I do have the book back and could deny anything he might say. All conjecture. It was quite clear to me that you two had been talking together."

"But we weren't. We never talked about the book. I didn't even remember the title."

"Then you lied in the note. I don't take chances."

If she did not feel in such danger, Jill thought she might actually find all this funny. Dr. Berne preferred murder to taking any chances. More than droll.

"Professor Platz?" Jill inquired, desperate for time. Somebody must come by soon.

"What kind of victim was he, Dr. Berne? Did he dare question the existence of your Paul?" There. She had put it out there.

The existence of Paul! She noticed Erica's face turning bright red with fury and denial.

Silence as she slowly regained her composure. "Jeffry? That's a long story, rather a boring one. I don't think you need to hear it," she managed with ice in her voice.

"Oh, but I do want to hear it. Surely Dr. Platz was not a gossip like your other 'victims,' or was he? I can't believe that of him. We all thought of him as detached and he certainly made it clear that he was having nothing to do with you."

"You say that with such approval, Miss Lake. Is that why you admired him? Because he would have nothing to do with me? You are more malicious than I had even imagined."

"I'm malicious? You murdered him in cold blood!"

"Not in cold blood, my dear, not at all. Hot blood. Do you hear me? Hot blood."

She was beginning to sound like a vampire, Jill thought. She almost didn't want to hear Erica's motive for the brutal murder or to encourage her "hot blood." But she must stall for time. "We all noticed that the two of you never seemed to admit the other existed."

Erica laughed. "Oh I do exist, Miss Lake. And Jeffry must be pondering my existence in hell this very moment. Did you know that he and Bill Brown were having an affair? Did you know how many affairs with students Jeffry has had over the years? I thought not. I walked in on Jeffry and one of those students some years ago. Since then we have never talked. I could have had him fired on the spot, so don't look at me as if I'm some sort of heartless villain. I did expect a certain amount of courtesy for my silence, as you can well imagine."

Jill felt sick to her stomach. She could barely stop herself from throwing up. So that was what Bill had wanted to discuss with her in the student lounge. Poor Bill. And poor Dr. Platz, to be under the thumb for years of a woman like Erica Berne! Her own guilt over her affair with David only intensified her feelings. Quite an ivory tower, this one, she thought to herself, allowing the macabre humor to steady her.

"And what discourtesy led you to stab the poor man?" Jill managed to get out.

"If you must know. I went to his office. He was surprised to see me. I closed the door behind me so that we could talk undisturbed. I asked him why he had voted against my wishes about the issue concerning you, my dear, the issue of whether my course was to be optional or obligatory as it has been for years. He laughed at me. He said, 'I'm tired of this game, Erica. Whatever you wish to report about me, feel free to do so. I no longer care.' I was about to leave his office and do just that, march into Black's office and report him for the scoundrel that he is. Then he rose to his feet and said, 'Poor Paul.'"

Erica was so excited by her tale that she had risen to her feet. Jill almost said, you should have been an actress, but she merely echoed the professor's words. "Poor Paul? What did he mean?"

"Exactly," Erica went on. "What do you mean, 'Poor Paul'? I demanded. Then he said, 'There is no Paul, Erica. There never was a Paul. You're pathetic. Having to invent a fiancé to make yourself seem desirable. And then killing him off so the truth won't come out? Absolutely pathetic!' Then he started laughing, your detached mentor, laughing. He was so doubled over with laughter that it was easy for me to move behind him, take his famous Italian letter opener from his desk, remove it from its leather holder, and stab him. That's just what I did and I'm proud of it."

"Am I the only one who believed you?" Jill asked.

"There was and is nothing to not believe," Erica insisted, using what Jill thought might be a double negative. She wondered if she would die now with that thought in her head. Erica using a double negative. Erica, she thought, *is* a double negative. Whatever that might mean. "It is enough that Paul is dead," Erica continued. "I will not have him maligned. Do you understand?"

"I understand perfectly," Jill replied. She was experiencing a surge of strength. She made a decision right then. She refused to be murdered by this malicious, pathetic, mad woman. No way.

Erica had moved behind Jill. "When they find you, my dear, floating in the lake—Miss Lake in a lake, imagine that-- they will doubtless have their suspicions. But they will not have any evidence. No motive, no evidence." With unbelievable strength, Erica pulled one of Jill's arms painfully behind her back with one hand, putting her other hand over the scream which Jill had finally found the desperation to let loose, but which was muffled by the woman's grasp. Jill felt that her arm was breaking as Erica moved her expertly toward the water. Her dream came back to Jill, the one in which she was running from somebody who wanted to drown her.

Perhaps, though, she still had a chance, Jill thought to herself. Erica might be able to throw her into the lake, but as soon as she released her she would start screaming, and she was a perfectly good swimmer; she would get away. The woman was not so clever after all. She had taken advantage of Jill's state of shock, but Jill was, she thought, younger and stronger.

But Erica wasn't thrusting her into the lake. She had pushed her down to her knees at the edge of the lake and was clearly getting ready to hold Jill's head under the water. Then she would thrust her in, after she had very carefully seen to it that she was drowned. But as she pressed her face down to the water, Jill mustered up all her strength and threw the woman off of her. Rising to her feet, she pulled Erica up and using the woman's own technique put her arm behind her in an iron grip.

"I feel sorry for you, Dr. Berne," Jill announced, panting to get her breath back. "Inventing somebody to love you because clearly noone does."

"How dare you," Erica muttered, astounded by the girl's strength. Then both of them heard a voice.

"That will do, Professor Berne," Detective Halloway shouted. "Magnificent, Miss Lake, I'll take it from here." He helped remove Erica from Jill's grasp and handed her over to Sergeant Kheel, who put Erica's hands behind her back in order to put on handcuffs.

Suddenly there were people everywhere. It was like the end of an adventure film in which everyone emerged from hiding as they came to rescue the heroine. Almost everyone Jill knew appeared from behind trees! Dizzy with fear and relief, the sobs that had mingled with her suppressed scream burst forth and Jill fell over sideways into David's arms, the tears pouring down her cheeks. Jim was standing back a few feet with Michael! Several police officers had emerged from behind the trees as well.

"That was a lousy, stupid, unforgivable thing you did!" David said to Jim who had approached to see how Jill was doing, Michael trailing behind.

Jim made no response to David's accusations but asked Jill if she was alright. "No thanks to you," David added, leading Jill, who was leaning on him heavily, over to the bench to sit down.

"I thought it was cool," Michael chimed in. "You were cool, Jill, I godda admit. Wait until I tell this at home!"

"What on earth are you doing here?" Jill asked. She could only imagine the look on her father's face if Michael told the story of what happened, what still was happening.

Sergeant Kheel ushered Erica to a police car which was parked slightly down the path. Inspector Halloway helped her into the car as if she were a visiting dignitary, not the deranged killer that she had turned out to be. Stony-faced, Erica sat in the car and seemed to look beyond the scene at hand.

"Where were you? Where did you come from?" Jill asked through her tears, which were subsiding considerably, although she was still shaking in David's arms.

"We'll tell you all about it, Jill, but I want to get you away from here first. Did you think I just casually left school without you when it was clear you were in danger? We followed you from the moment you left the building to go home, and then back."

Halloway approached and asked if he could give them a ride but David thought it better for Jill not to be near Erica. They would walk or he would bring his car there if the others would wait with Jill. Jill, however, said she wanted to walk and Halloway was released to take care of things with Erica at his end.

"I'm sorry to ask this of you, Jill, but as soon as you have recovered and maybe had some dinner, we'll need your statement." Halloway said before departing. "Do you think you'd be up to it this evening? Tomorrow morning would be okay as well."

Jill responded affirmatively and David said he would have her at the station after she felt better and ate something, maybe by 8:00. Jim tried to apologize, which confused Jill, and then at Jill's request he went off to the library to find the waiting Susie. David was going to take Jill and her brother out for dinner if she was up to it.

CHAPTER XXIII

Susie was getting quite concerned. She had been waiting on a bench in front of the library for over twenty minutes, and it was not like Jill to be late. She was relieved when she saw Jim approach.

"I bring messages from your dinner date. She has instructed you to dine with me and I will such a tale unfold as will your worries end, although I'm afraid I have put myself into a bit of trouble." Mystified, Susie let herself be led off to the corner café where Jim reassured her that Jill was just fine and began to tell the tale.

He began by identifying Erica as the murderer. "I've known for a long time that Erica was our man," Jim assured Susie, "but I didn't know why. You see, I thought Halloway was really stalling around, so I decided to do a bit of investigation on my own. What I found on my foray through the good lady's office was a stupid secret hiding place in her desk which held a little volume of intrigue called *The Wrong Victim*. I might not have looked twice at it if it had been lying about on her desk, but since it was so artfully hidden, I knew I had a clue. Forced to leave my academic studies behind, I dedicated an entire evening to the perusal of this little known volume and found that it was but a grade C thriller:

nobody in the book, you see, died of poisoning in their Sweet and Low. Nobody's car had brakes that had been tampered with. And to the best of my recollection, no bombs exploding either. But the central thesis, or should I say situation, or plot of the novel was truly of value."

"And what, pray tell, was that?" Susie asked, shaken herself by the tale that Jim unraveled, although she was enjoying bites of a large hamburger as he spoke.

"There was this beautiful broad who was in terrible danger. Or so the police were led to believe. Each time someone attempted to kill her, another died by mistake. Four people were killed in the book. Unlike our Dr. Berne, the killer in the book was effective on all counts, neatly killing off each of the four victims. Finally some dumb policeman realized that the dead were the real victims and the killer was the beautiful broad just making it look as if she herself was the one the murderer sought to kill."

"I see," Susie said, trying to digest the information, along with the hamburger.

"Now," Jim continued, "our little mad lady of bibliographical and historiological fame thought that Jill had seen her get the book, so Jill was in danger right along. Of course, I imagine it didn't help Jill that she was lovely and in love, and what's more, loved in return. That in itself made her an ideal victim for our Erica.

"At any rate," Jim continued, "before returning the little volume, which I only did because Jasper was looming as victim number three unless I acted quickly, I took it to Detective Halloway and outlined my theory. Unfortunately, especially for

Jeffry, and I can't tell you how awful I feel about that, Halloway didn't think he could build a case on it. He said he had a motive, but he wouldn't share it with me. And he said it wasn't enough. He needed evidence. The book might work as evidence if we could find something more."

"Well?" Susie asked between bites.

"You supplied the motive, Susie, and for that we may all thank you."

"I did?"

"You see, there is no Paul. There was no Paul. There never, ever was a Paul. You said at our investigative dinner that Erica probably overheard you and Nora talking about Paul being too good to be true in the ladies' room. She didn't hear enough to know that it was mere conjecture about Erica's descriptions of Paul. Nora was too close to the facts. To the psychology. Erica would have died of embarrassment if such an idea had circulated among the students and faculty. She had to act fast."

"But that's crazy. I mean, how could he have been made up? What about all the gifts he sent?"

"She had them sent to her, no doubt."

"What about the letters she showed Nora?"

"The same."

"What about the wedding plans? The wedding itself?"

"But you see, Susie, that was her first murder. Paul had to die."

Susie stopped eating and took a long drink of her water. "Then that must be the secret that Nora was going to tell me before she went to have that fatal cup of coffee! She must have found out that Paul truly was too good to be true, that he didn't exist!"

"Exactly."

"But how could Nora have found out the truth?"

"That I can't say, Susie. We may never know."

"But that's pathetic," Susie said, suddenly losing her appetite. "I mean, if you really think about it, that's about the saddest thing I've ever heard of."

"Well, it would be, Susie, if Nora and Jeffry were still alive. That takes a bit of the pity out of it. And your friend Jill was high on the list. In fact, tonight was the night."

"What do you mean? Where is Jill now? What happened? I want to go to her!"

"Hold tight. Finish up and I will lead you to her. At this moment David isn't feeling too kindly disposed toward me, but we shall all get together at the police station at 8:00 and you will see that Jill is fine. She is presently with her brother and David.

"You see, once I had the motive, I knew I still needed to get evidence. And there wasn't any. None, other than the book. All rather in the head. But the book gave me an idea. It took me back to the days when I had time to read that kind of thing. And in those books inevitably if one wanted to catch the criminal in the act, one used a decoy. I knew David would never agree to using Jill, but she was the logical choice."

"Oh, you didn't! But that's awful. What if Erica had killed her? What did you do?"

"Would you care for some coffee?"

"I would care for an answer to my questions. What happened just now? Is Jill really all right?"

"I know it sounds bad, Susie, but I think that if I hadn't done something, Jill and possibly others, you included, might have been in more danger. The woman really had to be stopped."

"Would you please tell me what happened? Now!"

"I sent Erica a note. Typed, of course. I told her that I had noticed that she had selected *The Wrong Victim* at the bookstore early in April and that I had recently read it and found it most interesting. I signed Jill's name and left it in Erica's box."

"And you knew that would make Erica act? And how did you plan to protect Jill?" Susie asked indignantly.

"Having sent the note, I didn't plan to act the hero myself. I went back to Halloway and told him. He was already having Erica followed. She had asked that Halloway remove the men who had been watching her and didn't seem to be aware that she was under surveillance. I also contacted Michael Lake, since I knew he was here for the weekend to guard Jill and take her home. He was totally willing to cooperate."

"Jill's father will kill him. And you for that matter. Jim Strand, you're days are numbered," Susie laughed.

"I also followed Jill," Jim continued. "I've even decided that I might be in the wrong profession. She never noticed and it was quite exciting. A little too exciting there at the end, I must admit, but exciting nevertheless. Halloway, I might add, wasn't too thrilled with my strategy, but he was decent enough to listen to the conversation Jill and Erica had behind the trees at the lake."

"What was Jill doing down at the lake with Erica?"

"I gather Erica wrote Jill a note to meet there and signed it David, typewritten. Jill had tried to reach you to tell you she'd be a little late. Michael had met me as soon as Jill left the house, so we both followed her. I have to tell you, Susie, it was all like a Hitchcock film. Jill and Erica were so engrossed in conversation, that they never heard everyone sneaking up behind trees or noticed those already there. Halloway's men were behind trees when Mike and I arrived, just before Jill did. And Erica was there, staring into the lake. Halloway didn't get there until just about then as he had stopped to pick up David and fill him in. In fact I heard the car off down the path, and I was afraid he had ruined the whole thing, but Erica and Jill were too engrossed in playing their little scene to hear."

"I'm with David on this, Jim," Susie announced. "Erica could have had a knife–after all she stabbed Jeffry Platz. She could have moved quickly even with all of you there. But never mind, go on. You still haven't told me what happened."

"I had some trouble hearing it all, but I heard enough. Erica started out casually–I must say the woman, aside from being generally mad, is quite crazy besides. I mean it was entirely possible that somebody could have passed by at any time. The fact that eight men were hidden in the vicinity was staged, but how she thought she could be sure of carrying it off without any interruption beats me."

"Jim, I am going to kill *you* if you don't tell me what happened."

"Okay, okay. She began by pumping Jill. Who else, she demanded, knew about the book? Then she said it didn't matter because she knew there was no evidence, and all that. Even Erica isn't looney enough to think of herself as the gorgeous vixen of the novel, so perhaps she thought she was safe on that count. Okay, okay, I know, what happened? There's nothing much more to tell, Susie. She said enough to damn herself in court and just for clinchers, she made a good, decent attempt to drown Jill in the lake."

"And you all stood there and watched?"

"No, no. As soon as it was quite clear what she was up to, Halloway and his men moved in. But it turned out not to be necessary. Jill turned the tables on Erica. At first it looked as if Erica was the stronger. After all, she took Jill by surprise. But as we all moved in Jill had Erica in a vice-like grip all ready for Halloway to arrest her."

"Go Jill!" Susie rose from her chair and threw her arms around Jim in delight at the news. Then she drew back in embarrassment. "Sorry about that."

"No need. Best moment of my week. Why don't you do that again?"

Susie blushed and sat back down. "Keep going, more details please."

"I actually thought Halloway waited a bit long. He must have been holding David by main force."

"How could puny Erica hope to have drowned Jill?"

"Surprise factor, I suppose. And terror. Erica knew just what she was up to. And she was watching Jill closely. Jill was taken by surprise to find her there in the first place and her reflexes must have been nil. At any rate, you needn't waste too much sympathy on Erica. Apparently her plan was to hold Jill's head under water until she was quite drowned and then toss her in. Nice lady."

"Oh, Jim, I just can't believe it."

"I know, Susie. I can hardly believe it myself, but there it is.

And it's over, now."

By now Susie had completely lost her appetite. "What about the car accident?"

"She bragged about that to Jill. I guess she loved her car a lot, but she wanted you out of the way. Again, it was taking a considerable chance, but she was betting that if she played sick and hung onto Kheel for support that Black would send you for the car. I guess she figured if he sent somebody else it didn't matter."

"And all in the name of a made-up Paul. Sick. What will happen to her now?"

"I don't know. Let's go down to the station and find out. It's almost 8:00."

Jim payed the check and then took Susie's hand as they left the restaurant. "Susie, my love," he said to her gently, "I know you don't approve of my tactics, but here we all are, safe and sound."

My love? Susie could hardly believe her ears. She guessed she would have to forgive him if she were to be his love. Or was it just an expression? From the way he grasped her hand she thought perhaps not.

Chapter XXIV

Detective Halloway took Jill, David, Michael, Susie and Jim into his office and made everybody as comfortable as possible. The Pastor at Erica's church had been over and had managed to find a lawyer who was willing to represent Erica. Some distant relations of hers were notified and a cousin was coming to look into things the following day. Meanwhile, the detective explained, Erica had been taken to the psychiatric ward of the local hospital where she was going to undergo a battery of tests over the next few days.

Halloway served coffee and called in his assistant to record the proceedings. "I know you are angry with Professor Strand for putting Jill in danger this evening, David, but I hope you will listen carefully and find it possible to understand what he did, what we all did for that matter. I admit that I didn't approve of it myself, and I may even be in hot water for going along with the whole affair. You see, I have known for some time that Erica Berne was Nora's killer, Susie's would-be killer and that she was responsible for the death of Jeffry Platz. If I had acted sooner with Jim we may have prevented that death and for that I will always feel guilty."

Still shaken from the evening's events, Jill could hardly believe her ears. All were shocked, except Jim who knew that Halloway had been onto Erica.

"Let me explain," Halloway continued. "I know it appears that we haven't been active in this investigation, but actually we have been working on it continuously behind the scenes. Let's face it, this is the biggest case I've ever had to work on. What we found out a couple of weeks ago after extensive investigation is exactly what you found out from questioning Susie the other night. No Paul."

"How did you find out?" Susie asked.

"We began by investigating the deaths of American citizens in London the day and even the week that Paul was supposed to have been murdered there. No such murder. We didn't question Erica at any great length about Paul because we didn't want her to know we were suspicious, but we found out enough details about his supposed business, his origins, his family, etc. to look into the whole affair and we found nothing. He was pure invention. And of course no funeral. I have no idea what Erica Berne was doing in New York when she was supposedly attending his funeral."

"If it was all so obvious, why didn't you do something about it?" David demanded, still angry with Jim and Halloway. "Erica wasn't all that clever about her invention if you were able to unmask it so easily. Why couldn't you arrest her?"

"There was the matter of motive. I didn't know that Nora and Susie were speculating about Paul's existence. And I gather that they weren't really; Erica just surmised that they were. I just thought the invention of Paul was mad and had a gut feeling that she was the guilty one, not the victim. But I had no evidence.

Making up a fiancé and killing people off are not necessarily related actions. I was even more suspicious when Erica, after pretending to be so frightened, asked for an end to surveillance on her. I imagined she would be up to more tricks. But we really had no choice but to wait and watch."

"If you were watching so well," David asked, "how did she manage to rig the breaks on her car? And how could she plant a bomb without being noticed? I still don't get it."

"Sergeant Kheel didn't think she could accomplish much on her way to school and met her there, stopping for a donut on the way. Erica had plenty of time to fix her brakes and walk down the hill to school. Kheel said he arrived just as she did."

"And the bomb?" Jill asked.

"That's a bit more tricky. The woman is a strange combination of diabolically clever and fantastically careless and daring. The bomb was apparently a hand-made baby that she put together at home. I have no idea whether she learned how to do this from some book or television program, any more than I know how she became an expert on cars. The bomb was small, as you may remember, and she must have transported it in her purse or in her briefcase. She stayed to work late the night before the bomb went off. When we questioned Mary, who was on night duty for cleaning up that evening, we found that Erica saw her in the hall and asked her to clean her office while she was out for dinner since she planned to return and work late–she said she didn't want to be disturbed. So I gather she calmly went out to eat, returned, pretended to work for an hour or more and set her bomb, closed the door and hoped Mary wouldn't stop back in for anything since the bomb was meant for Jasper. Again, she was desperate enough to take the chance--if Mary was blown up, too bad."

"But if Erica thought Jill and Jasper knew about the book, surely Erica would have assumed they told others. Why would killing them off help?" This from the still confused Susie.

"I don't know how rationally Erica was thinking at any point along the way, Susie," Halloway explained. "But I do know one thing. We still didn't have any evidence for an arrest, and if Jim hadn't come up with the idea of using Jill as a decoy, no matter how dangerous that may seem to all of you, she might have been in far greater danger than she was tonight with all of us there aware of Erica's moves. I do believe she would have made a move this weekend, before Jill left for home."

Michael felt he shouldn't intrude on the conversation, but he couldn't help himself. "Detective Halloway," he asked, "did you find out who the driver was who was spying on Jill and David? I had written down the license number."

"Oh, yes, Michael. Jim gave me the number. And our thanks. The license was from the rental car Dr. Berne was driving. That almost provided us with the evidence we needed for Erica at least as a stalker, but not quite enough. You are surely going to be a detective one day."

Michael beamed and Jill leaned over and gave him a kiss, after which he turned bright red. "My hero," Jill said, and everyone felt just a little more relaxed after the evening's ordeal. "I guess I really have to thank you as well, Jim," Jill said, turning and smiling at him. "David, it makes sense. And if Jim had told us what he was up to, I never could have acted the part. And I don't think you would have let me."

"Maybe," David conceded. "Sorry, Jim, but I still can't sort it all out. And I still think you should have told me about it. Even if I had stopped you. But let's forget it. It's over now. And Jill's safe."

"What about the others at school?" Susie asked. "I kept thinking my boss was the murderer. I wonder what was bugging him? He certainly was acting strangely."

"Well, Susie, we can't solve all mysteries here. I've been on the phone with Black. He said he would contact the other members of the faculty and the whole thing will be in the papers tomorrow. While you were at dinner, I spoke with the press as well. After my assistant here takes Jill's statement, why don't you kids all go home and get some rest. I think I need to go home and get reacquainted with my family myself," Halloway said.

———— ⊰⊙⊱ ————

By the time they all left Halloway's office it was past nine. Exhausted though they were, they weren't quite ready to part. Jill invited everyone to her apartment for a drink. She wanted to go to her place because she knew she had to call home to report before her parents read the news in the paper tomorrow. Jim offered to take Susie and Mike so that David could take Jill and have a moment or two alone with her.

Riding home in the car with David, Jill snuggled close. "I know she tried to kill me, David, but I do feel sorry for her."

"You do? I guess she is pathetic. Since she's safely packed away I can feel a little sorry for her too. But not very. Too dangerous. What I can't figure out, though, is why I didn't figure it out. Seems to me I offered to be your protector, Jill. I honestly don't know if I'm still mad at Jim because he risked your life or because he put the whole thing together, which may mean in the long run, he saved your life."

"You don't need to be jealous, David. I admire Jim's detecting in a way, and I even think he may have saved me and Susie, but in all honesty I don't like being used as a decoy. And I'm glad you were furious." There was something just a bit like her father in David, Jill thought as they rode on. Fiercely, even irrationally protective. Perhaps, when she told her father the whole story, he would appreciate David's attitude about it all and decide that he was the perfect husband for his daughter. What sometimes irritated her in her father seemed just right in David. She snuggled closer.

"It's so Beckett," Jill almost muttered.

"Beckett? How so?"

"You said that nothing *happens* in *Waiting for Godot*. Paul is the nothing that happened here. And the results are devastating. Our lovely campus might just as well have been a Godot wasteland."

"Clearly you have become the teacher here, Jill," David said, nodding. "A little more comedy mixed into the tragedy in Beckett though. But it's certainly Erica's Endgame, and unfortunately Nora's and Jeffry's too."

"But I'm feeling like a Pinter survivor. Do you think Pinter knows he's a feminist?"

"I have no idea. You should write and tell him."

David had reached a red light and he leaned over and kissed Jill. He was still kissing her when the light turned green, and then red again. And then green. "We better get there, darling," Jill said, reluctantly pulling away. "I have the key."

━━━◆◆◆◆◆◆◆◆◆◆◆◆◆◆━━━

Jim had stopped to pick up some bottles of wine, which all were imbibing. Even Mike. He was only allowed one glass but seemed high on the whole situation, if not the wine. Jill had called her mother and father and told them the murderer was in custody, and that they could relax. She decided not to tell them how she was used as a decoy. Her father might have a stroke! Maybe the full story would not come out in the paper. If it did, well, she would deal with that later.

"I have some news to share with you all," Jim declared, "some news and an invitation." Everyone listened intently although they weren't sure they could take much more on this particular evening.

"Shoot," Mike said. We're all ears. And I'm up for any and all invitations."

"I quit," Jim announced.

"You what?" David asked.

"I quit my job. The department is decimated anyway. I have no idea how they will go on, or if Huston College will even go on, but I don't plan to wait around to see. As for being your adviser, Jill, my advice to you is to quit as well, and to you too David, and you too Susie."

"But what will you do?" Susie asked as she felt a deep disappointment. Jim would not be here? Then if there was a relationship to be developed, how could that happen?

"That's where the invitation comes in," Jim declared with a smile. "I find I like this detecting work. I plan either to open my own agency, especially if you will join me, or I might go to work for an agency if you won't. I would specialize in crimes committed on campuses, college or high schools, but would be open to other work as well. Susie, you could start out as a secretary, but maybe move into investigative work if we make enough money to hire somebody else to do the secretarial work. Jill, you could finish your degree someplace else, wherever we locate and work for us part time. David, you could join us if you toughen up a bit. We would all be entering a field where there is danger, and you would have to allow for that in your life."

Jim's statement was greeted with silence. Each person in the room made an effort to digest the idea. David spoke first. "You're right, Jim. Who knows whether Huston will even open next year. But if it does and Jill returns after the summer, I do too. If it doesn't reopen, I will take your offer under consideration. On one condition. Jill is never again to be a decoy."

"Okay," Jim said. "I could live with that."

"What would I live on?" Susie inquired. "If you start up an agency, you wouldn't have any money for a while."

"Oh, we'd find a way. A loan perhaps, to get started. Or we might become a branch of an existing agency. I plan to spend the summer investigating all the possibilities."

"As long as I can continue studying someplace," Jill chimed in. "I can't just drop Pinter on his head after getting so involved with him."

"And I want to go to college," Susie chimed in. "Before I get too old to remember stuff."

Everyone laughed. The conversation went on for another hour and then Susie, Jim and David departed. Michael and Jill were so exhausted that they didn't have any further discussion and were asleep before they could even discuss Jim's proposal. As he lingered awake for a moment, curled up on the floor in the sleeping bag he had brought along, Mike did say to his sister, "As soon as I graduate from college, I'm in."

CHAPTER XXV

Detective Halloway finally felt free to discuss the case in detail with his wife. He needed her help with the guilt he was feeling over Jeffry Platz's death. "You see, he explained, I knew Erica was the guilty party days before she killed Jeffry, but I couldn't arrest her. At least I felt I couldn't arrest her because I had no evidence. I just couldn't imagine her striking like that right in the building with everyone about."

"That's an awful burden to carry around," his wife responded. "But my dear, you couldn't have anticipated that action. You mustn't blame yourself." As he went on to try to create Erica's outer and inner life for her, the way she listened helped him to feel calmer.

"I'm also worried about the way we used Jill Lake as a decoy. It wasn't my idea, but I felt I had to go along with it or risk other deaths. Still, I was risking Jill's life. What if Erica had used a knife again as she did with Jeffry? I suppose I should feel immense relief."

"You had to do that," his wife agreed. I'm sure you will be a hero for solving the case and that nobody will blame you for that risk. But what will happen to the college now?"

"I have no idea. The publicity may close the place down. Or

now that the case is closed, all may return to normal. If there is such a thing," he added, kissing his wife goodnight and falling asleep almost immediately.

⎯⎯◦«◉»◦⎯⎯

Leslie Podmonk listened to Black's tale on the telephone with disbelief, thanked him for his call and poured herself a huge bourbon and soda. Erica! It had been Erica all along! She knew Erica had become colder and colder, meaner and meaner. She had figured Erica would come around, but as time passed, she showed no signs of their old friendship. Well, it was a shock. But let her rot in jail. Maybe she would even visit her there, just to annoy her.

No Paul? Not possible. It had been Paul who had come between them. No Paul. No Paul for Erica, perhaps, Leslie thought as she sipped her drink. Paul was never meant for Erica, after all. He was hers. Later in the night they would meet again. Good riddance to Erica. He was hers.

⎯⎯◦«◉»◦⎯⎯

Margaret Lambert had been napping when Halloway called, and after she hung up the phone she wasn't sure that she was awake. She made herself a cup of tea and sat down at the kitchen table to mull it over. Then she rose from the chair and took a lovely red apple out of the refrigerator.

Yes, she thought, yes. Made perfect sense. They were all going to wake up now from the nightmare of the last several weeks. She wondered how they all could have been so fooled by the delusions of the unpopular, lonely professor. She had not received an invitation to the wedding because she had carefully kept her distance from Erica, but for the professor to have gone that far with her delusion, to actually have sent out invitations, seemed somehow over the top.

The baby seemed to be doing a bit of a dance. It made Margaret smile. You'll be safe now, little one, she said, patting her belly. Back to the minor crazies of academia. Perhaps, now all would be well. "Feel free," she said out loud to her unborn child, "to arrive any time. The coast is clear!"

⸺◈⸺

Jill's parents could not let the subject go. Of course they were thrilled and relieved to know that the murderer was in custody. But Jill had been very unclear about what led to the arrest, and when they asked to talk to Mike to get a better picture, she had said he was out and about. But she had indicated that he had been involved. He had played some sort of heroic role. Out and about? His instructions had been to never leave Jill's side. How heroic could that be?

Jill had mentioned that her new boyfriend would be visiting soon. They worried about that. He seemed a nice enough chap, but if Mike had played some kind of heroic role in the arrest, why hadn't David? And wasn't this a little soon in a relationship to invite him home. And what would the relationship do to both of their roles at Huston? It seems that even with the murderer under arrest they could find plenty to worry about.

Maybe, however, Mike had not gone out and about until after the murderer was arrested. They would apparently have to wait until Jill and Mike returned home on Monday to get all the details. That would be a challenge. Still, it felt as if a huge weight had been lifted from their shoulders and that night, they slept the sleep of the relieved.

———⫸《◉》⫷———

Jasper thanked Professor Black for calling him. Very nice man, he thought. He actually considers me a human being. He could easily have told me in person. And why am I not surprised? I knew she was a nut case. Everyone knew that. All that business about a book I knew nothing about. Her hunt for dust just to get on my case. I'll have to sit down and figure out the way she pulled all this off, but I'm just not surprised.

It's been a hell of a spring, he thought, as he prepared for bed. Enough going on to fill a book. Maybe I should write it. A mystery maybe. Some dame sets herself up as a victim when she's really the killer on the hunt. Maybe put in some of my military tales. Make Paul a soldier rather than a whatever he was. Hmmm. Does that all go together? Maybe I really will. Give me something to do in my spare time. Too bad, though about Nora and Platz. Nora was always pleasant and Platz was always polite. Maybe if I write it I can make myself the hero, the one who figures it all out. I like that idea.

No, I'm just not surprised.

———⫸《◉》⫷———

Jim delivered Susie to her door. Leaning over, he gave her a kiss on the cheek. He then departed, whistling quietly to himself.

He felt as if he were truly free for the first time in his life. He had almost no regrets about quitting his job and felt that he was on his way to a career which would provide the kind of challenges he would enjoy. And he had to admit that, despite his inability to avoid Platz's death, he thought he had seen what he considered his first case through rather brilliantly. Well, maybe not brilliantly, but… well, whatever. And Susie. He couldn't get her out of his mind. But why in the world should he?

As she readied herself for bed, Susie couldn't decide whether Jim's kiss had been fatherly, big brotherly, or the kind of kiss she found she wanted from him. She would have to wait and see. And working in a detective agency? Well, why the hell not?

Erica Berne did not say a word. She would not speak to the nurse who was trying to be kind. Or the doctor. She was very tired. She lay back on the pillow.

The knife penetrated the flesh, reached the bone, twisted…

His body turned, inadvertently forcing the assailant's knife to twist as it entered his flesh…

Several short jabs of the knife, in-out, in-out, in…

No matter that the details were hazy. The fact was that Paul was dead. The fact was that his unknown assailant, either unaware or uncaring that Paul would gladly have parted with whatever money he had carried on that rainy night in London, had coupled robbery with murder.

Or had Paul actually courted death? Had he protested, refused, taken on his adversary at that midnight hour, bringing down his heavy destiny and oh hers, her heavy destiny on them both? If so, it had been cruel, the very first cruel gesture he had made toward her, a gesture which reached across the ocean and touched her life so that she was not sure that she could ever repress the rage which mingled with her self-pitying tears. He surely had not risked his life so soon before their marriage, only six short days. No, she could not believe that of him. It must have been from behind. He was taken unawares–the pain was brief.

But Erica could not stop her pain. She lay prostrate and taut on the bed. Paul's death scene, played out in all of its possible forms, kept moving on the ceiling before her half-closed, tear-filled eyes and mingled hazily with her dreams of their future life together. Finally, her eyes closed, her muscles relaxed slightly, and her angular body seemed to lift, then float, then sink into a sleep of grief.

CPSIA information can be obtained
at www.ICGtesting.com
Printed in the USA
FSOW01n1127281215
15030FS

101 Relaxation Games for Children

SmartFun Books from Hunter House

101 Music Games for Children by Jerry Storms

101 More Music Games for Children by Jerry Storms

101 Dance Games for Children by Paul Rooyackers

101 More Dance Games for Children by Paul Rooyackers

101 Drama Games for Children by Paul Rooyackers

101 More Drama Games for Children by Paul Rooyackers

101 Movement Games for Children by Huberta Wiertsema

101 Language Games for Children by Paul Rooyackers

101 Improv Games for Children by Bob Bedore

Yoga Games for Children by Danielle Bersma and Marjoke Visscher

The Yoga Adventure for Children by Helen Purperhart

101 Life Skills Games for Children by Bernie Badegruber

101 More Life Skills Games for Children by Bernie Badegruber

101 Cool Pool Games for Children by Kim Rodomista

101 Family Vacation Games by Shando Varda

404 Deskside Activities for Energetic Kids by Barbara Davis

101 Relaxation Games for Children by Allison Bartl

101 Pep-Up Games for Children by Allison Bartl

101 Quick-Thinking Games + Riddles for Children by Allison Bartl

1_01

Relaxation Games
for Children

Finding a Little Peace and Quiet
In Between

Allison Bartl

Illustrations by Klaus Puth

A Hunter House SmartFun Book

Ordering

Trade bookstores in the U.S. and Canada please contact:

Publishers Group West
1700 Fourth St., Berkeley CA 94710
Phone: (800) 788-3123   Fax: (510) 528-3444

Hunter House books are available at bulk discounts for textbook course adoptions;
to qualifying community, health-care, and government organizations;
and for special promotions and fund-raising. For details please contact:

Special Sales Department
Hunter House Inc., PO Box 2914, Alameda CA 94501-0914
Phone: (510) 865-5282   Fax: (510) 865-4295
E-mail: ordering@hunterhouse.com

Individuals can order our books from most bookstores,
by calling **(800) 266-5592**, or from our website at
www.hunterhouse.com

Project Credits

Cover Design	Stefanie Gold
Illustration	Klaus Puth
Book Production	John McKercher
Translator	Emily Banwell
Developmental & Copy Editor	Kelley Blewster
Proofreader	Herman Leung
Acquisitions Editor	Jeanne Brondino
Editor	Alexandra Mummery
Senior Marketing Associate	Reina Santana
Publicity Assistant	Alexi Ueltzen
Rights Coordinator	Candace Groskreutz
Interns	Amy Hagelin, Julia Wang
Customer Service Manager	Christina Sverdrup
Order Fulfillment	Washul Lakdhon
Administrator	Theresa Nelson
Computer Support	Peter Eichelberger
Publisher	Kiran S. Rana

Hunter House Inc., Publishers
PO Box 2914
Alameda CA 94501-0914

Library of Congress Cataloging-in-Publication Data

Bartl, Almuth.
[Kleine Stille zwischendurch. English]
101 relaxation games for children : finding a little peace and quiet in between /
Allison Bartl. — 1st ed.
p. cm. — (SmartFun activity books)
Translation of: Kleine Stille zwischendurch.
ISBN-13: 978-0-89793-493-0 (pbk.)
ISBN-10: 0-89793-493-8 (pbk.)
ISBN-13: 978-0-89793-494-7 (spiral bound)
ISBN-10: 0-89793-494-6 (spiral bound)
1. Games. 2. School children—Recreation. 3. Relaxation. I. Title.
II. Title: One hundred one relaxation games for children. III. Title:
One hundred and one relaxation games for children.
GV1203.B35313 2007
790.1'922—dc22   2007025123

Printed and Bound by Bang Printing, Brainerd, Minnesota

Manufactured in the United States of America

9 8 7 6 5 4 3 2 1   First Edition   08 09 10 11 12

Contents

List of Games

Silence is tranquility but never emptiness;
it is clarity but never absence of color;
it is rhythm like a healthy heartbeat;
it is the foundation of all thought,
and therefore every creative thing of value depends upon it.

YEHUDI MENUHIN, AMERICAN VIOLINIST AND CONDUCTOR, 1916–1999

Introduction

Why Relaxation Games?

Children need security, love, freedom, recognition, support, and a lot of fun in order to achieve balance and inner peace. At the same time, they want to be taken seriously as people, to have their feelings, needs, and dreams acknowledged. For teachers, this means creating a balance between protection and trust, between support and challenge, between class community and individuality. Only then can the classroom feel like home to the children—a place where they can largely be free of fear and stress.

Unfortunately, this is not the reality for many children. In recent years, chronic stress has become a part of our culture, and the result is an increase in developmental disorders in children. More and more school-age children suffer from speech difficulties, poor social interactions, physical illnesses, and emotional problems.

In general, stress has increased in many different areas of children's lives; for example:

Family. The growing number of divorces means that children's guardians and role models change frequently, making it hard for children to decide where their loyalties lie. Other problems that create pressure for many children include a parent's unemployment, or a parent's dependence on the child as a "partner replacement" or for help in raising younger siblings.

Free time. Children can become overwhelmed by an overcrowded schedule. Between homework, commitments to activities like soccer, excessive TV watching, and time spent playing computer games, many children have little or no downtime. The lack of exercise that accompanies an overexposure to electronic media worsens the negative effects of stress.

School. The wrong kind of schooling can cause a lack of intellectual stimulation and/or performance pressure. Other stressors that should be taken seriously are pressure from parents to achieve, abuse by a teacher (e.g., humiliation, cynicism), bullying, verbal and nonverbal violence among students, peer pressure, noise in the classroom, and frequent changing of teachers or classrooms. Children need a teacher who will calmly take steps to prevent or solve conflicts among the students. Relaxation games can assist these efforts by providing a peaceful, fun atmosphere.

The activities in this book are designed to release tension and promote relaxation. Use them any time you have a few extra minutes of classroom time. They are especially useful at the beginning of class, to help children settle down and refocus on learning. Or when your class is especially fidgety and distracted, you may find it productive to stop your regular lesson and play one or two of the games. Then everyone can resume the lesson feeling refreshed and calmed.

Teacher, be sure to join in. Your participation will help increase the sense of fun and community in your classroom. Most important of all, relax and enjoy yourself!

Key to the Icons Used in the Games

To help you find activities suitable for a particular situation, each one is coded with symbols or icons that tell you some things about it at a glance:

- The size of the group needed
- Appropriate for older children
- If props are required
- If a large space is needed
- If music is required
- If physical contact is or might be involved
- If the activity involves going outdoors

These are explained in more detail below.

The size of the group needed. Most of the games can be played by the whole group, but a few require pairs or small groups, and some can be done individually. All games are marked with one of the following icons:

 = The whole group plays together

 = The children play individually, so any size group can play

 = The children play in small groups of three or more

 = The children play in pairs

Suitability in terms of age. The games are designed for children ages six to ten, and the higher the number of the game, the more challenging it is marked.

If a game is specifically suitable for children age eight or over, it is marked with the following icon:

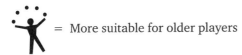 = More suitable for older players

If props are required. Many of the games require no special props. In some cases, though, items such as paper and pens, blindfolds, or other materials are integral to leading or playing a game. Games requiring props are flagged with the icon below, and the necessary materials are listed under the Props heading.

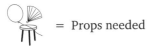 = Props needed

If a large space is needed. A large space is required for a few of the games, such as when the whole group is required to form a circle or to walk around the room. These are marked with the following icon:

 = May require a larger space

If music is required. Only a few games in this book require recorded music. If the music is optional, it is noted as such; if it is required, the icon below is used:

 = Music required

If physical contact is or might be involved. Although a certain amount of body contact might be acceptable in certain environments, the following icon has been inserted at the top of any exercises that might involve anywhere from a small amount of contact to minor collisions. You can figure out in advance if the game is suitable for your participants and/or environment.

 = Physical contact likely

If the activity involves going outdoors. A few games require going outdoors. These are marked with the following icon:

 = Involves going outdoors

The Games

My Partner's Hands

How to Play: The children stand opposite each other in pairs; they put their palms together and close their eyes. They stand like this for a while and feel the warmth of each other's hands. When the leader gives the sign—by ringing a little bell, for example—each child turns around once and then tries to find the other's hands, all while still keeping their eyes closed.

2

whole group

Multiplying Vampires

Props: Folded slips of paper with the word "vampire" written on only one

How to Play: At the beginning of this "scary" game, each child is handed a folded slip of paper. Only one of them says "vampire" on it, while the others are blank. After the children find out whether or not they are the vampire, they keep that information a secret and walk slowly and quietly around the room. When two people meet, they ask each other, "Vampire?" If both whisper "No," they continue on their way; if one whispers "Yes," the other becomes a vampire, too, and turns everyone he meets into a vampire as well. After five minutes the game ends, and the remaining nonvampires identify themselves.

Back to Back

How to Play: One child stands in front of the room, turned sideways, with her eyes closed. The leader points to a second child, who then creeps forward on his tiptoes and leans against the "blind" one, back to back. The first child, using her back sensors but not her hands, tries to feel the body of the second and guess who it is. If the "blind" child cannot guess who it is, she can order the mystery person to quack, chirp, or bark. This should make the guessing easier. Now it's the next person's turn!

Silence is not just the absence of noise, but a quietness that allows people to open their eyes and ears for another world.

SERGE POLIAKOFF, RUSSIAN ARTIST, 1906–1969

Ghostly Voices

Props: A cassette, CD, or MP3 player; recorded music

Preparation: Hide the music player somewhere in the room.

How to Play: Before the children arrive, a tape, CD, or MP3 player playing very soft music is hidden somewhere in the room. At first, only a few children notice the music. Eventually, more and more people notice it. The room grows quieter and quieter, until finally everyone is listening closely to figure out where the sounds are coming from. If someone thinks they've found the hiding place, they may guess. There is a small prize for guessing correctly.

5

Wilma the Wicked Witch

How to Play: Wilma (or Walter) the Wicked Witch (the adult leader) stands in front of the group and says, "I don't want to see any ears!" Immediately, all the children cover their ears with their hands. The witch looks closely at all the children, and anyone whose ears are showing is out and has to put their heads down on their desk until the game is over. Next, the leader says, "I don't want to see any hands," and immediately the children sit on their hands or hide them under their shirts. The next time, the witch may not want to see any faces. In that case, the children could make a nest with their arms on the desk and put their heads down, or pull their sweaters up over their faces.

The witch continues to croak out her wishes before finally saying, "I don't want to see any children at all!" Presto—all the remaining children disappear under the tables or behind the curtains, waiting to see what happens next. The child—or children—who hide the best get to be the witch(es) or wizard(s) the next time. To wrap up the game, the witch mutters that she would like to see all the children again, along with their pencil cases, binders, or whatever is needed for the next activity.

whole group

Things I Can Do with My Hands

How to Play: One child begins the game by saying, "With my hands, I can wave hello." The child demonstrates by waving. The second child repeats the phrase and the action: "With my hands, I can wave hello," and adds (for example), "and pet a kitten," demonstrating the new action. The next child repeats both actions and names a third; for example, scratching, getting dressed, washing, putting on sunblock. If someone gets stuck or can't think of anything else, they can call on another child to help. (The order can be determined by seat assignments or called out by the leader.)

Imagination is more important than knowledge...

ALBERT EINSTEIN

Snail Gymnastics

How to Play: The children stand at their places and breathe calmly from their bellies. The leader transforms them into snails who get to do gymnastics together. First, moving at a snail's pace, they stretch their arms way up into the air, and then use them to draw a big circle, taking at least a minute to complete the activity. A snail-paced knee bend might be next. Finish by having the snail children *very slowly* sit down. The leader also performs the movements so that the children can follow his pace.

any size

Grow in the Dark

How to Play: First, the classroom is darkened. All the children crouch on the floor; they are teeny-tiny plants. Then the light is switched on and off, five times in a row. In each phase of darkness, the little plants grow a tiny bit. As soon as the light is switched back on, everyone stands still. The children may peek at their fellow plants to see how much they have grown. By the end of the fifth "night," all the little plants should have grown into big, strong plants. If desired, a second round of the game can be added in which the plants slowly, slowly wilt and finally end up back on the floor, curled into a little ball.

any size

The Gorilla Game

How to Play: All the children stand at their seats. With their fingertips, they softly beat on their chests. At the same time, their mouths fall open and they let out a deep gorilla sound. The noise grows louder and louder, then fades; it grows quieter, then quieter still, and finally stops. The children's fingertips should move faster and then more slowly, depending on the sound level. Finally, everyone's arms should fall limply to their sides.

Note: The leader should by all means play along (and guide the players as needed)—and can also ask a child to "conduct."

10

Angry Spaghetti

How to Play: Instead of spaghetti with sauce, we've got spaghetti with anger. Each person thinks of something that upset him or her today. It could be a shove from the person sitting next to him, a bad grade, the fact that she wasn't invited to a classmate's birthday party, or the stupid green sweater that his mom made him wear.

First, the children shake their heads to loosen up the angry spaghetti. Then they slowly pull one long noodle after another out of their ears, imagining that each strand is a bit of their anger, wad them all up into an angry spaghetti ball, and throw the ball out the open window with gusto. Whew, what a relief! Children can tell the class what they threw away, if they would like, but don't push them to.

any size

Conveyor Belt

How to Play: All the children and the leader stand at their places and breathe deeply and calmly from their bellies. Then they close their eyes and imagine standing at one end of a long conveyor belt. The other end of the conveyor belt is so far away that you can't see it. Without speaking, each person puts everything on the conveyor belt that bothered her today, or that made him sad. They enact or mime this, still keeping silent. Perhaps Jenny imagines loading Michael onto the belt since he threw all those snowballs at her on the way to school. What a great feeling to see your problems being dragged away on the conveyor belt, getting smaller and smaller, and finally disappearing in the distance. When they are finished, the children can act out their relief and quietly sit down.

* * * * * * * * *

**We should not try to untangle our problems,
but instead untangle ourselves from our problems.**

KIRPAL SINGH, INDIAN SPIRITUAL TEACHER, 1894–1974

any size

Washing Day

How to Play: Everyone imagines the following scenario and accompanies it with the appropriate motions:

Everyone has been working hard washing lots of sheets. Now there's a soaking-wet sheet lying in front of each child. The children bend down and grab their sheets with both hands. Boy, they're heavy! Each person hoists a sheet and swings it over one shoulder. Then they smack the sheets onto the ground in front of them as hard as they can. Wow, there's water everywhere! Again, they lift the sheet, swing it over their shoulder, and then slam it onto the ground as hard as they can. Suddenly they notice how light the sheets have gotten. They let them flutter in the breeze for a minute, then fold them up. One child walks through the room, collecting the imaginary sheets in an imaginary basket.

Trust Seesaw

How to Play: This game requires a certain amount of courage and trust in one's fellow players. But any child armed with those qualities can relax and enjoy this wonderful seesawing exercise.

Divide the children into groups of six. One child stands in the middle, and the other members of his group make a tight circle around him. Once they are all positioned correctly, the child closes his eyes and falls in any direction he chooses. He is immediately caught by the circle of players and gently pushed back upright. Using his momentum, the child now falls in a different direction, and again he is safely caught. He continues falling back and forth, keeping his feet in the same spot.

After a while, the catchers can perhaps take a small step backward. By now the seesawer has learned to trust his playmates.

Give everyone in the group a chance to be the player who falls and then is caught. Is the leader brave enough to try being caught, too?

Note: If the children are very small, extra care should be taken to make sure the falling child can be caught properly.

The Gummy-Bear Talk Show

Props: A bag of gummy bears or other treats (e.g., raisins, peanuts, cookies)

How to Play: For this activity, the children make a circle with their chairs. Taking turns, one child gets to tell the others one thing about herself: how many siblings she has, if she owns any pets, what her favorite food or drink or game is, and so on, and then it's the next child's turn.

Since some children find it hard to talk, the following rule applies: For every statement made, the talker gets to take a gummy bear from the bag.

The leader should stop the children when five minutes are up. Whoever is talking at that moment finds a stopping point, and the other children each get a gummy bear as a reward for their patient listening!

15

 whole group

Push the Wall Down

How to Play: All the children stand in a row with their backs against a wall. As soon as the leader gives the signal to start, they collectively push against the wall as hard as they can. The leader takes part enthusiastically, too. After this display of strength, they all shake out their arms and legs, make some loose circles with their shoulders, and go back to their seats. If they would like, children can share with the group how they felt when pushing and how they felt when they stopped.

Even the wisest man can learn immeasurable amounts from children.

RUDOLF STEINER, AUSTRIAN PHILOSOPHER
AND FOUNDER OF THE WALDORF EDUCATIONAL SYSTEM, 1861–1925

any size

Angels by Candlelight

Props: At least one candle for each table or desk

How to Play: During the holiday season it's easy to transform hyper children into a band of angels, simply by lighting a candle on each table. The candles should be blown out after about five minutes, though, or the effect begins to wear off and an experimental spirit sets in: What happens if I hold the point of my pen (or Laura's sandwich) over the flame?

Tip: The children breathe in deeply through their noses, hold their breath for three seconds, and then breathe out through their mouths with a hissing sound. The candles are extinguished as the air is blown out.

Note: Before playing this game make sure open flames are permitted in your play area and be sure to take any other necessary safety precautions.

Deep-Breathing Stroll

How to Play: The children and the leader stand comfortably at their places. They all breathe in deeply through their noses for four counts, hold the air in for one or two counts, and then breathe out fully through their mouths, again for a count of four. The children are told to make a hissing sound as they breathe out. At first, the leader counts along: "One, two, three, four (hold); one, two, three, four." Once a rhythm is established, everyone starts moving slowly. Calmly and in time with the rhythm of their flowing breath, they choose a partner and go for a stroll through the room. When the leader gives the sign, the children return to their places and sit down.

In the Land of Smiles

How to Play: One child stands up and smiles at another child, who he chooses at random. This child "catches" the smile, stands up, and smiles at a third child. The smiling epidemic continues until finally all the children—and of course the leader, too—are standing up and smiling at each other and everyone.

The last child to catch the smile now greets another child: "Good morning, Tim!" and sits back down, smiling. Tim in turn greets a standing child and sits down, too. When all the children are finally sitting back down, you can move on to the next activity.

19

Painting with Sunlight

Props: A small mirror (or a flashlight, if it isn't sunny)

How to Play: The leader holds a small mirror so that the sun shines onto the mirror, reflecting its rays onto one wall of the room. Then the leader slowly moves the mirror, using the ray of light to draw a symbol or a simple object on the wall, or to write a letter of the alphabet. The children pay close attention to what they see on the wall. Whoever is the first to name the correct object or letter receives the mirror and gets to be the next person to draw a picture with sunlight on the wall. The solutions should not be shouted out loud; the children should raise their hands to be called on. Real pros can write whole words or math problems on the wall!

20

any size

Flashbulb Storm

How to Play: All the children are famous actors and actresses and are standing on the red carpet having their picture taken. Whether they feel like it or not, they have to smile! They endure the bright lights of the red carpet for at least a minute, all the while flashing their best "toothpaste-commercial" smiles. Finally, the leader gives the sign that they are relieved of this terribly strenuous job, and everyone sits back down. They can then tell the class who—and where—they were.

Don't make the mirror responsible for your face.

ALLISON BARTL

whole group

Don't Wake Me Up!

Props: Various objects that make noise (e.g., bicycle bell, handbell, percussion instruments, etc.)

How to Play: On a table place various noisemakers—for example, a handbell, a bicycle bell, a cup with a spoon in it, a squeaky toy, a key ring, etc. One child is chosen to be the "alarm clock" and is sent out of the room. The others decide which noise they want to be woken by—for example, the squeaky toy. The children lay their heads down on their folded arms on the table, and the leader calls the "alarm clock" back into the room. He tries making different noises to wake the others up: tapping the spoon on the edge of the cup, rattling the key ring—but the children keep sleeping soundly. Only when he makes the right sound, by squeezing the toy, do all the children wake up. Then they stretch out their arms and legs and are now ready for the next task. Once the children know how the game works, they can send the adult leader out of the room to be the alarm clock and discuss which noise they want to have wake them up.

Indoor Forest

How to Play: Each child represents a tree, anchored to the spot with strong roots. The leader plays along, too, so she can guide the children through the activity. Their arms, as the branches, are stretched up into the air, and their fingers move gently like thin twigs in a barely noticeable breath of wind. Now the wind grows stronger. Everyone makes whooshing wind sounds and moves accordingly. The twigs move faster, and the branches begin to bend in the wind. The wind grows even stronger, becoming a storm that whips through the trees. It rushes and whooshes through the indoor forest. Fortunately, the storm calms down quickly. It gets quieter and finally stops altogether. What a wonderful feeling for the poor, battered trees! Now it's completely calm in the forest, and the leader and the children all take their seats.

any
size

Headphones

How to Play: All players, including the leader, prop their elbows up on the table, close their eyes, and hold their hands over their ears like headphones. At first, you don't hear anything; then you begin to hear various sounds—a rushing noise, then your own breath, swallowing, etc. After a few minutes, the leader gives the sign for everyone to take off their headphones, perhaps by striking a bell or gong. Afterward, the children report on the sounds they heard.

* * * * * * * * * *

The greatest revelation is silence.

TAO TE CHING

Ghosts Knocking

Props: A blindfold and pencils

How to Play: A few children (the "ghosts") sit in a circle on the floor, each holding two pencils. Another child who would like to be a ghost, too, sits in the middle of the circle wearing a blindfold. If she can prove how good her ears are, she may join the ghosts. Once the room is completely silent, the leader points at one of the ghosts. This ghost taps its pencils together several times. The child in the middle listens carefully to see where the sound is coming from and then points in that direction. If she correctly identifies the noisy ghost, she is accepted into the exalted ranks of the ghosts and gets to choose the next candidate to sit in the middle.

The Shadow Game

How to Play: All but three children sit in a circle on the floor and close their eyes. The three children scurry around the circle of players in their sock feet, quiet as mice, then stand behind three players as their shadows. The leader reminds the children to keep their eyes closed. Children who think they have shadows should now raise their hands. Then everyone may open their eyes and see who guessed right. If a child has guessed correctly that there was a shadow standing behind them, that child gets to be a shadow in the next round. If a shadow escapes discovery, they continue to be a shadow.

Tip-of-the-Nose Meeting

How to Play: In pairs, the children stand approximately one step apart and look at each other. When the leader gives the sign, they all close their eyes and lean in toward their partners, trying to bring the tips of their noses together.

After several attempts, players can swap partners.

Temple Rub

How to Play: The children and the leader stand in a circle and calmly breathe in and out a few times. Then they create a "temple-rubbing" train by turning to the right, closing their eyes, and placing the tips of their index and middle fingers against the temples of the child in front of them. Applying gentle pressure, the children use their fingertips to make small circles on the temples, ten times in each direction. Then everyone opens their eyes again, stands up, and quietly takes their seats.

If they choose to, the children can take a few minutes to share what the experience felt like.

I have never let my schooling interfere with my education.

MARK TWAIN, 1835–1910

any
size

Slow Motion

How to Play: This is a fun, quiet game that is perfect for calming children who are wound up. When the words "slow motion" are called out, everyone in the room is required to move very, very slowly. After recess, for example, children might have to take off their jackets at a snail's pace. Or one child might walk in slow motion to the board and draw something. Or the leader might move slowly through the room. Everyone simply does what they would be doing anyway—just in slow motion.

If you feel the need to laugh during this game, make sure that happens in slow motion too: Ha...ha...ha...!

I'm Tired

How to Play: One child stands at the front of the room. It is her job to make the rest of the children yawn. First, she has a good long stretch, and the others imitate everything she does. Then she breathes in deeply through her mouth, closes her eyes, and lets out a long, deep yawn from the pit of her stomach. She keeps stretching until the first yawns can be heard from the group. How long will it take before the leader yawns, too?

Lumberjacks

How to Play: The children play in pairs. One child, playing the part of the log, lies down on his stomach with his arms at his sides. His partner is a lumberjack whose only job is to roll the log over onto its back. But the log is unbelievably heavy and seems to be rooted in the ground. The strong lumberjack doesn't give up, though. She keeps trying with all her might to roll the log over. After two minutes, a bell is rung. If the lumberjack has not yet succeeded, then the "log" wins. Then the roles are reversed, and the new lumberjack gets to discover how hard the task really is.

Honor as a teacher anyone who increases your knowledge.

JEWISH PROVERB

African Back Drums

How to Play: Children team up with a partner. If one child does not have a partner, the leader can also play. One child sits in a chair, closes her eyes, and rests her head on her crossed arms on the table. Her partner stands behind her and drums gently on her back with both hands. The "drummee" relaxes, opens her mouth, and lets out a low sound that sounds funny because of the drumming on her back. Finally, the drummer calmly lays his hands on his partner's back for thirty seconds while both children breathe deeply and relax. Then they switch roles.

Witch's Fingers

How to Play: Children team up with a partner. One child stands behind his partner and gently taps on her head with, for example, three fingers. While doing so, he quietly whispers, "One, two, three, four, five, and six, how many witch's fingers itch?" At the end of the rhyme he lets his fingers rest on the other child's head. Then the partner must guess how many witch's fingers were used. If she is right, they switch. If not, the witch repeats the game with the same number of fingers.

any
size

One Minute of Silence

How to Play: Each child stands behind a chair and waits for the leader's signal to start. The assignment is for each child to sit down quietly after they think exactly one minute has passed. The leader then checks her watch to see whose time estimate was closest.

Tip: Give especially antsy children something to hold in their hands during this activity: a smooth stone, a chestnut, or a wooden ball; let them hold their worry "stones" during other activities, too.

Never be afraid to sit awhile and think.

LORRAINE HANSBERRY, AMERICAN PLAYWRIGHT AND PAINTER, 1930–1965

34

any size

The Candy-Sucking Endurance Challenge

Props: A piece of hard candy for each child

How to Play: This is an emergency game for those times when you desperately need some peace and quiet. Each child gets a piece of hard candy; at the leader's signal, they put the candy in their mouths. Then they suck on the candy as slowly as possible. The winner is whoever has a sliver of candy left when all the other candies have dissolved. The best strategy is to avoid moving the candy around in your mouth at all; that way it will last longer. The winner receives another piece of candy to take home.

Caution: Make sure all the children are allowed to have candy, or consider a sugar-free candy.

whole group

Eagle Eyes

Props: Two identical objects

Preparation: Hide one of the identical objects.

How to Play: This is a good way to calm down a rowdy group of children who are storming into the room. The leader stops the children at the door and shows them an object, like an apple, whose "twin" is hiding somewhere in the room. The leader tells the children that the object is hiding in plain view, so they will not need to look behind curtains, under books, etc. The children line up against a wall and use only their eyes to look for the object. When a child finds it, he shouldn't say anything and should quietly sit down. The game continues for a set amount of time (say, three minutes) or until all the children have spotted the object.

36

any size

Classroom Mobile

Props: Photos of the children; other images; clear tape; nylon fishing line; pipe cleaners; swizzle sticks

How to Play: A mobile that gently twirls in the air can be relaxing and relieve stress. Children can even make their own mobiles. A fun way to do this is with photos of the children. Use wallet-size school photos, and tape two together back to back. Hang them by nylon thread (i.e., fishing line) from a mobile structure, which can be constructed from pipe cleaners, brightly colored plastic swizzle sticks, etc.

any
size

Listen!

How to Play: All the windows in the room are opened wide. The children and the adult leader all sit down, relax, and listen to the sounds coming from outside. The longer you concentrate, the more sounds you can distinguish: a car door slamming shut, rustling leaves, the maintenance man sweeping the yard and muttering to himself. Somewhere there are children singing, birds chirping.... After a while the children can share what they have heard.

If the children write down what they hear, the leader

Variation: If the children write down what they hear, the leader can check their lists to which children hear the most and which don't hear too well.

Tip: Most people hear even better with their eyes closed.

whole group

Ghost Hour

Props: A blindfold

How to Play: One child is the head ghost. She sits in the middle of the class-room, wearing a blindfold. Then the clock tower chimes, letting the children know it's the witching hour! Now all the other ghosts, including the leader, dance noiselessly through the room. If the head ghost hears a sound, she points in that direction, and the ghost who has been "caught" must return to his seat. When the head ghost claps her hands, everyone freezes in place. When she claps them again, the dance continues. But soon the bell chimes again; it's one o'clock, the witching hour is over, and all the spirits float back to their seats.

If a man insisted always on being serious,
and never allowed himself a bit of fun and relaxation,
he would go mad or become unstable without knowing it.

HERODOTUS, 484–430 B.C.

Magic Note

How to Play: The leader sings, hums, growls, or whistles a single note, and all the children do the same, echoing the magic note. When the leader hums quietly, it transforms normal children into tiny gnomes crouching on the floor. When the leader's hand is raised, the sound gets louder and the gnomes grow, getting bigger and bigger. Soon they are gigantic. When the leader's hand is lowered again, the sound gets quieter again and the children grow smaller. The leader's hand position, along with the volume, switches faster and faster. At one point, the magic note is so loud it sounds almost like a siren. Finally, it grows quieter again until it is barely audible, and the gnomes silently sit down.

Food for the Stork

How to Play: Anyone can turn into a stork by bending one leg until the foot is next to the buttocks and then grabbing the ankle with his hand. It's comfortable to stand like this on one leg, but suddenly the stork gets hungry. Fortunately, there is a tasty frog sitting a couple of feet in front of him. (Assuming a shortage of amphibians in your classroom, imagine erasers or pencil sharpeners as the frogs.) Slowly and carefully, the stork leans down and picks up a frog with his free hand. Once a stork has managed this task, he can sit down.

Note: Children should not force this action if it causes them any pain.

any
size

Pretend Shampoo

How to Play: A pretend shampoo can be relaxing and refreshing, and can free up space for new ideas. The leader walks through the room and, from an imaginary bottle, squeezes a dab of shampoo into each child's hand. Now everyone can wash their hair. First everyone sudses up; then they massage their scalps vigorously using all ten fingers. The leader slowly walks though the room again, this time with an imaginary watering can, and "rinses" the children's heads.

whole group

Shadow Children

Props: A blindfold

How to Play: One child sits on a chair in the middle of the room, wearing a blindfold. The leader points to one or more children. On their tippy-toes, these children sneak up to the one in the middle and stand behind her, acting as shadows. Can the blindfolded child guess how many shadows are standing behind her? Can she maybe even guess the names of the shadow children?

If they guess correctly they choose the next "guesser"; if not, one of the shadow children is the next child to be blindfolded.

You can learn a lot from your students—
for example, how much patience you have.

ALLISON BARTL

What's That Sound?

Props: A blindfold

How to Play: One child stands in front of the room wearing a blindfold. When the room is completely silent, the leader points to one child who then makes a noise; for example, closing a book, dropping his pencil case, or loudly blowing his nose. The blindfolded child has three guesses to figure out who made the noise and how it was made.

Royal Visit

How to Play: One child leaves the room and then reenters it as a beloved king (or queen). The door opens, and the king enters the hall with head held high. He moves slowly, smiles graciously, and greets a few people. Hands reach out to the monarch; some subjects wave, and some bow when the king passes by. His Majesty moves through the room and is seated on the throne. Children particularly enjoy it when the leader plays along, demonstrating obedience to the king.

45

small
groups

Blowing Troubles Away

Props: Plenty of bottles of soap bubbles; bubble wands

How to Play: The children are divided into small groups. Each group gets one bottle of bubble solution. In turn, each child in the group gets the bottle, thinks of something that is bothering her, and blows those troubles away along with the iridescent bubbles. Children who have already had a turn can quietly sit down. The leader gets a turn, too.

If you want to be able to appreciate a rainbow,
you have to accept rain along with sunshine.

ALLISON BARTL

whole
group

Sticky Soap Bubbles

Props: A bottle of long-lasting soap-bubble solution; a bubble wand

How to Play: In toy stores and novelty shops, you can sometimes find a soap-bubble mixture that makes bubbles that don't pop as fast as regular bubbles. Instead, the bubbles stick wherever they land, giant shimmering pearls that last for a good long while. Children then take turns blowing some of these special bubbles, and everyone watches to see where they land. After a round of doing this, the children can try to make bubble sculptures by adding to previous bubbles.

Magic Breath

How to Play: This is played with a partner. One child has magic powers, and the other unfortunately does not. As soon as the magician blows on his partner, she slowly collapses. The magician blows and blows until his "victim" is lying flat on the floor. But the magician also has the power to reverse the effect! Slowly, he sucks in air as though through a straw, until his partner starts to stand back up, finally returning to her full height. It's really great to have such strong magic powers! Have the children take turns being the magician in the pair.

Variation: Have the children think of different things the magician can do with his breath.

48

Friendship Circle

How to Play: The class is divided into two circles of chairs. The game begins in each circle as follows: One child thinks of something nice to do for the person on his right. He might stroke her arm, pat her shoulder, or say, "I like you." The child receiving this friendly treatment passes the same gesture along to the person on her right; he does the same, and so on until the kind gesture makes it back around to the first child.

Next, the second child thinks of a different kind gesture that can be passed along from child to child.

Ideally, each child gets a turn. If they run out of ideas, the leader can help.

Hand Massage

Props: Plenty of hand lotion

How to Play: Small children's hands, having spent all day writing and working, deserve a little break. The leader goes from child to child, squeezing a pea-sized dollop of hand lotion into each one's outstretched palm, and finally into her own. Everyone rubs their palms together, as if washing their hands, and massages the lotion in generously. Each finger gets special treatment, with special attention to the fingertips.

Conductor

Props: A CD or MP3 player; recordings of some orchestral classical music

How to Play: Everyone gets to be a conductor today. The children stand, hold a pencil in one hand, close their eyes, and conduct the orchestra, which is playing quiet classical music.

Life is a great big canvas,
and you should throw all the paint on it you can.

DANNY KAYE, ACTOR AND SINGER, 1913–1987

Zero to Sixty

How to Play: The easiest time to relax is after the muscles in the body have been completely tensed. The children are all in their seats, resting their arms loosely on the table.

Saying a magic word, the adult leader transforms all the children into race-car drivers who will drive as fast or as slow as the leader decides. Once the children are ready, the leader tells them to flex their right arms—in other words, to let all the engine's power flow only into that arm. The level of tension will vary from zero (completely relaxed) to sixty (as tight as possible). To start with, the leader might say "twenty." The children tense their right arms just a little, and maintain this tension until they get new instructions: "thirty." Then the racecars take a sharp curve, and have to reduce their speed to ten. The level of tension continues to go up and down; make sure the children are really only flexing their right arms, not their whole bodies. After the right arm comes the left one; after that it might be their legs, then their shoulders, back, and belly.

52

whole group

At the Campfire

Props: A sturdy candle and shades for the windows to darken the classroom, if possible

How to Play: Everyone sits in a circle on the floor around a burning candle. The room is dark, and only the fire in the middle gives a little light.

Together, the leader and the children reminisce about their day so far, recalling as many small details as possible. The leader begins, modeling a slow and calm way of talking. At the end, everyone takes hands. The leader squeezes the hand of the child to his right, and the silent signal is passed from child to child. Once the squeeze comes back around to the leader, the last child to pass it along may blow out the "campfire."

Note: Before playing this game make sure open flames are permitted in your play area and be sure to take any other necessary safety precautions.

Massage Circle

How to Play: All the children and the leader sit in a circle. When the sign is given, everyone turns to the right so that each child is facing their neighbor's back, which now gets the celebrity treatment: Each child kneads, rubs, and pats the back in front of them while enjoying the same treatment from someone else.

**We do not have to get our children to learn;
only to allow and encourage them in their learning.**

POLLY BERRIEN BERENDS, AUTHOR OF *WHOLE CHILD/WHOLE PARENT*

Mystery Categories

How to Play: One child silently decides how she will divide up the group—for example, into children with glasses and those without. Then she slowly calls the names of all the children with glasses and asks them to stand up. The children look at each other and try to guess what the criterion was. If someone thinks he knows it, he raises his hand. If he is right, it's his turn to divide the group.

Other criteria might be: hair color, hair length, people who take the bus, people wearing jeans, first letter of the first or last name, children with and without siblings, children wearing T-shirts. The leader makes sure no hurtful categories are chosen.

whole group

Inflate-a-Kid

How to Play: All the children except for one squat on the floor, pretending to be deflated balloons. The child left standing has an air pump, and quickly she starts to inflate her companions. The more the balloons are blown up, the more they expand and unfold, until finally they are all standing up straight. Then the air pumper runs through the room and gently pulls on an earlobe here and there. These children immediately deflate, growing smaller and smaller until finally they are all folded back up on the floor.

Musical Rhythms

How to Play: One child thinks of a song that all the others will know. Then he taps out the rhythm of the song by knocking on the table. The other children listen carefully and try to guess the song. Whoever wants to guess raises his hand. The musician stops tapping and calls on the guesser. If the guess is correct, there's a round of applause for quick guessing. If it is incorrect, the guesser is out and cannot make any more guesses. This is a strict rule because otherwise children start randomly listing all the songs they know.

Where's Wendy?

How to Play: All the children walk slowly around the room with their eyes closed. They quietly whisper their names as they walk: "My name is…(Miriam)." The leader taps one child on the shoulder, turning her into "Wendy" (or "Willy" for a boy). She is allowed to open her eyes, and from now on she starts muttering, "My name is Wendy (or Willy)." The other players listen carefully to the names they hear. If a player hears "Wendy/Willy," he follows her closely and stops saying his own name. In this way, the number of voices gets to be fewer and fewer, and the line behind Wendy/Willy grows longer and longer. At some point, the leader claps their hands to signal that everyone can open their eyes again.

pairs

Caboose

How to Play: The children form pairs. One partner, the "engine," stands in front with the other partner right behind her. As soon as the leader claps, the partners start walking; the "caboose" must copy the engine's actions exactly. If the first one stretches her arm out to the right, for example, or tilts her head to the side, her partner does the same. In this fashion, the pairs wander through the room or across the yard at varying speeds. When the leader claps a second time, the children all switch positions; i.e., the caboose becomes the engine.

**If you are being criticized,
you must be doing something right.
Because people only attack the person who has the ball.**

BRUCE LEE, CHINESE-AMERICAN MARTIAL ARTIST, 1940–1973

pairs

I Feel So Green Today

Props: A glass of water and a paintbox for each child

How to Play: For this game, everyone gets to color the water in their glass according to their mood. This should be done slowly and carefully so the children can enjoy the ribbons of color floating through the water. Once all the children have mixed their mood cocktails, each tries to explain to a partner why they have chosen this particular color and what its significance is.

any size

Cuckoo Eggs

Props: An index card with the same short text on it for each child; the leader's sheet has words underlined at random that, when the text is read aloud, can be replaced by other words

How to Play: The children all have the text in front of them. The leader reads the text aloud, replacing the underlined words. For example, "blue bicycle" might be replaced by "green bicycle," and so on. Each child reads along silently, without making any sign when there is a mistake; each keeps track of how many substituted "cuckoo eggs" there were. At the end, compare notes to see who found all the mistakes.

Good-Vibe Alley

Props: Background music (optional)

How to Play: The children stand in two rows facing each other, creating an alley. One participant at a time, beginning with the leader, walks through the alley. As each person passes through, the children pet or massage the person's arm or back. Once the person reaches the end of the alley, a child from the end of one row follows, strolling through the alley. This should allow each person to go through the "good-vibe alley" at least once.

The stroll can be especially relaxing if suitable music is playing softly in the background.

The Echo

How to Play: "Whatever you call into the forest will come back to you," says a proverb, and there's something to that. In this game, one child stands in front of the group and calls out all kinds of things he himself would like to hear—for example, "Good job!" "Bravo!" or "I like you!" The others repeat it back as a chorus. The leader is a member of the chorus, too. At first the echo comes back as a loud yell; then it grows quieter and quieter until the last phrase is just a whisper.

Take rest; a field that has rested gives a bountiful crop.

OVID, 43 B.C.–17 A.D.

whole group

What Smells So Good?

Props: An oil burner with fragrant oils or scented candles

How to Play: Not only do scented oils and candles provide a pleasant smell, they also promote a sense of well-being and relaxation. The use of a scented-oil burner is particularly recommended during stressful times. Every so often, the leader can draw the children's attention to the lamp. Then everyone should sit quietly and see whether they can smell the scent; they determine what it smells like and whether they like it.

Variation: To make this activity more of a game, choose three to four relatively easily identifiable and distinct scents (e.g., lavender, strawberry, vanilla, eucalyptus) to disperse in the different corners of the room or play area. The children should smell each scent, keep their guesses to themselves, and sit down quietly. The leader then announces what scents were in which corners. Who made the most correct identifications?

Notes
- Some people—both children and adults—may be sensitive or allergic to scents, so if this may be of concern in your environment, check with all relevant parties (e.g., parents, students, administrators, and other leaders working in a shared space) before undertaking this activity.
- Before playing this game make sure open flames are permitted in your play area and be sure to take any other necessary safety precautions.

Pencil Pal

Props: Ten pencils for each pair of children

How to Play: One child lies on the floor, and her partner places pencils all over her body. One might be on her forehead, one on her upper arm, one on her left hand, etc. Her partner should try to balance about ten pencils on different parts of her body (i.e., none of the pencils should be touching other pencils) without letting any roll off. Naturally, the "pencil pal" must lie absolutely still in order for this to work.

Once all the pencils have been balanced, the balancer counts loudly to three. At the count of three, the pencil pal gets to jump up, shake herself off, and then help collect all the pencils. Now it's her partner's turn to lie still.

Birds' Nests

Props: A piece of paper for each child; pens or pencils for drawing

How to Play: Each child takes a piece of paper and draws ten circles of varying sizes, representing birds' nests. The circles can be arranged however they like. Then each person trades sheets with a partner. Each little bird now has a minute's time to memorize the location of the nests before closing their eyes and drawing an egg in each nest. Then everyone opens their eyes again. Who managed to lay the most eggs inside the nests? Even if an egg is only touching the outside of the circle, it counts as a hit.

any
size

Mandalas

Props: Plenty of mandalas or other pictures that can be colored; colored pencils, markers, or crayons

How to Play: Because of the calming effect mandalas can have on children, coloring them has become a popular free-time activity in schools. Even pictures from regular coloring books are popular with young children; as long as coloring outside the lines is allowed, this can be a very de-stressing and calming exercise.

Variations

- Instead of having each child color their own mandala, break the children into small groups of two to four in which the children will work together on the same mandala at the same time. This requires some communication and organization.
- After all of the mandalas are completed, post them on a blackboard or wall and have the children say which mandalas are their favorites and why.

- Each child sits in a circle, facing the center, and colors one mandala for two minutes. When the leader announces that time is up, each child must pass their mandala to the child on their right and continue coloring.

Back Massage

How to Play: The children play this with a partner. The adult leader can participate, too, if there is an odd number of children in the group. One child bends forward, letting his head and arms hang down loosely. His partner stands behind him and thumps on his back with both palms—not too hard, but emphatically.

After about a minute, once every part of the recipient's back has been patted down, the massaging partner strokes his partner's back from top to bottom. Gradually, the child receiving the massage straightens up, finally standing upright, and tells their partner and/or the rest of the group how the massage felt. This exercise provides wonderful sensations for tense shoulders and backs.

**People will forget how fast you worked,
but they will remember how well you worked.**

ALLISON BARTL

Undercover

Prop: A blanket or big sweater

How to Play: All the children and the leader sit in chairs with their eyes closed. One child goes around the room and collects approximately twenty small objects—for example, a pencil, the cap from a marker, a watch, a key, a piece of chalk, etc. The items are spread out on a table and covered with a blanket (or a big sweater, if nothing else is available). Then—based on an order chosen by the leader—one child at a time comes forward; each has thirty seconds to feel the objects. The children may not reach under the blanket, so they must try to recognize the objects through the fabric. Once the thirty seconds are up, the child quickly sits and writes down what they detected. While the rest of the children take their turns identifying the objects, the "hider" can start correcting the finished lists. Finally, the leader gets to feel the objects and make a list too. Children get one point for each object correctly identified; the one with the most points wins.

whole group

Tea Party

Props: A cup and a teabag for each child, plus honey and lemon juice; also, if no kitchen is available, an electric teakettle so you can prepare tea in the classroom

How to Play: Warm peppermint or chamomile tea is not necessarily a child's favorite beverage. However, when they have it with a group of other children and the tea is served by an adult, they all like to drink it. Whoever wants to can sweeten the tea with honey and drizzle a little lemon juice into it. Even just feeling the warmth of the cup in one's hands and inhaling the fragrance of the tea can have a relaxing effect and trigger a feeling of well-being.

Variation: The leader can introduce the children to different types of tea services that are important in other cultures, such as the Japanese (*Chado* or *Chanoyu*), Chinese (*Gong Fu*), and Korean (*Panyaro* or *DaDo*) tea ceremonies and the British/Victorian tradition of having a tea break in the afternoon during which small sandwiches, scones, and other tasty snacks are served.

Interested children can do further research and try to perform a traditional tea service from one of the cultures above for the class.

Scouting Expedition

How to Play: All the little scouts tiptoe quietly along behind their leader (a child chosen by the adult leader), who chooses a route through the room and out into the yard. The group should move as quietly and secretively as possible. They might, for example, creep out of the room, down the hall, down the stairs, past an open door, through a lobby, and then, one by one, sneak out to the playground. Whew, we made it—that was close! Now they quietly choose a new leader, whom they follow silently as she leads them back to the room. The teacher tiptoes along with them, of course!

Even if you are on your way to your gold mine,
don't forget to pick up the silver dollars lying along the wayside!

ALLISON BARTL

River of Cares

How to Play: All the children scoot their chairs back a little bit, fold their arms on their table or desk, and lean forward, resting their heads on their folded arms. Each imagines that they are stretched like a bridge across a calmly flowing stream. This river of cares takes with it everything that is weighing on the children's minds. It might be a bad grade, a fight with a best friend, worries about a lost hat, or any number of other things. Each worry is mentally placed on a water-lily leaf, and the child watches as they float away.

whole group

Cat and Mouse

Prop: A blindfold

How to Play: Each corner of the room is assigned a number. Then one child is turned into a mouse, and one into a cat. The cat is blindfolded. She stands in the middle of the room while the other children, including the mouse, spread out into the four corners. The cat guesses which corner the mouse might be in, and calls out the number of that corner. If the mouse is indeed there, the game is over, and a new mouse is chosen.

If the mouse is not in that corner, however, the game continues. All the children who were in the corner the cat named must go back to their seats. The remaining players spread out again into the four corners, and the cat "pounces" again, calling out a new number. The game continues until only three children besides the cat are left. If the mouse has not been caught at this point, he can proudly claim to have bested the cat. The leader can play, too!

whole group

Queen Sharp Ears

How to Play: Queen (or King) Sharp Ears sits in the middle of the room and "sleeps" (closes her eyes) while her underlings perform a task. They might be cleaning up art supplies, getting ready for snack time, or coming in from the playground. Queen Sharp Ears is a light sleeper, and no one wants to wake her, so the task is done very quietly and on tiptoes. If Queen Sharp Ears hears a noise, she immediately points in that direction, and the guilty party is banished to his seat. Of the extra-quiet workers who are left at the end, the queen chooses her successor.

Teaching kids to count is fine,
but teaching them what counts is best.

BOB TALBERT, AMERICAN JOURNALIST, 1936–1999

74

Laugh!

How to Play: A hearty laugh relaxes your muscles, frees up your mind and spirit, and is immediately calming. Get the whole group to start laughing, not in a helpless giggle or a furtive chuckle, but in a free, hearty laugh. If the mood is not quite right for laughing, two or three children can tell their favorite jokes. Who is the best at making everyone laugh?

In case they ask you for your favorite jokes, here are a few suggestions:

Fred walks into the classroom, loaded down with sandwiches and soda. The teacher yells, "What do you think you're doing? This isn't a restaurant!" Fred replies, "I know, that's why I brought my own lunch."

Teacher: "Whose hat is this?
Student: "It looks like mine, but it can't be, because mine is lost."

"Do you always have to have the last word, Lisa?"
"Well, how am I supposed to know when you're going to stop talking?"

"Hey, Tom! Wow, you've really changed—new haircut, new clothes, even a new backpack!"
"My name isn't Tom, it's Alvin."
"What, a new name, too? Isn't that taking it a bit far?"

whole group

The Magic Book

Prop: A book

How to Play: The leader shakes a book, and something falls out from between its pages. Now she takes this something and pets it very carefully with one finger. It seems to be an animal. A dog, maybe, or a cat? No, it's much smaller than that. Hey, it jumped up on her shoulder! It could be a mouse, but the way this animal jumps makes it seem more like a frog, don't you think?

The first child to guess the right animal gets to take a turn shaking the magic book. This time, maybe an alarm clock will fall out, or a toothbrush; it might be a parrot, or a sandwich, or a lawnmower. The "mime's" actions toward the imaginary object will help the others guess what it is.

Burbling Lips

How to Play: All the children stand by their seats. Together, they take a deep breath and hold it while the leader counts to four. Then the children breathe out through their slightly open mouths in such a way that their lips gently "burble"; in other words, they vibrate just a little. They might even make a funny noise; but if they start laughing, they are out and have to sit down. As they do this, the leader counts to eight. Then everyone takes a deep breath again—one, two, three, four—and slowly lets the air burble back out. This breathing cycle is repeated at least five times. Who will stay relaxed and focused enough to finish the exercise?

Petting Zoo

Props: Various objects that have pleasant textures; a box to put them in

How to Play: A secret box contains various objects that can be used to "pet" another person in the group. One child closes her eyes, and another player touches her arm or hand with one of the objects. Can she guess which item from the petting zoo is being used? If she guesses incorrectly, she continues guessing until she gets it right, at which point she becomes the next "toucher" and gets to choose the next "guesser."

Examples
- a cotton ball
- a feather
- a scrap of fur
- a fleece glove
- a wooden ball
- a ball of yarn

The Outsider

How to Play: One child, designated as the guesser, leaves the room. The others think up a particular pose or facial expression that all but one of them, the "outsider," will make. For example, the participants might cross their right legs over the left, while the outsider does not; in this case, he could even cross his left leg over his right. There is no talking during this game, and all the children need to be careful to maintain their poses or expressions throughout, so that the guesser is not led astray.

Once the children are ready, the guesser comes back into the room. She then has three minutes to make five guesses as to who the outsider is. If she does not guess the correct answer or runs out of time, it is revealed by the leader. Either way, the guesser then gets to pick a new guesser to leave the room.

The wisest mind has something yet to learn.

GEORGE SANTAYANA, PHILOSOPHER AND AUTHOR, 1863–1952

whole group

Good Neighbors

How to Play: All the children sit in a circle and close their eyes. The leader calls one child by name—Drew, for example. Drew does not move, but the children on either side of him must react quickly. Whichever neighbor is the first to raise their hand gets a point. The leader calls out names faster and faster, requiring the children's utmost concentration. Of course, the leader can also join the circle and choose a child to lead the game. Whoever has the most points at the end wins.

Word Order

How to Play: This little game is great for occupying fast readers until slower readers have a chance to get to the end of the text. While all the children are reading, choose about ten different words that appear in the text only once, and write them on the board in random order. The readers' assignment is to write down the words in the order in which they appear in the text.

whole
group

Feelers

Props: A blindfold and two long pencils

How to Play: One child is blindfolded and handed two long pencils to use as feelers. The other players pick a random object, not too small—a sneaker, for example, or a hole punch. Can the child, using her pencil feelers, figure out what the object is?

Learning is like paddling against the stream.
If you stop, you will drift backward.

CHINESE SAYING

Mental Journey

How to Play: The children and the leader all close their eyes. One child is chosen to be the tour guide. He thinks of a place that everyone knows, and describes it without mentioning its name. He describes what he sees and hears, smells and feels there. It could be the zoo, for example, the local playground, or the skating rink. The first player to guess correctly gets to be the guide for the next trip.

Flight School

How to Play: All the children stand at their seats and let their arms hang loosely at their sides. As the leader slowly counts to four, the children lift their arms until their hands are at shoulder level. Then they slowly lower their arms as the leader counts to four again. Next, the children close their eyes and imagine they are birds flying way up high in the sky, in the warm sunshine. They evenly and smoothly move their arms up and down.

Sometimes I sits and thinks, and sometimes I just sits.

SATCHEL PAIGE, BASEBALL PLAYER, 1906–1982

Look Around You

Props: Paper; pens and pencils

How to Play: Each child takes a piece of paper and writes the letters of the alphabet down the left-hand side. Then they look around the room for things that start with each letter of the alphabet.

Examples
- apple
- blackboard
- Christina
- door
- eraser
- fingerpaint

(If necessary, leave out Q and X.)

Around the Circle

How to Play: The children are divided into two groups. The children in group A sit in a circle on the floor and close their eyes. The children in group B wait quietly in one corner of the room until they are called up. The leader points to one of the children in group B. This child walks once around the circle of kids in group A and then goes back to her corner. The members of group A now open their eyes, and together they try to guess which child from group B just walked around them. If they guess correctly, the teams alternate roles. If they guess incorrectly, another round is played. The game gets both harder and funnier if two children from group B walk in different directions around the circle, or if someone decides to crawl around the circle, hop around it, or even wiggle like a seal.

86

whole group

Who Are You?

Prop: A blindfold

How to Play: One child is blindfolded while another sits in a chair in front of the group. Carefully, a third player guides the blindfolded child's hands to the seated child's face. By feeling this person's face, how quickly can the guesser tell who it is?

After a few rounds, you can discuss the game: Who was easy to guess and who was hard? Why?

Nothing is permanent in this wicked world— not even our troubles.

CHARLIE CHAPLIN, 1889–1977

Sentence Rhythms

Props: Pencils and paper

How to Play: One child thinks up any short phrase; for example: "Michael eats cake and cookies." He does not tell it to the others, but instead claps out the syllables of the words. In our example, this would be:

— — — — — — —

The leader, using dashes or another convenient symbol, draws the syllables on the board as a visual aid. The other children get out pencils and paper and try to think of complete sentences that match the syllable pattern—maybe, "Anna sits on the sofa," or "Charlie Frog's car is speedy," or "Lizards have big fat fingers." The first child to come up with five sentences yells "stop!" reads her sentences to the group, and then gets to call on five others, who each read one of their own sentences. At the end, the first child reads his original sentence.

Vending Machine

Props: Assorted coins; paper; pens or pencils

How to Play: This game requires a lot of concentration, and it's good for logic and addition skills. Each child gets out a piece of paper and draws three rows of three circles each. These sets of circles will be enough for three games. Then the children rest their heads on their folded arms and close their eyes. The leader slowly drops three coins onto a flat surface, then gives their combined value (e.g., "fifty-one cents").

The children open their eyes and write the values of the three coins in the first three circles. In this case, the solution would be: quarter, quarter, penny.

Before too long, the next three coins are falling to the table. Whoever guesses all three combinations correctly gets a small prize. The game gets harder if you increase the number of coins to four, then five.

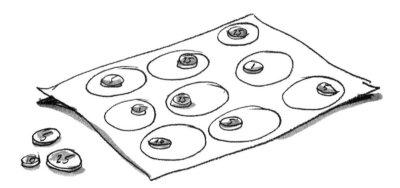

whole group

Story Time

Props: A tape recorder and some blank cassettes on hand for recording stories while you read them aloud

How to Play: If you set a tape recorder to record you while you are reading stories aloud, you will be prepared for any eventuality. While children are doing some other activity—drawing or crafts, for example—they enjoy listening to stories, even if they already know them, and the room will be quiet.

Tip: You can send tapes of recorded stories to children who are sick at home or in the hospital.

Variation: Set the tape recorder to record children reading stories. These recordings can be used later (as above) or sent to grandparents, family members living far away, etc.

True joy is relaxed.

SENECA, ROMAN STATESMAN, DRAMATIST, AND PHILOSOPHER, 3 B.C.–65 A.D.

90

One Chicken, Two Ducks

How to Play: Here's a variation on a well-known game. The leader says, "One chicken," and pauses so the children can mentally repeat the phrase. Then he repeats the words and adds to them: "One chicken, two ducks." Again there is a pause, long enough for the children to silently repeat the phrase and commit it to memory.

Then: "One chicken, two ducks, three geese." One animal after another is added to the list until it reaches five; for example, "One chicken, two ducks, three geese, four cats, five dogs." Then one child gets to demonstrate her powers of recollection by repeating the whole list. Animals are just one example of a category that can be listed, of course. Others might include types of fruit or articles of clothing.

Variation: To make this memory game more competitive, each child can write their list down after the leader stops speaking. The leader then checks each list, and whoever has made a mistake is out. The game is played repeatedly, with new list items, until every player but one, the winner, has been knocked out. If a few players have strong memories, lengthen the lists they must memorize.

Variations

Any of the following can make the game more challenging:

- Add another element in each round, up to ten.
- The numbers are out of order, so the list might be, "Seven apples, four pears, two lemons...."
- The items on the list do not belong to a single category; for example, "Six balls, three bicycles, nine carrots...."
- Each concept is described more specifically; for example, "Three rusty watering cans, five striped T-shirts, two pounds of dried figs...."

Feet Tables

Props: Two books per child except one, and three additional smaller objects

How to Play: All the children but one lie in a circle on the floor, their feet pointing inward. Then they all stretch their legs up into the air, and the leader places a book on each pair of feet. The children close their eyes and try to keep balancing the books on their feet. The remaining child stands in the middle of the circle, holding three notebooks (or sneakers, or lunchboxes, etc.). He tries to get rid of these as quickly as possible by sneakily balancing them on top of a child's book. If the overloaded child notices, though, she raises her hand, and the balancer has to take the object back. The game is over when the balancer manages to get rid of all three burdens at once, at least for a moment.

Little Dots

Props: Pens or markers with washable ink

How to Play: Children play this with a partner. One closes her eyes, and the other takes a pen or marker (with washable ink) and draws a tiny dot somewhere on the first child's arm, on the back of her hand, or on a finger. Without opening her eyes, the child who received the dot tries to touch it with her index finger. This is much harder than it sounds. For every dot she locates, she gets a point. After five rounds, the winner is the one with the most points.

Before you try to change the world,
go three times through your own house.

CHINESE PROVERB

93

Activity Jar

Props: Paper slips prepared in advance (see below); straws or rubber bands

Preparation: On small colored pieces of paper, write down riddles, mind puzzles, and word problems that the children can solve in about five minutes. For suggestions, see my book *101 Quick-Thinking Games + Riddles for Children* (publication information is provided at back of this book). Roll up each slip of paper and wedge it into one end of a drinking straw or secure it with a rubber band. Keep the activities in a jar until needed.

How to Play: You can use this whenever an extra activity is needed: If a child finishes an assignment early, for example, he gets to draw an activity from the jar and get to work.

Examples

- If two rabbits weigh as much as a fox, and a fox and a rabbit together weigh as much as a dog, how many rabbits will it take to equal the weight of the dog? (Solution: three.)

- A crate full of flour weighs 15 pounds. A baker takes out half of the flour and sees that the crate with the rest of the flour weighs 9 pounds. How much would the empty crate weigh? (Solution: The crate weighs 3 pounds. 15 lbs. – 9 lbs. = 6 lbs; 6 lbs × 2 = 12 lbs; 15 lbs. – 12 lbs. = 3 lbs.)

whole group

Squeezing Oranges

How to Play: For these two tensing/relaxation exercises, the children imagine they are squeezing oranges.

The children and the leader, standing up, fold their hands in front of them at chest level. Now they imagine they are trying to squeeze the juice out of a small orange. They squeeze their hands together with increasing pressure, especially at the bases of the fingers, then relax. They squeeze and release the orange five times, until the orange has been thoroughly juiced; then the children shake out their hands to loosen them up.

Next, the children and leader stand at their places and take calm, deep breaths in and out. Now they imagine they have to squeeze an orange that is stuck between their shoulder blades. They bend their elbows and push them firmly backward for five seconds at a time. Then they let their arms hang loosely at their sides, and they shake off the imaginary juice droplets.

Repeat this exercise three times in a row, and enjoy the sense of relaxation it creates.

whole group

Fingertip Cargo

Props: Small objects like pennies, erasers, or pencil sharpeners

How to Play: The first child stands against a wall and holds out his hands, palms up and fingers spread apart. Then a helper places a small object or scrap of paper on each of the first child's fingertips. His job now is to walk across the room to the opposite wall, losing as few objects as possible. If something happens to fall, his helper, who accompanies him on the walk, picks it up while the "transporter" continues to walk calmly. Who will have the best balance and avoid being thrown off when objects fall? Who will get the most objects to the other side? The spectators are quiet as mice. The leader, too, can become a transporter for one round, and be amazed at how much fine motor control is needed for this light transport.

The Knocking Rule

How to Play: Children love this game. It is useful, too, so you can be glad the next time an outsider knocks on the door. At that instant, the children all turn to stone. Someone who was about to say something stops with her mouth open, while someone on his way across the room instantly freezes in that position. No one moves, no one makes a sound. It's not really that easy, since after all you can still move your eyeballs to look around, and the other frozen children look pretty funny. The spell is broken only when the visitor has left the room and the door is closed; then the children can get all the bottled-up laughter out of their systems.

Life is tough, and if you have the ability to laugh at it
you have the ability to enjoy it.

SALMA HAYEK, ACTRESS

whole group

Escape

Props: Five blindfolds

How to Play: Five children are blindfolded; the rest form a circle around them and hold hands. The five children inside the circle are robbers who have been languishing in prison for a long time. Today, however, they've heard about a hole in the wall that could let them escape to freedom. They only have three minutes before the hole closes up again.

Before the game begins, the leader gives two of the "wall-children" a sign to let go of each other's hands. This will be the hole through which the robbers can escape to the outside. Then the whistle is blown, and the robbers know the clock is running down!

It's completely silent in the cell while the jailbreakers look feverishly for the hole. If one of them finds it, she says nothing and simply disappears from the jail without a trace. After three minutes, the whistle is blown again; the hole closes up, and the rest of the robbers may take off their blindfolds. They'll never know how close they were to freedom!

whole group

Miniature Kingdoms

Props: Plenty of string

How to Play: Each child becomes a king or queen and gets a piece of string, about three feet long. They tie the ends together to make a loop and lay the circle of string down somewhere on a piece of ground outside to mark the boundaries of their "kingdom." Then each king (or queen) kneels or lies down next to the tiny kingdom and gets to know the landscape and its inhabitants. Carefully, they push stalks of grass aside and are amazed by beetles, ants, grasshoppers, and many other insects they have never seen before. The longer they observe their kingdoms, the more they discover. If they see something especially cool, they can make a note of it on a pad of paper. After a while, the monarchs meet for a short comparison of their experiences. If time allows, the rulers can pay an official visit to another kingdom.

99

pairs

Balance

Props: Two books for each pair of children

How to Play: Children play in twos. One lies on his back and lifts his feet in the air, and his partner places a light book on each of his feet.

Once the child lying down is able to balance the books without difficulty, he can start moving his legs up and down. As he stretches his legs he breathes in deeply, and as he bends them he breathes out. If this doesn't seem too hard, the game advances: Now he moves his legs as if riding a bike—first very slowly, then a little faster. He continues breathing slowly and rhythmically the whole time. If a book happens to fall, his partner puts it back. After a few rounds of bike riding, the partners switch.

whole group

Silent Keys

Prop: A large key ring containing many keys

How to Play: Here's a good activity for promoting more peace and quiet in the group. Have the children pass around the ring of keys. The goal is to do so absolutely silently. Whoever clinks the keys is knocked out of the game, but then they get to be a clink detective, listening carefully for the slightest sound from the others.

Three Good Things

Props: Pens and paper

How to Play: At the end of the day the children are asked to think back over all the things they have experienced. On a piece of paper, each child writes down the three best things that happened—for example, the poem she managed to memorize this afternoon, or the fun game the group played earlier in the day, or the fact that it was Tim's birthday and he brought cupcakes. Ask a few children to volunteer to read their lists aloud before it's time for everyone to go home.

Know how to listen,
and you will profit even from those who talk badly.

PLUTARCH, 46–120 A.D.

Alphabetical List of Games

Games with Special Requirements

Games in Which Physical Contact Might Be Involved

Games Requiring a Large Space

Games Suitable for Older Children

Games Requiring Going Outdoors

Games Requiring Musical Accompaniment

SmartFun *activity books encourage imagination, social interaction, and self-expression in children. Games are organized by the skills they develop and simple icons indicate appropriate age levels, times of play, and group size. Most games are noncompetitive and require no special training. The series is widely used in schools, homes, and summer camps.*

101 MUSIC GAMES FOR CHILDREN: Fun and Learning with Rhythm and Song *by* Jerry Storms

All you need to play these games are music CDs and simple instruments, many of which kids can make from common household items. Many games are good for large group settings, such as birthday parties, others are easily adapted to classroom needs. No musical knowledge is required.

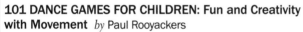

>> 160 pages ... 30 illus. ... Paperback $14.95 ... Spiral bound $19.95

101 MORE MUSIC GAMES FOR CHILDREN: New Fun and Learning with Rhythm and Song *by* Jerry Storms

This action-packed compendium offers musical activities that children can play while developing a love for music. Besides concentration and expression games, this book includes relaxation games, card and board games, and musical projects. **A multicultural section** includes songs and music from Mexico, Turkey, Surinam, Morocco, and the Middle East.

>> 176 pages ... 78 illus. ... Paperback $14.95 ... Spiral bound $19.95

101 DANCE GAMES FOR CHILDREN: Fun and Creativity with Movement *by* Paul Rooyackers

These games encourage children to interact and express how they feel in creative ways, without words. They include meeting and greeting games, cooperation games, story dances, party dances, "musical puzzles," dances with props, and more. No dance training or athletic skills are required.

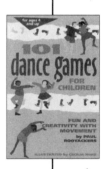

>> 160 pages ... 36 illus. ... Paperback $14.95 ... Spiral bound $19.95

101 MORE DANCE GAMES FOR CHILDREN: New Fun and Creativity with Movement *by* Paul Rooyackers

Designed to help children develop spontaneity and cultural awareness, the games in this book include Animal Dances, Painting Dances, Dance Maps, and Dance a Story. The **Dance Projects from Around the World** include Hula dancing, Caribbean Carnival, Chinese Dragon Dance, and Capoeira.

>> 176 pages ... 44 b/w photos. ... Paperback $14.95 ... Spiral bound $19.95

101 MOVEMENT GAMES FOR CHILDREN: Fun and Learning with Playful Movement *by* Huberta Wiertsema

Movement games help children develop sensory awareness, ease of movement, and using movement for self-expression. Games are organized in sections including reaction games, cooperation games, and expression games, and include variations on old favorites such as Duck, Duck, Goose as well as new games such as Mirroring, Equal Pacing, and Moving Joints.

>> 160 pages ... 49 illus. ... Paperback $14.95 ... Spiral bound $19.95

101 DRAMA GAMES FOR CHILDREN: Fun and Learning with Acting and Make-Believe by Paul Rooyackers

Drama games are a fun, dynamic form of play that help children explore their imagination and creativity. These noncompetitive games include introduction games, sensory games, pantomime games, story games, sound games, games with masks, games with costumes, and more. The "play-ful" exercises help to develop self-esteem, improvisation, communication, and trust; children also learn confidence in speaking in front of peers.

>> 160 pages ... 30 illus. ... Paperback $14.95 ... Spiral bound $19.95

101 MORE DRAMA GAMES FOR CHILDREN: New Fun and Learning with Acting and Make-Believe by Paul Rooyackers

These drama games require no acting skills—just an active imagination. The selection includes morphing games, observation games, dialog games, living video games, and game projects. **A special multicultural section** includes games on Greek drama, African storytelling, Southeast Asian puppetry, Pacific Northwest transformation masks, and Latino folk theater.

>> 144 pages ... 35 illus. ... Paperback $14.95 ... Spiral bound $19.95

101 IMPROV GAMES FOR CHILDREN AND ADULTS by Bob Bedore

Improv comedy has become wildly popular, and this book offers the next step in drama and play skills: a guide to creating something out of nothing, for reaching people using talents you didn't know you possessed. Contains instructions and exercises for teaching improv to children, advanced improv techniques, and tips for thinking on your feet—all from an acknowledged master of the improv form.

>> 192 pages ... 65 b/w photos ... Paperback $14.95 ... Spiral bound $19.95

101 LANGUAGE GAMES FOR CHILDREN: Fun and Learning with Words, Stories and Poems by Paul Rooyackers

Language is perhaps the most important human skill, and a sense of fun and word play can make language more creative and memorable. This book contains over one hundred games that have been tested in classrooms around the world. They range from letter games and word games to story-writing; there are also several poetry games including Hidden Word and Haiku Arguments.

>> 144 pages ... 27 illus. ... Paperback $14.95 ... Spiral bound $19.95

101 FAMILY VACATION GAMES: Having Fun while Traveling, Camping or Celebrating at Home *by* Shando Varda

This wonderful collection of games from around the world helps parents to connect with their children. Full of games to play at the beach, on camping trips, in the car, and in loads of other places, including Word Tennis, Treasure Hunt, and Storytelling Starters.

>> 160 pages ... 7 b/w photos ... 43 illus. ... Paperback $14.95 ... Spiral bound $19.95

101 COOL POOL GAMES FOR CHILDREN: Fun and Fitness for Swimmers of All Levels *by* Kim Rodomista

It's never too early to begin enjoying the benefits of water exercise and play. These games for children ages 4 and up can be played again and again. Best of all, they burn calories and improve a child's overall fitness level. A special section covers exercises, including water walking, jumping, and balance activities.

>> 128 pages ... 39 illus. ... Paperback $14.95 ... Spiral bound $19.95

THE YOGA ADVENTURE FOR CHILDREN : Playing, Dancing, Moving, Breathing, Relaxing *by* Helen Purperhart

Offers an opportunity for the whole family to laugh, play, and have fun together. This book for children 4–12 years old explains yoga stretches and postures as well as the philosophy behind yoga. The exercises are good for a child's mental and physical development, and also improve concentration and self-esteem.

>> 144 pages ... 75 illus. ... Paperback $14.95 ... Spiral bound $19.95

YOGA GAMES FOR CHILDREN: Fun and Fitness with Postures, Movements and Breath

by Danielle Bersma and Marjoke Visscher

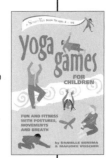

An introduction to yoga for children ages 6–12, these games help young people develop body awareness, physical strength, and flexibility. The 54 activities are variations on traditional yoga exercises, adjusted for children and clearly illustrated. Ideal for warm-ups and relaxing time-outs.

>> 160 pages ... 57 illus. ... Paperback $14.95 ... Spiral bound $19.95

101 LIFE SKILLS GAMES FOR CHILDREN: Learning, Growing, Getting Along (Ages 6–12) *by* Bernie Badegruber

How do you teach tolerance and responsibility or help children deal with fear, mistrust, or aggression? Play a Life Skills game with them! You can help children learn social and emotional skills; for example, how to integrate the new girl into the group, how to cope with aggression, and safe ways of letting off steam.

>> 192 pages ... 40 illus. ... Paperback $14.95 ... Spiral bound $19.95

101 MORE LIFE SKILLS GAMES FOR CHILDREN:
Learning, Growing, Getting Along (Ages 9–15)
by Bernie Badegruber

Schools are under increasing pressure to find ways to teach a core vocabulary of social skills to pre-teens and teens. The games in this book tackle issues such as learning patience, self-confidence, love, and respect; having good boundaries; and being fair. An explanation of the difference between play therapy and game pedagogy—using games with children—sets up the actual games, which are illustrated with lively drawings.

>> 176 pages ... 39 illus. ... Paperback $14.95 ... Spiral bound $19.95

42 MANDALA PATTERNS COLORING BOOK
by Wolfgang Hund

The mandalas in this book mix traditional designs with modern themes. Nature elements such as trees and stars reflect the environment, while animals such as fish, doves, and butterflies remind us we are all part of a universal life. Motifs repeat within mandalas in a soothing way that encourages us to revisit the images, finding new shapes and meanings in them each time. A perfect introduction to the joy of coloring mandalas.

>> 96 pages ... 42 illus. ... Paperback $11.95

42 INDIAN MANDALAS COLORING BOOK
by Monika Helwig

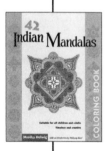

Traditionally made of colored rice powder, flowers, leaves, or colored sand, mandalas such as the ones in this book have been used to decorate homes, temples, and meeting places. They may be used daily as well as on special occasions, and are found in the homes of people of all faiths. Each pattern is different and special, increasing the delight of all who see them.

>> 96 pages ... 42 illus. ... Paperback $11.95

42 SEASONAL MANDALAS COLORING BOOK
by Wolfgang Hund

The seasonal and holiday mandalas in this book will appeal to both the sophisticated and the primal in all of us. Luscious fruit, delicate flowers, and detailed leaves and snowflakes are among the nature designs. Holiday themes include bunnies and jack-o-lanterns, Christmas scenes, and New Year's noise-makers. Children can learn about the seasons and celebrate familiar holidays with these playful designs!

>> 96 pages ... 42 illus. ... Paperback $11.95